a Novel by Melanie Kerr

Mary Green

a Novel by Melanie Kerr

Mary Green

Stonehouse Publishing
www.stonehousepublishing.ca
Alberta, Canada

Stonehouse Publishing Inc is an independent publishing house, incorporated in 2014.

Cover design and layout by Janet King
Printed in Canada

National Library of Canada Cataloguing in Publication Data
Kerr, Melanie
Mary Green
Novel
ISBN: 978-0-9866494-5-5 (bound)
ISBN 978-0-9866494-4-8 (paperback)
First Edition

Dedicated to my parents who, quite by accident and possibly to my detriment, instilled in me a belief that I could do anything.

Chapter One

The name of Mary Green was so far beneath the notice of Miss Hargreaves and her sister that its bearer hardly heard it spoken except in rare occasions of company. When forced to address the poor girl, it was therefore as simply 'Polly,' and most often uttered with resentment at being required to acknowledge her existence at all.

The three young ladies lived at Challey Hall in Oxfordshire, with the late Mrs. Hargreaves' younger sister, Miss Preston. The house was by no means the largest in the county, but it was not so small that a lady on one floor in the east wing might be expected to hear the call of her cousin on another floor in the west.

"Polly!" cried Miss Augusta from the seat of her dressing table. Though she was a little more friendly than her sister, she was neither so humble as to call Mary by her proper name, nor so selfless as to go in search of her rather than sit and grow angry at Mary's being so careless of the feelings of others as to be out of hearing distance when she was required.

Augusta called for Polly again, drawing out the sounds in an insistent and desperate holler, unequal to imagining that Mary may have any other engagement but to wait, out of sight of her cousins, for the moment she may be needed by either of them. Augusta let go an impatient sigh, glared into the mirror and drew a great breath to call again for that wretched little creature when the door of her chamber flew open.

"What on earth do you do, Gussy?" was the indignant reply, for it was not Polly who had burst in, and indeed, she never burst anywhere, but Dorothea, the elder Hargreaves girl, gliding across the carpet to stand over her sister in breathless elegance. "Do not you think how ill it becomes you to shout the whole house down like that? Do you wish people to think you savage?"

"I know not what people there are in this house whose opinions might concern me, unless you mean Aunt Preston or the servants. Clearly Polly does not hear me."

Dorothea, catching sight of herself in the mirror was instantly distracted and calmed by the thought that she must have a new day gown made, one just like Lady Darlington had brought back from Paris. It would suit her figure so much better than Lady Darlington's. She lowered her eyes to her sister's surly reflection.

"Well, go and fetch her then," she said, "if you need her so." She raised her eyebrows at Augusta's image then turned and strode back across the room. Stopping to look the door frame up and down as if in disapproval, she added, "And if you think the talk of servants benign, I could tell you a sobering tale or two," and left the room.

Augusta watched her sister in the mirror as she departed, then sat in furious silence. She would not give Dorothea the satisfaction of seeing her follow her instruction to go and find Mary, but neither would she expose herself to further insult by calling out again. After a few moments of internal debate, she gave up and threw herself onto her bed, taking up a novel from the nightstand and attempting to read it while her mind replayed every act of insolent superiority ever perpetrated against her by her sister.

On hearing a knock, Augusta looked up over the book to see the figure of Mary, standing just outside the open door, which Dorothea had not deigned to close upon her departure. "Your sister said you were calling for me," she said.

"Did *she* go and fetch you?" asked Augusta. "How like her." She threw down her book and slipped off the bed and back into place before the mirror. "Will you *please* come and help me, Polly," she said, beckoning to Mary, who came and stood beside her. "I am utterly distraught over the Westley Ball. All three of the Ingles brothers are going to be there, even Lord Marsden. You do remember him? Of course you do. One does not forget Lord Marsden." She heaved a great sigh at the thought of being noticed or–dare she even hope?–asked to dance by such a gentleman as the unparalleled Lord Marsden. "But what am I going to wear that can possibly draw the attention of any of the gentlemen away from Dorothea?" She shook her head. "I could not tolerate being outdone by her again. She has allowed me to borrow any of her pieces that I should like," she indicated a selection of jewels laid out on the table, "yet I know they shall all be of no use to me."

"That was very kind of her," Mary offered. "Several of these are among her favourites, I am sure."

"It is nothing like kindness," Augusta spat. "It is a twisted sort of conceit. She knows I shall never look as well in any of them as she does, and she only proves her own supremacy by allowing me to demonstrate as much. And of course she is right. She shall wrap herself in some torn old rags with a fishing net on her head, and everyone shall announce her the most natural and unaffected beauty in the kingdom. She is so blessed tall, she might wear anything to advantage, just like you. I am the only poor dwarf in this house. I am no less deserving than her and yet I get none of the attention."

"I may be tall, it is true," said Mary, choosing the most delicate necklace from the table and fastening it around Augusta's neck, "but I will always want Dorothea's grace. I am rather plodding I am afraid, and shall never be as dainty as yourself."

"Well that is true, I suppose," Augusta conceded, touching the necklace and turning her head to admire it from both sides.

"Gentlemen like a dainty lady, or so I am told." Mary took down the gowns that had been hung beside the mirror.

"Let your sister envy you for a change," she said, "and regret her great, towering form. Here," she held out a white sprigged muslin. "The subtlety of this fabric would be lost on her, and will flatter you very well I think."

"But it is so plain," complained Augusta, who, though not quite so handsome as her sister, was still rather pretty. "I am already so plain. I shall draw no attention in that."

"Take a little of the lace from *this* gown," said Mary, picking out an elaborately embellished silk "and add it to the muslin. You have several days until the ball. I am sure Ellie will be able to accomplish something very pretty in plenty of time."

"That is a thought," said Augusta, looking over the two gowns.

"And I am sure we can make good use of some of your ribbon for your hair, and there are some charming little flowers in the gardens just now. No doubt they would be quite happy to be liberated for your adornment."

"Oh Polly, would you do that for me?" she simpered. "And please tell Ellie just how the gown should be made up. I know I should make a mess of it, and before such company, I should be mortified. I simply *cannot* allow Dorothea to keep all the gentlemen to herself."

"Only one gentleman may marry Dorothea," said Mary, taking up the two gowns. "There will be others left for you, you know."

"Perhaps, but I should like to be *somebody's* first choice, and besides, who is to say they shall not all squander their lives in pining for her if they cannot find her equal."

"Let us not despair of that quite yet," said Mary, as she gathered up the gowns.

Augusta eyed her ruffled burden. "I would loan you something to wear but I just do not think anything I have would fit you without irreversible adjustment. I am afraid you must look to Dorothea for that."

"Something to wear?" said Mary.

"Well, you cannot go in your old house dress. It would reflect badly on us. I am sure Aunt Preston will see it that way."

"I am to go to the ball?" Mary was all confusion. She was never invited to join the Hargreaves girls on social outings. She was not even a blood relation, after all, though she was always referred to as a cousin. Mary was, in fact, a nobody, and only permitted to remain in their house out of what the sisters regarded as a misplaced senti-mentality on the part of their ever absent father.

"I should hope so!" said Augusta. "You were particularly men-tioned in the invitation, and I do not think Aunt Preston would take it very well if you were to refuse. It would look like ingratitude."

"No, of course, I should not wish to give offence, and I have no cause to refuse. I am merely surprised to have been invited." The honour of an invitation to Westley Park was more than she ever expected to receive, and she felt the thrill and the apprehension of attending such a great occasion as such a humble character. Already she began to think how she might make over a tattered cast-off of Dorothea's which hung in her closet, though next to the sisters Hargreaves, she knew she would always look the penniless orphan that she was.

"Well, you must not make yourself too pretty," Augusta scowled. "It is one thing to be outdone by Dorothea, but if you were *both* to appear more handsome, it would be quite intolerable and I should never forgive you."

Mary knew Augusta too well to think her in jest, though the notion that Mary could ever be more remarkable than either of her cousins was most ridiculous. "I do not think you need worry about that," she said. "I shall be the one in rags and no one has ever called *me* a natural beauty."

"Oh do not be so self-pitying. It does not become you." Augusta turned and waved Mary away. The latter bit her tongue as she always did, recounted to herself all her many blessings, and made her way from the room, leaving the other girl to herself and to the misery of her sister's jewels.

Chapter Two

"That is a very pretty gown," said Mary, who was already dressed and waiting in the drawing room when Dorothea joined her. "I do not think I have seen it before. Is it new?" Dorothea wore neither old rags nor a fishing net, but a pale blue silk and a dishevelled coiffage, the effortless effect of which no doubt took some hours to achieve.

"No," she said, floating into an armchair. "Not entirely new. I believe I have had it nearly two months already, though I have not had the opportunity to wear it." She opened and closed her fan a few times and then stared out of the window, or rather at her own perfection in the pane. After a minute or two of silence, she must have seen Mary in the glass, for she turned to her and, noticing her dress for the first time, remarked, "You are wearing my old muslin."

"Yes," answered Mary. "It was a little worn, but the holes were small, and with this ribbon of Augusta's and a little ruffling, I managed to hide the worst of it. I believe it is quite passable, for me at least."

"Hmm," said Dorothea, not moving her gaze from Mary's gown, unconcerned by the awkwardness which her silent observations caused to its wearer. After some minutes, Mary was saved from her discomfort by the arrival of Aunt Preston, flushed and plump in her usual grey taffeta. Shuffling into the room, she stopped and gasped on espying Dorothea, a broad smile erupting across her face.

"Oh my dear!" she exclaimed. "How marvellous you look. Why, the colour of that gown is exquisite. I do not believe I have ever seen your complexion so radiant. And your eyes, why they are so deep as to drown every gentleman in Middle England, I shouldn't wonder. Do stand and let me see the whole of it."

Dorothea merely sighed. "I shall stand the whole night at the ball, Aunt," she replied, tilting her head back to rest upon the chair. "Let me have a little ease now, while I may. I am sure Augusta will be quite happy to jump up and twirl for you if you wish."

"But where is your sister?" Aunt Preston asked sharply. Dorothea merely shrugged and resumed playing with her fan. Turning to Mary with impatient accusation, she repeated, "Where is she?"

"I am sorry Madam," replied Mary. "I do not know. I expect she is still in her room."

Huffing, Aunt Preston spun about and bustled back out into the hall, muttering impatiently to herself. She stood at the bottom of the staircase with her foot on the first step, contemplating the height of the ascent, when she heard the creak of a door above. "Come, come my dear," she called up. "We do not want to keep the Ingles waiting. Everyone shall be quite accounted for by the time we arrive if we do not make haste."

Augusta came bursting into view of her aunt, who did not fail to gasp and fuss over her as she descended the remainder of the stairs. With unceasing delight, she took the beaming Augusta by the hand and presented her to the drawing room. "Oh girls, what do you say?" she said in raptures. "Could not she pass for the Queen of France?"

"Certainly, Aunt," replied Dorothea, rising from her chair. As she passed them in the doorway she added, without stopping, "if the Queen of France is a novel term for a whipped syllabub."

Aunt Preston's gaze followed Dorothea out of the room and into the hall where a servant waited with her cloak. "Oh Dorothea, you are always so droll," she said, walking away from Augusta. It was therefore only Mary who saw the younger girl's face harden and her eyes turn red with the threat of tears.

"Oh Gussy," she sighed, rising from her chair and hastening to take her cousin's hand. "You mustn't pay her any mind." It appeared as though Augusta had embellished the muslin with all the trim from the silk gown as well as several others, for the lace rose in layers from the hem to above the knee, and around the neckline. The sleeves seemed to have been replaced entirely as they were twice the size of the originals, and drowning in bows, gathers and, indeed, more lace. Augusta's hair extended at least six inches above the crown of her head and teemed with every variety of flower grown on the estate. She also wore a bright red sash, tied at her back in an enormous bow, and Mary guessed by the size of her skirt that she was wearing numerous petticoats.

"I know not why she must be so cruel," stammered Augusta, looking away from Mary towards the windows. "She is already everything to everyone. Why must she trample me so? It is merely because she can. I know it is."

"I do not think she can know how she affects you," said Mary tenderly, reaching for a handkerchief. "She simply says whatever comes into her head, whether true or not." She held out the handkerchief. "And besides, I am rather fond of a syllabub." Augusta looked Mary in the face.

"Thank you, I do not need a handkerchief," she said coldly, pulling away her hand and turning to join the others in the hall. Taking her cloak and muff roughly from the servant, she added, "and I do not believe I gave you permission to call me 'Gussy.' 'Augusta' or 'Cousin' is quite familiar enough."

The servant had to rush forward to open the door for her, for she did not wait to take her place behind her aunt and her sister, but with her chin high, marched first out of the house.

As she bolted into the night air, she was nearly thrown clear onto her back, colliding as she did with a tall, broad figure who was just approaching the front doors. His great, gloved hand caught her before she was in any danger, and looking up into his face, all her present feelings gave way to delight and relief.

"Papa!" she cried and leapt up to embrace her father.

"My darling girl!" he replied, kissing her cheek with enthusiastic affection. "How sweet it is to see you. You cannot know how I have missed you."

"Papa?" came Dorothea's voice as she emerged through the doors behind her sister.

"Dorothea, my love," he said as he took her face in his hands and kissed it with as much sincerity and tenderness, if not as much vigour as he had her sister's.

"Why did not you tell us you were coming?" asked Augusta, "and what brings you back to England? You must tell us all about the Indies. Are they still just as hot and as dreadful as they always are? How long can you stay this time? You always go away too soon. It is not fair. But I know you will have brought us presents. You never come home without presents. Will you give them to us tonight? It is so good to see you."

"Please, Gussy," said Dorothea. "Let him at least come inside his own house before you begin your assault."

"One man's assault is another man's delight," said Sir Richard, taking Augusta's hand and squeezing it. "But it is indeed a chilly night for a man just returned from the tropics, and I am eager to re-acquaint myself with the comforts of my home."

Mary had just begun to fasten her cloak when the commotion began. Aunt Preston had stepped forward to follow the girls out when she thought the better of it. Her eyes narrowed as she turned towards Mary, raising her finger at her and saying in a malevolent whisper–

"If that is Sir Richard, I do hope you shall be on good behaviour. Do not forget that you are here at his pleasure. If you show yourself ungrateful for all his kindness to you I shouldn't wonder if he would take his first chance at being rid of the burden of you."

Before Mary could compose a reply, Sir Richard was ushering his daughters back into the house, laughing with the tanned exuberance of a traveler delighting in the return to all things familiar and much missed, including, apparently, Mary and Aunt Preston, who forgot, or at least set aside, her anxiety for the Ingles and their ball.

"My dear girl," he said to Mary as he embraced her. "Let me look at you." She blushed and looked at the floor as he stepped back to take her in. "I do believe you have grown. You are almost as tall as Dorothea, if I am not mistaken." Turning to the older lady he said, "Miss Preston, it gives me such comfort to know what care you always take of my young charges while I am gone. I could never sleep at night if I did not trust so wholly in your love for my girls." He gestured towards his daughters. "And here is proof that I have not mislaid my trust."

"Come, sir," said Miss Preston, uneasy with his praise. "You must wish to sit."

"I am so sorry," said Sir Richard when once he was installed in the drawing room with a cup of brandy in his hand. "I have been so distracted with the joy of seeing you all that I am only just beginning to realize that you were on your way out when I arrived. Please, do not let me keep you from your evening."

"But you have only just got here!" protested Augusta. "We cannot simply leave you."

"You are too kind, my dear," said Sir Richard "but I am terribly fatigued, and the pleasure of being home again has quite done me in. I shall go directly to bed in any event, and I know how indispensable a ball is in the country, especially to ladies. I shall still be here in the morning, and all the better company for having slept, and in my own bed too. What an enticing prospect!"

"Your father is quite right, girls," said Aunt Preston, happy to be relieved of the choice between offending the Ingles and offending her brother-in-law. "Let us leave him in peace. You shall quite wear him out with your talk."

The girls wished Sir Richard a good night, and followed their aunt into the carriage with many promises of enjoying themselves and of having much to say in the morning.

Chapter Three

"You will sit with me if I have not a partner, won't you?" said Augusta to Mary as the carriage rolled out of the drive, all previous offence now utterly forgot. "What could be more sorry than a young lady with only a spinster aunt for company? But if you will sit with me, I shall not seem so wretched. What a pretty pair we shall make." Augusta smiled at Mary, who understood very well that Augusta would be only too happy to be seen with her, as Augusta would always be the finer of the two and appear all the more lovely for the comparison.

"If you should wish," answered Mary, returning the smile rather weakly. It did not signify to her whom she sat with. Had she not been particularly named in the invitation, she doubted anyone would have considered her included. She did not anticipate dancing many dances, and Augusta's company would at least interrupt the monotony of solitude. Augusta was nothing if not distracting. "Of course I shall sit with you. Though I do not think you shall have much need of me, not if all three Ingles brothers are to be there. I heard even Lord Marsden has condescended to join in his parents' country ball."

Aunt Preston leaned forward and gripped Augusta's hand, saying, "Imagine if Lord Marsden should ask you to dance! I am certain he shall, and then you shall not want for partners."

This sent Augusta into a flurried exposition of all the merits of Lord and Lady Rosborough, Lord Marsden, the Ingles family generally, and Westley Park, as well as every gentleman in the county who might be supposed to have been invited, and every possible combination of partners. So thorough were her musings that she spared all her fellow passengers the pain of making any sort of conversation until cut short by the dumb excitement precipitated by the Park itself as they turned into the drive.

"Well now, girls," offered Aunt Preston. "Is not this the world on a platter?"

Sir Richard's arrival had, indeed, delayed the party past the first two dances, and Aunt Preston was quick to allay her own fears in that regard. "Our lateness may be an accidental advantage you know," she remarked through her panting as they conquered the front steps. "After all, a gentleman always grows more fond of a lady who keeps him waiting a little. And now the rooms shall be quite full when we are announced, which is certainly to be preferred."

The party was presented to the room, to the noise and the crowd, and to no response whatever. Dorothea slipped through the multitude to the punch table. Aunt Preston forced her way around the edge of the room to a seat with all the power of her rotund self-importance. Augusta and Mary followed in her wake, the former on tiptoes, willing herself tall enough to take in all the guests and rattling off all the gossip about every one of them she could see. Although there was a seat free, Augusta did not sit. She stood, instead, in front of her relations, keeping her eyes on the crowd, attempting to catch the eye of a gentleman who may yet want for a partner. She succeeded with one who stood near enough as to make it awkward for him not to address her once their eyes met. With some uncertainty, he approached, a dark-eyed fellow in tidy regimentals. Augusta sallied boldly forth with outstretched hand and beaming smiles.

"Mr. Briggs," she said as she approached. "Or should I say Colonel Briggs? What a delight! I did not expect to see you here." Colonel Briggs kissed her hand, which she allowed to linger in his a little longer than he knew what to do with. Seeing Aunt Preston behind her, he nodded to her.

"Good evening, madam," he said. Seeing Mary beside her, he nodded to her also. Augusta did not introduce them, but continued without a pause.

"You do not dance, sir," she remarked. "Are you injured? I cannot think that you could want for a partner, not a gentleman in uniform. I have only just arrived myself, or I expect I should be dancing myself giddy by now." Colonel Briggs considered her giddiness entirely unconnected with her dancing, but felt it poor manners to disregard such an obvious plea.

"Might you do me the honour of joining me in the next?" he asked. "It is a minuet, I believe." Augusta made a show of checking her card, taking care not to let him see that it was quite empty.

"Well, how could I refuse such a gentlemanly offer," she replied with a swish of her skirt. "And I am excessively fond of a minuet. But I am dreadfully parched. Do let us get a drop of punch before we begin." With that she took his arm, though it was not offered, and led him the long way around the room to the punch bowl, promenading in such a way as to allow everyone to see that she was on the arm of a gentleman, and more than that, a red-coat.

Aunt Preston spoke not a word to Mary, but made as much idle chat as she could with her neighbours. The dance soon began, and Mary was thereby spared more than the occasional remark from her companion regarding the elegance or the style of her nieces' dancing.

Augusta seemed vastly contented with her partner, the soldier, and Dorothea looked much as she always did. Her partner was the third and youngest son of Lord and Lady Rosborough, Mr. George

Ingles, a man of no particular profession, but very fashionable and of an artistic persuasion and hair that clung defiantly to the gold of its youth. It was generally accepted by everyone, though never formally announced, that he was to marry Dorothea, who herself never expressed any objection to the idea, nor any enthusiasm for it. Watching the pair of them dance, both handsome, tall and accomplished, it seemed to Mary that Dorothea was rather as indifferent about matrimony as she was about dancing, and her partner in either made not so much difference to her so long as he was moderately agreeable and did not demand anything of her beyond her wont. Being so beautiful, and so natural in all her accomplishments, surely it would be a rare gentleman that would expect more of her.

"Good evening, madam," a familiar voice drew Mary's attention from the dancers. Mr William Ingles, the second son of the family, bowed a greeting to Miss Preston and then to Mary. "Miss Green, how do you do?"

"How do you do, sir," she replied with an honest smile, cheered at the sound of her proper name. "Please, do join us." She indicated a place beside herself, which he took with alacrity.

"I am so very pleased you accepted our invitation this evening," he said as he sat. Mary was convinced that it was rather *his* invitation than that of his family in general, who, no doubt, failed to recall her existence unless pressed. "I am afraid these affairs are not much to my taste in general; I was never one for pageantry, you know, and I do not dance. So there is little enjoyment in it for me, unless I may partake of your company and conversation for some part of it, in which case I shall have a very pleasant time."

"I shall endeavour to satisfy your expectations," she responded, "and I have very high hopes of doing so, for I have such news to share that might fill an entire evening." She paused, hoping to increase his suspense. She had few gifts in the world, but a decent bit of news enriched her as much as any jewel, and this information was as valuable as any. "Sir Richard has come home," she announced.

"Oh yes!" he returned enthusiastically. "I heard that from your cousin just now. What a great surprise that must have been." Mary was crestfallen at being robbed of her only prize.

"Quite, quite" she managed to utter, determined not to be disappointed. Sir Richard's return was indeed a joyful occasion unto itself, whoever was first to spread word of it. "We were just on our way here when he appeared in the doorway. He nearly knocked Augusta over on the threshold."

"What a happy commotion that must have caused! I imagine you were all delighted." Mary thought of Aunt Preston's less than delightful words of warning to her, but could see no cause to relate them, especially as she sat in the adjacent chair.

"Indeed," she answered. "We are always quite beside ourselves when he comes home, especially his daughters, as you might expect."

"And what brings him home this time? Will it be a long stay?"

Mary was quite gratified to give as many particulars as she had learned in the few minutes between Sir Richard's arrival and their departure, and to make of them as much conversation, whether speculation or fact, as she could.

The dance ended, and Mr. Ingles looked around the room.

"Well, Miss Green," he said, "I fear I may be required to make myself agreeable to a few more of our guests or I shall be in very bad stead with Mama. And besides," he added, rising from his seat, "whatever my preferences, I am sure it would not be very generous of me if I were to stay here with you the whole evening. I promise I shall return a little later."

"I look forward to it," she said, adding with a look across the room, "I do not think Dorothea or Augusta intend to sit out any dances."

"Oh, but you must not sit here all the evening," he urged. "You must dance also. I do not enjoy the activity myself, as I have never known any proficiency in it, but you need not be held back on such an account."

Mary felt suddenly awkward. There were at least twice as many ladies as gentlemen, and all infinitely better dressed than herself. Although she had done a commendable job of making herself presentable enough to sit at the edge of the room without disgracing her company, she knew there was not a gentleman present who would be inclined to wish to dance with her above anyone else.

"If I am asked, I shall certainly accept," she replied, forcing a smile as she lowered her gaze to her lap, where she clasped and unclasped her hands. She did not approve of seeking compliments by self-deprecation, but nor could she express any legitimate anticipation of a partner.

"But of course you shall be asked," insisted Mr. Ingles. Looking about himself, he saw his younger brother walking somewhat in their direction with Dorothea. "Here comes George now," he said. "Why, he was just saying before this last set how he was looking forward to dancing with you tonight. Is not that right, George?" he called out, though his brother was so far away as not to have had any chance of hearing their exchange.

Mary began to blush, for she was certain he had said no such thing, and that this was William's doing, forcing his brother into asking her to dance. She did love to dance, and often longed in vain to be asked, but she would be mortified to be the object of pity, or to be forced on anyone.

"What is that you say, Billy?" said George, walking more directly towards his brother on hearing his name.

"I was just relaying to Miss Green the wish you earlier expressed of dancing with her tonight. Do not I speak true?" Mary attempted to look up at Mr. George Ingles, but had not the courage, and so smiled in apology to Dorothea, who was occupied in adjusting her gloves.

"Quite so!" replied George. "In fact, I am not engaged for the next, which is a waltz I believe. Would you do me the honour of joining me?"

A timid "thank-you" was all she could manage as she took the hand he proffered and allowed herself to be led out into the set. Meanwhile, William took his leave of Dorothea, and left her to sit with her aunt. She was barely into her seat before she was whisked out of it again by the prompt invitation of a sprightly young gentleman in a green coat.

George was surprisingly affable throughout the dance, and Mary thought his breeding served him well that he should treat the likes of her with such condescension. He even went so far as to attempt to convince her that it had been his idea to include her expressly in the invitation, against his brother William's insistence that the inclusion was understood. As far as lies went, Mary thought this was rather a pretty one. And the consequence lent her by George's notice went so far as to encourage at least two other gentleman to invite her for a turn in the set. Though modestly attired, she was a lively and gracious partner once given the opportunity to exhibit. It was an uncommon evening of untainted delight and Mary fell upon her bed that night dizzy with the thrill of dancing, flirting, and elderberry punch.

Chapter Four

Mary did not hasten to breakfast in the morning. The taste of the previous evening's enjoyment was still fresh, and she was not keen to replace it with whatever bitter reflections the sisters might fling her way over tea and toast. She stayed, therefore, with her sweet memories and her charcoal crayons in the nursery from which she had never moved, sketching her recollections of the ball. Her pictures were better company than the living creatures awaiting her downstairs.

She could often be found avoiding the scorn of her cousins and Aunt Preston, closeted in her room with her paper–the one indulgence she was permitted. Her favourite subject was portraits, though she never had the benefit of a model, and was forced to work mostly from memory, occasionally drawing her own likeness from the glass. But the image she most often attempted was that of Mrs. Markham, of whom her memories were faint but precious. She was the only person who had ever shown Mary real affection.

Captain and Mrs. Markham had brought four-year-old Mary home with the intention of raising her as their own, but were prevented on account of their mutual deaths just before Mary's fifth birthday. Before bringing Mary home, Mrs. Markham had been frequently at the orphanage, and Mary remembered, if not the details of her features, at least the warmth of her demeanour and the love she always expressed.

As Sir Richard's sister, Mrs. Markham's portrait hung in the gallery upstairs, but Mary had never sought it out, lest her memory be tainted by the artist's impression which may not be as true as her recollections. These she attempted to render in her pictures and preferred to keep as they were. She never showed her sketches to anyone, much as one may choose to keep a diary private, though she sometimes dreamed they would be seen by someone who might judge them excessively valuable and thereby free her from her condition of dependency on the family of Hargreaves.

She remained in her room for well over an hour, perfecting one image of Augusta in her enormous white gown, until her wish for food and drink outweighed her wish for solitude and she reluctantly made her way to the breakfast room. Aunt Preston and Augusta were already deep in animated chatter, repeating with enthusiasm and embellishment all the events, the gowns and the partners of the previous night. Dorothea was present, and was the subject of much of the talk, though not one of its primary contributors. Mary slid quietly into a chair and took a piece of toast. She was able to ignore the others for several minutes, until her name was eventually mentioned.

"You must have been very disappointed, Dorothea, to relinquish your partner to Polly," said Augusta, suppressing a grin.

"No," was Dorothea's only reply, as she stirred her tea but did not drink it.

"No, of course not," interjected Aunt Preston. "Mr. Ingles cannot dance every dance with Dorothea, nor sit out the entire evening. Surely, if he must dance with someone else, better it should be Polly, whom he should forget in a moment, rather than any other young lady on whom he might be expected to dwell."

"Well, I should have been vexed to be in your position, Dorothea," Augusta continued. "Fortunately, none of *my* partners deserted *me*."

Dorothea broke off a piece of toast and looked at her sister.

"Do you really doubt the constancy of George Ingles?" she asked flatly.

"Nobody could doubt his constancy," replied Aunt Preston. "I should not doubt the constancy of any gentleman to lay eyes on you, much less one so well acquainted with your person."

"I suppose if he *must* dance with someone else, it might as well be Polly," remarked Augusta.

"Did he never ask you?" Dorothea asked, placing a morsel in her mouth. Augusta put down her tea cup.

"I expect my card would have been quite full," she returned. "I hardly sat down all evening."

"Still," sighed Dorothea, "not to be asked…" She did not complete her thought, but sipped her tea and turned her gaze to the window.

Mary could see that Augusta was hurt, and tried to give her a sympathetic look, but could not catch her eye.

"I was asked!" Augusta retorted. "I was asked by many gentlemen. I do not see that it should signify whether one particular gentleman did or did not ask me, particularly when I was occupied the entire evening with others."

"You were very much admired, my dear," offered Aunt Preston. "I daresay there were several gentlemen who were very taken with you, and how could they not be? And I am sure Mr. George Ingles would have been very keen to dance with you if he had not been preceded by so many others."

Dorothea was unmoved by these observations, and was still looking calmly out the window when something there caught her attention, and she sat up a little in her chair.

"Papa is coming back," she remarked. The others presently followed her line of sight but had missed the prospect of Sir Richard, who was now approaching the door. In a moment he was in the breakfast room and taking his place at the head of the table. Augusta's countenance instantly transformed from sour gloom to radiant smiles. Even Dorothea deigned to face her company and don a cheerful expression upon his entrance.

"Good morning, ladies," he said brightly, helping himself to tea. "I am so pleased I did not entirely miss breakfast. I was awake at rather a ghastly hour this morning, and I thought I might make use of the fact by touring the gardens and some of the grounds, just to see how everything has been getting on in my absence, you know. I am afraid I walked a good deal farther than I intended. It was only when I reached the old millers' cottages that I realized just how far I had gone, and I have only got back this moment. I was glad of the bit of bread and cheese I lifted from the kitchen in my hunger this morning, but I am afraid that was hardly sufficient for such a long walk in such fresh air."

"Good morning," said the ladies, more or less in unison. Augusta laughed awkwardly.

"You four seem in good spirits this morning," responded Sir Richard. "Do I take it you had an enjoyable evening last night?"

All answered in the affirmative, Augusta and Aunt Preston giving more details than Dorothea and Mary, the latter merely nodding in silence. The ladies reviewed again for the benefit of Sir Richard every detail of the ball, not failing to emphasize all the flattery paid to themselves.

"Well, you all looked charming," offered Sir Richard. "I am very glad to hear you enjoyed yourselves so well, and only regret I could not have joined you."

"Oh Papa," said Augusta with the sudden rush of a fresh idea. "What if we were to have a ball here? Truly we must. You are here so rarely, it would be such an offence not to invite our neighbours. What would they think if you would not host them all when you have the chance of it?"

Sir Richard chewed his toast, nodding in contemplation. Dorothea rolled her eyes up and sat back in her chair.

"Now, Augusta," said Aunt Preston, "do not burden your father with such requests. He has only just arrived, and he does not stay long. I am sure he wishes for peace, not the chaos of social obligations. I am as fond as anyone of a ball, but you do not seem to appreciate the amount of work involved. We must look after your father while he is here, not expect him to look after the neighbourhood."

"There is no time for a ball," added Dorothea with a look of impatience, "not one that I should not be ashamed to host."

"Is that what *you* think, Mary?" asked Sir Richard, he being the only one in the family ever to use her name. Pleased as she was by the rare honour of being asked her opinion, she did not enjoy being positioned between the sisters in a disagreement. She felt the hard stare of Aunt Preston, cautioning her not to give offence to anyone, as she looked about the table and gathered her thoughts.

"The ball last night was delightful," she said, "but very grand. I do not think such an affair could be repeated in the few weeks allowed. It might, however, be possible still to invite some of the neighbours, perhaps for something less ambitious. I do not think anyone would be affronted only to be invited, say, for dinner."

Aunt Preston's eyes shifted about as she considered whether this reply was satisfactory. Finding no fault with it, and indeed liking the suggestion more than she should wish to like anything coming from the neighbourhood of Polly, she voiced her approbation as vociferously as if it had been her own idea.

"You know, Sir Richard, I think it would be vastly preferable if we merely invited a few people for a quiet dinner, rather than a ball. We simply do not have time to put on the sort of evening that would do you credit, but if we contain our ambitions, we might do something very satisfactory in the time we have. I do know everyone is very keen to see you. They spoke of little else all yesterday evening. And the girls could play for us. They do not have so many opportunities to perform, you know, and it would be so much to their benefit and our delight, I am sure." Aunt Preston looked from one niece to the other in a flush of smug adulation.

"It seems settled then," said Sir Richard. "A dinner it shall be. You may choose the date, Miss Preston, and take care of the invitations, as you will know far better than I who is about at this time, and what might be got at the markets."

"Quite so, sir," she answered, her stout form puffing with pride. "You may leave everything to me. It shall all be done without any need of your troubling yourself."

"There shall not be time to order new gowns," remarked Dorothea, rising from her chair. "So I suppose I had better begin at making something over."

"No doubt it will look enchanting, my dear. You always astonish me with what you can do with an old gown to make it new again," said Aunt Preston to Dorothea, who did not acknowledge her but walked clear out the room before her aunt was quite finished. "Well, I suppose there is much to do," she added, without permitting her smile to fade. Augusta rose from the table, saying–

"I, too, shall find a gown I might do over. It is not only Dorothea can make something pretty you know."

"Of course not dearest," responded Aunt Preston, rising to follow her. "Come, come, come; let us all get about our business." She made to leave the table, but seeing that neither Sir Richard nor Mary were moving to go, she changed her mind and watched Augusta huff her way out of the door. Sitting back down, she said, "I suppose I should finish my tea first," and looked anxiously between her companions.

"I very much look forward to hearing you girls play at this dinner," said Sir Richard to Mary, who choked on her tea and began to cough.

"You do not expect Polly to perform!" said Aunt Preston before Mary could regain her breath.

"Why ever not?" returned Sir Richard. Aunt Preston looked to Mary to answer, but the girl continued coughing in deliberate evasion. Aunt Preston was therefore forced to give some explanation.

"You know how shy she is, sir. I hope to invite Lord and Lady Rosborough and all three of their sons, including Lord Marsden. Surely it would be an unkindness to ask her to play in front of such grand guests, and so many of them relative strangers."

"But why is that?" asked Sir Richard. "If she is so shy, she ought to be encouraged to overcome the fact, and there shall be no strangers present. It shall all be friends. What say you, Mary?"

Sir Richard and Aunt Preston now both looked at Mary for her reply, and she knew she must give one.

"I am afraid I do not possess the same skill as your daughters, sir," she managed.

"Nonsense!" exclaimed Sir Richard. "You have always had rather a talent for music. This must be some sort of false modesty, which I did not expect from you, Mary. No, I insist you play at dinner, and we shall all see how unjustified is your inferior opinion of your own skill."

Neither Mary nor Aunt Preston could argue with such a final

declaration, and both excused themselves from the table, the latter with a pretext of a busy day and the former with a heart full of dreadful apprehension.

Chapter Five

Later in the morning the ladies were gathered in the drawing room. Dorothea practiced on the pianoforte and Augusta sat embellishing a bonnet while Mary worked on a bit of embroidery. Their relative tranquility was then suddenly rent by the bustling in of Sir Richard, carrying several boxes. Augusta ceased her playing.

"Well, girls," said Sir Richard. "Did you think I would come back without presents?"

Augusta burst forth from behind the table and threw herself towards her father, who was just setting down the boxes. He laughed and ruffled her hair, a gesture which, at any other time, from any other person, would have elicited a dreadful reprimand in defence of her vanity, but on this occasion, her anticipation outweighed her concern for her appearance and she only asked which one was for her.

Sir Richard handed one box to each girl, including a rather surprised Mary, who accepted her parcel with a wide-eyed "thank you." All three young ladies opened their boxes at once to discover identical pairs of nankeen boots. "I do hope they shall fit," said Sir Richard. "I had your aunt send me the measurements, and she is not usually wrong in such matters." The girls all put them on, to confirm that they were well sized, which they were, with the exception of Mary's, which fit a little large, as did all her shoes since they were previously owned by Dorothea, whose feet were just a little longer than hers. Mary had never had her feet measured, and was certain Aunt Preston had simply used Dorothea's measurements. She was delighted nonetheless and assured Sir Richard that they were quite perfect.

Aunt Preston, who had come to see what all the noise was for, gasped when she saw that Mary had received the same gifts as her cousins.

"And do not think I would forget you, Miss Preston," said Sir Richard, handing her another box of the same description. "I am afraid I had to guess at your size, as it would have ruined the surprise to have asked for your measurements."

"You are too generous!" she exclaimed, taking out the boots and trying them for size, which was very near exact.

"But there is more!" he said, his face gleaming as he passed round several more boxes of various sizes, each containing trinkets and ribbons and lace, over which all four ladies in turns went into raptures. Much of the remainder of the day was thus taken up in trying things on, and choosing which pieces of what to attach to gowns and bonnets and the like.

Mary followed Augusta to her room, on request, to help her choose which gown to wear for the upcoming dinner and how best to adorn it with her new trims. Together they chose a blue gown which was trimmed with a white ribbon. Augusta felt her new gold ribbon would suit it very well and picked off the old white one, casting it to the ground as she began to pin the new one in place. Mary picked up the ribbon. "Do you not mean to keep this one?" she said, not liking anything to be wasted.

"Oh no," replied Augusta. "You can see how worn it is. And this one is so much finer. You may throw that in the basket."

"May I keep it then," asked Mary, "if you have no other use for it?"

Augusta scoffed, "If you wish."

Mary folded the ribbon neatly and made to leave, when Augusta sighed loudly and turned to her. "Oh, Polly," she said. "I simply cannot make this lie straight. Would you ask Ellie if she might fix it for me?" She handed the gown and the ribbon to Mary, who walked back across the room and took them for her, feeling a little pity for Augusta's incompetence and her laziness, so complete as to prevent her knowing even the satisfaction of sewing a ribbon to a skirt.

The next morning Mary rose early, eager to try her new boots outside before breakfast. She laced them on over thick stockings so they would not be so loose, tied Augusta's old white ribbon in her hair, and feeling rather more elegant than was her wont, slipped out of the sleeping house into the crisp and dewy sunlight. She would keep to the paths to spare her boots, which she would not dare expose to the mud and damp of her usual walking route through the woods behind the house. If she were not anxious to preserve her new gift for her own sake, she would certainly take care not to offend her aunt with her ingratitude by ruining them on her first day of ownership.

She wandered out into the park in no particular direction, imagining, as she often did on her outdoor ramblings, what her future might hold. Her musings were of rather an optimistic turn this particular morning, and while she sometimes dwelt on the misery which might await her, today she permitted herself to imagine her favourite fantasy. She dreamt of meeting with a pilgrim of some description, and that he might fall in love with her and take her as his bride, to travel together in blissful poverty. Or perhaps they might be taken in by a wealthy and pious family in the North who would give them a small living by which they could minister to the needy. It was not a grand dream, nor likely to come true, but in it her life had some worth. In it she was loved and exceedingly happy, and to it she thus frequently returned. If it should come true this very morning, at least she was well shod for traveling by foot.

There had not been much rain in the last few days, and she had an easy time making her way through the park. Fond of a brisk walk, and accustomed to rougher terrain, she had soon covered all the pathways of the garden and found herself coming out the other side of it. Here the path followed the edge of a small forest which bordered the main road. Hearing a snap in the trees, she turned in sudden fear to see what was there. Peering into the dark of the shade, she could see a small child, a girl it seemed, staring back at her. Both of them stood a moment, frozen in apprehension.

The child seemed quite alone, however, and Mary decided after a few panicked heartbeats that she must be lost. She could not have been more than six years old. Mary crouched down and beckoned the little girl forward, smiling to dissipate any fear. The girl came slowly forward into the light, exposing her ruddy dress and haystack of hair.

"Good morning, miss," said Mary gently. "What is your name?" But the girl kept her head down and would not speak. "My name is Mary," she continued, at which the girl raised her head suddenly with a smile, saying–

"Mine is too!"

"Is not that too great a coincidence?" said Mary with an exaggerated expression of amazement. "I am Mary Green. How about you?"

"Mary Potts," said the girl with a curtsey and a shy giggle.

"And how did you, Miss Mary Potts, come to find yourself alone here in this wood?"

"Oh, I am not alone," said the girl quite plainly. "My parents are only back there." She pointed through the trees, then bent down to pick a flower from the edge of the path. She handed it to Mary, who took it with a gracious nod of the head. The girl then picked a second flower and, smiling up at Mary, took an unembarrassed bite from it. Mary blinked in surprise.

"Are you eating that dandelion?" she said. The girl nodded.

"They are not so bad, if you only eat the yellow parts," she said. Mary's sentiments turned instantly from shock to compassion. She longed to do something for this child, but what could she do?

"Are you hungry?" she asked, to which the girl shrugged.

"Not especially," she said. "I mean, no more than usual."

Mary's heart ached for this little creature, and her parents, who had nothing to feed her but wildflowers. "Do you think you could wait here a few minutes?" she asked. "If you wait right here, I will bring you something." The girl shifted on her feet and looked over her shoulder into the forest. "You need not fear," said Mary. "You are Mary and I am Mary, and so you may trust me."

The girl seemed to follow this ill-reasoned logic and nodded her head. "I shall be right back," said Mary, rising and darting off at a run along a direct route back towards the house.

Panting, she entered the breakfast room, where the others were already seated. Mary took her seat and began to gather as many items as would fit on her plate. "I am rather famished this morning," she said, by way of explanation. "I went for quite a long walk. In fact," she paused, gathering her courage, "it is such a beautiful day, I think I should like to take my breakfast out of doors. That is, if you do not mind, Sir Richard."

"Not at all," replied Sir Richard. "Shall I have the kitchen make you up a basket?"

"Oh, that is quite all right," she answered hastily, opening up her napkin and piling her food onto it, adding a few lumps of sugar on the top and folding into a precarious parcel. "I shall do very well with just this." As she rose from the table, she caught the suspicious and warning glare of Aunt Preston, at whom she simply smiled awkwardly, and left the room. Once out of the door, she set off again at a run, and with pounding heart and burning breath, arrived back at the edge of the forest where the younger Mary now sat, building a tower of pebbles beside the path.

Assured that she was not too late to help her new little friend, she stopped, bent over, gripping the napkin full of breakfast in one hand, and her side with the other. She began to hear a noise from the forest–footsteps and a woman's voice calling, "Mary!"

Not yet master enough of herself to speak, she looked at the child, who rose to her feet and turned back to the forest and then again to Mary, unsure what to do. Mary straightened herself up, and the girl called to her mother, waving her arms, "I'm over here!" The child's mother came into view and, seeing Mary on the path, stopped, gesturing to her child to come away.

"It's all right," Mary managed to call out. "I-I just brought a little something," she stuttered, holding out the napkin. The girl's mother rushed forward and pulled the little child towards her, looking to either side of Mary to see if anyone else was there. Mary took a step forward and set the napkin down on the grass beside the path, opening it to reveal three pieces of toast, some cake, and two eggs–as much as Mary could fit in the little parcel, and as much as she felt was hers to take. "I am sorry it is not more," she said. The girl burst out from her mother's grip, and rushed forward to collect the lumps of sugar. She put one in her pocket and handed two more to her mother.

"One for you and one for Papa," she said, then returned to the pile of food, sat down and began to eat from the cake. The mother smiled shyly and came forward to join her daughter.

"Thank you," she said, taking a piece of toast and an egg and placing them in her pocket. "For my husband," she explained. He would be too proud to take it from you, but he will take it from me." She then took the other egg and began to remove the shell. Mary watched, a multitude of questions tugging at her mind, but politeness preventing her from asking any of them. Seeing her expression, the girl's mother volunteered their story. "We are on our way to Wycombe," she said. "I have a brother there who says there is work to be had in some new factory. My husband was a farm worker, but I am sure he can learn a trade. He is very clever."

"I am sure he is," said Mary, smiling at the little girl and her mouthful of cake. She reached up and took the white ribbon from her hair. It was a little worn, but shone like new when she tied it round the little girl's head, making a tidy little bow. The girl smiled brightly up at her mother, who stroked her cheek.

"Thank you," she said to Mary, without looking at her.

"I am sorry I have not more to give," she said. "I have nothing of my own." Mary looked at the woman's boots, which were coming apart at the toes. She wondered if her old boots might fit. They were very well used, but might do better than what this lady presently wore.

"We should be going," said the girl's mother, taking the last of the food from the napkin. "Thank you very much for this. We have a long way yet to go, and we must make use of the daylight. God bless you." She rose to her feet.

"Oh," said Mary, "but I have just thought of something. If you could just wait here, I would not be long. It would make me so happy to be able to be of some use." The woman shrugged her acquiescence and Mary set off again, running over the same stones for the third time that morning. She leapt up the stairs to her room to retrieve the old boots, stopped only to gulp a quick drink, and departed again. She was not as quick as she had been the first time, for her legs were growing tired, and she cursed her tardiness as she approached the spot where she had left them, for they were no-where to be seen. Seeing the napkin on the path ahead, she walked grudgingly over to retrieve it. As she leaned down to pick it up, she saw a message in the grass–a little pile of stones in the shape of a heart, and beside it a letter 'M' traced in the dirt with a stick. Her heart broke at the sight of this simple gesture, and she began to cry, though without quite understanding why.

Slowly she made her way back to the house, and as she did so, she thought about what else she could have done. Looking down on her feet, she watched her new boots crunch along the path. Had she been higher born, she might have seen no injustice in her having something so nice when someone else did not, but she had been raised to know her station as no better than that of the woman she had just met, and she began to wonder whether she ought to have given her the Nankeens. It would have been an immense gesture to give up something so treasured and new to one she had only just met, but the more she thought on it, the more she chastised herself that she had not done exactly that. It would have saved the time of another trip back to the house, and she would not have missed them on her return. She told herself it would have enraged her aunt and offended her uncle, but she knew it would more likely have gone entirely unnoticed. She felt convinced it was her own desire to retain the only thing she had ever had new. Was it so wrong to wish to keep them? Dorothea and Augusta would not dream of part-ing with theirs to a traveling farmer's wife. But Mary did not wish to judge herself by the standard of her cousins. They were not the mark by which she measured her own conduct, and she thought it would have been a far finer thing to have such generosity than to have a new pair of boots that nobody would ever see, though she was not certain she had such capacity for selflessness.

As she entered the house, she was greeted by the boisterous sound of Augusta, vigorously rehearsing her musical piece for next week's dinner. Mary's thoughts thus turned to that quickly approaching evening. She had only a few days to prepare for a performance for which she was entirely unqualified, and which threatened to embarrass not only herself but all the family and guests who would be forced to endure it. She climbed up to her room, threw her boots to the corner with a sigh, and took out Augusta's long-discarded and poorly copied musical dictation, which was Mary's only instruction in the art she loved so well.

Chapter Six

That week was an anxious one for Mary, though rendered a little less so by the unexpected attentions of Aunt Preston, who procured a little-used gown from Dorothea for her to wear, and even arranged for her to practice a few minutes on the Broadwood while Sir Richard was out. The result did little to allay her fears of playing in public. She traced the shape of the instrument's keys onto paper, which she then spread out on the dressing table in her room so that she could rehearse her fingering in silence. This expedient was not very effective, since she could not hear her mistakes to correct them.

On the day of the dinner, Mary was surprised to find that Aunt Preston had arranged to send Ellie to her to fix her hair. Ellie usually acted as lady's maid to the Hargreaves girls, but rarely attended Mary unless to ask her assistance or advice. Mary did not understand why Aunt Preston was so keen to show her to advantage in the presence of Sir Richard. She was usually so quick to belittle her as a means of aggrandizing her nieces. It was not, however, in Mary's nature to refuse any sort of privilege, and she welcomed Ellie's powers of beautification in hope that she might, for once, be more than tolerably presentable at a social occasion.

Ellie did not have a surplus of time to complete her task, but managed some very becoming curls and a pretty arrangement of ribbon before she was needed in the other end of the house.

"Oh, Ellie," said Mary as she took in her image in the glass, "I do believe you must have a little of the pixie in you to work such magic in so little time. Thank you, truly. With Dorothea's gown, I shall not be at all disgraced." She touched the simple cross which hung on a ribbon around her neck and added, "If only I had something more fitting in the way of jewels. My little necklace seems so out of place now."

"Did not Miss Preston tell you I was to give you these?" responded Ellie, taking a box from the basket in which she had brought all her tools. She handed the box to Mary, who took it with a look of uncertainty. Opening it, Mary gasped, for it contained a ruby and sapphire necklace and matching earrings belonging to Aunt Preston.

"Are you quite certain she meant for you to give these to me?" she asked in disbelief.

"Oh yes," answered Ellie. "She was very clear. She said she thought you might wish for something to wear to dinner. She did not mean for you to keep them, mind."

"No, of course not. Still, it is uncommonly generous of her."

Ellie simply shrugged and began to gather her things. "Perhaps she does not wish you to disgrace the family in front of the Ingles."

"Perhaps," said Mary as Ellie turned and departed.

Mary stared at the necklace. She did not trust this behaviour on the part of Aunt Preston. It could not be for the benefit of the Ingles. She knew Lord Marsden had gone back to town, much to the disappointment of Augusta who had failed to entice him into offering her a dance at the Westley Ball and who had been hoping for another opportunity of catching his eye. Mr. George Ingles was all but betrothed to Dorothea, and Mr. Ingles did not care for finery. What is more, Aunt Preston was always quite pleased for Mary to appear a little impoverished and pathetic, as she would never risk Mary's outshining her nieces.

She was certain there was some mischief behind the loan of the necklace, though she could not understand what that might be. Did Aunt Preston intend to accuse Mary of stealing the jewels? Would nobody believe Ellie's word that Aunt Preston gave them willingly? Was Ellie complicit in the plot? Could something so devious really be in Aunt Preston's nature? She had always been callous and dismissive, but never had there been anything to suggest she might be capable of such a level of willful deceit.

Unable to explain the offer, and even more unwilling to face Aunt Preston's wrath for her ingratitude, she put on the necklace and marvelled at her appearance. She felt she could pass for a princess of the realm and for a brief instant forgot about having to play the pianoforte. She remained most of the day in her room, anticipating some commotion amongst the family that she wished to avoid. She therefore occupied herself in rehearsing on her paper instrument until she heard footsteps coming down the hall in so flustered and tripping a way as could only signify that Augusta was approaching, followed by a pert knock upon her door.

Mary folded her paper keys, calling–

"Come in!" as she stuffed them into her drawing case. Augusta fluttered in, closing the door neatly behind her.

"And what are you secreting away there, Polly?" she asked, pointing to the case. "I hope it is something devilishly clandestine and surprising."

"I am sorry to disappoint, but it is nothing," replied Mary. "It is just my drawing case."

"Oh," said Augusta. "Well, you do keep them secret enough, though I do not see why you must conceal them from me, when I am the closest to a sister as you have." Augusta sat down upon the little bed.

"Did you come to ask about my pictures?" asked Mary, with

more than a hint of pleading in her voice. In truth, it was not entirely out of modesty that she did not show her pictures to anyone. It was also in part because she was never asked. Although she dreaded any criticism of what was to her an extension of her own self, she also longed to hear her work praised, to show off the skill she had honed with no instruction or assistance whatever. Given adequate assurance of kindness, Mary would not scruple to expose her entire life's work to a sincerely interested audience.

"Not exactly," Augusta answered and held out a copy of Ackermann's, turned to one of the fashion plates. "Ellie is attending to Dorothea just now, and I must make up my mind how I am to do my hair this evening. Will you tell me what you think of this?"

Mary took the picture from Augusta and examined it. It bore the image of rather a tall lady, wearing a turban with extensive, coloured feathers. She thought it would threaten to drown the poor girl, but doubted she could convince Augusta of her opinion.

"Will there be time to put this together?" she asked. "It is elegant, to be sure, but do you think Ellie can manage it? Would not it be better to do something simple that you know you can achieve? It is rather late to experiment. Guests will be arriving in only two hours. There shall not be time to do it over if you do not like it."

"I do not fear on that account. I know Ellie to be very skilled, and she shall make it look quite perfect, I am sure." Augusta took back the picture. Mary expected her to leave again in the same abrupt manner she entered, but instead she sat a moment on the bed, attempting to enter a new and possibly awkward subject.

"Polly," she began, "do you think there is any hope that a gentleman might prefer me to Dorothea? I know she is to marry Mr. George Ingles, but until they are formally engaged, she continues to draw everyone to her. Even Lord Marsden danced with her at the

Westley ball. Did you know that?" She did not give Mary time to respond. "I could not even catch his eye, a gentleman like that. He is so elegant, so handsome, and a title awaiting him. If only he would look at me, how happy I would be, and yet she dances with him, and does not care. She takes it so for granted that they all follow her like puppies. When she is done toying with them all, she shall have her beau, and I shall have lost my bloom and die an old maid."

"I doubt that very much," said Mary, sitting down beside her. "There were many gentlemen who asked you to dance also. When you forget your sister, and simply enjoy yourself, you are just as admired as she is. You shall not want for proposals, mark my word." Augusta looked up at her. "Were there no gentlemen at the ball who gave you any cause to hope? Speak truly."

"Well," a coy grin began to appear on Augusta's countenance, "there was one very handsome soldier."

"Go on," urged Mary.

"He is a colonel in the Militia. His name is Briggs, and we have met several times before. I did not at first detect any peculiar regard for me, but he did ask me to dance at the ball, and was very gallant. I asked Aunt Preston to invite him to the dinner, and he has agreed to come. Surely that must mean he wishes to see me. Do not you think? Why else would he accept? He could easily have invented an excuse if he did not."

"That is very promising," said Mary. "And doubtless, he was and is not your only prospect. If you can stir such a passion in one dance, then I am afraid I cannot share your fears of never inspiring a worthy gentleman to matrimony."

Augusta laughed. "I suppose you are right," she said with a sigh. "I suppose I must not allow Dorothea to discourage me." After a pause she added, "But Mary, what about you?" It may have been the first time Augusta had taken any interest in Mary's future, and she did not know how to respond. "How are you ever to find a husband? You have no dowry, nor any family."

It was said not in spite but as a passing, honest thought spoken mindlessly aloud, and it was not new to Mary, the assumption that there was little hope of her ever receiving an offer of marriage. No one had ever discussed Mary's future with her before, and when she thought of the subject, it was never with any grand expectations, though perhaps with some fond hopes.

"Oh, do not worry about me," she said. "Perhaps I shall stay here to keep Aunt Preston company when you both are married and moved away. Or, if I am very lucky, I might meet with some humble curate from a lowly family but with a kind heart. Such a man may not mind the obscurity of my birth and could carry me off to his remote parish. I think I would be quite happy with either destiny." Indeed, she would have been quite overjoyed with the latter possibility, though she knew it was by far the less likely.

Augusta nodded. Having never really wished to consider in any depth the future of her cousin, she abruptly returned to her favourite subject, being that of her own person. "Perhaps you might take my likeness some time," she said. "That is, you are so fond of drawing, and you must sometimes want for a subject, and I have never had my portrait done you know. I know you do not let others see your work, but I think it would do well enough for me. I thought perhaps Papa would like to take it with him when he goes, you know, to remember me by."

Mary considered for a moment the drawing she had recently done of Augusta at the ball. She was quite proud of it, and had wished there might be a way of hearing it praised. Augusta was just vain enough that she might extol anything bearing her own image.

"You know I am not accustomed to showing my drawings to anyone. They are so very private to me. But if you thought it might bring your father some joy, it is possible I might be convinced to make an exception. He has been so kind to me."

Augusta jumped off the bed, clapping her hands.

"Oh, Polly!" she cried. "You make me the happiest of women. I may sit for you any time you like."

"That may not be necessary," Mary replied, "for it happens that I have already completed a portrait of you."

"But that is not possible," Augusta mused, "for I have never sat for you before."

"If I required my subjects to sit for their portraits, I should have nothing but pictures of myself or the trees," said Mary, opening her case, careful to position herself between the drawings and Augusta so as not to reveal her other work. Finding the desired piece, she held it facing herself and closed the case. "You must promise to hide your opinion if it be not favourable."

"But of course!" she heartily agreed, gesturing for Mary to show her the picture. Mary passed it to her, facing the floor. Augusta took it and held it up to view it. "Polly!" she gasped. "It is perfection itself! You are so cruel to have kept such a treasure hidden for so long. If you have drawn this from mere memory, there must be no limit to what you might achieve." She paused and looked at Mary, whose modest countenance was turned down in a blushing grin. "You must not keep your talent secret any longer. Do allow me to show this to Mr. George Ingles."

Mary looked up in sudden confusion.

"Mr. George Ingles?" she repeated.

"Why, of course. He has the most thorough knowledge of art of anyone we know. He might do something for you, you know, for

I believe he knows all the painters in London, if not the whole of Europe." Augusta thought this a very good scheme for increasing her own standing in the eyes of the neighbourhood. She had always considered herself an expert in beauty, and if she were to discover a great artist, it could not fail of increasing her esteem. What is more, it was an excellent excuse to reacquaint everyone with the delights of her person, as shown in the portrait itself. "Please say I may show it to him. I should have it framed and hung in the front hall, where everyone might see it and remark on its beauty, but I shall limit myself to Mr. Ingles, if you insist upon it. Only do say he may see it."

Unaccustomed to flattery of any kind, Mary found herself powerless to resist such an appeal and agreed that Augusta might show the picture to Mr. George Ingles that evening, if chance should allow it, but to no one else. And if he should approve of it, and Mary become a celebrated artist, that Augusta should have her share of the credit.

appears as though they have not touched it for days. And the same is true of their dress. I assure you, Mary was merely trying her hand at this fashion. It is not something I approve of, but then I am an old spinster. I am not to be listened to, and I am certain my aunts did not approve the fashions of my youth." Aunt Preston was forever proclaiming herself to be aged when, in truth, she was barely ten years the senior of Dorothea.

"Is that really what fashions have come to in my absence?" Sir Richard responded with an incredulity that could not threaten to match that of Mary, hearing all this from the hallway. If Aunt Preston was to defend her, which was itself surprising enough, what need was there to invent this falsehood? Why not simply point out that Mary had not the means to attire herself to the standards of the Hargreaves girls?

The voices within the dining room grew louder as footsteps approached the door. Mary slipped her trembling self into the shadow of a doorway as Aunt Preston and Sir Richard strode off back to the drawing room.

It was several minutes before Mary could compose herself enough to return to the company, and she arrived just in time to welcome the first of the guests. She was so distracted by what she had overheard that she could hardly hear the compliments she received, nor make conversation with the neighbours who were introduced one by one. Matters did not improve much over dinner. Mary had long tolerated her inferior station within the household. She had always considered herself very fortunate in her situation, and received with gratitude what she was given by the Hargreaves girls, be it gowns, books, or odd bits of learning. To be housed, fed, and clothed, not to mention somewhat educated, and all without requiring any labour from herself was more than a penniless or-

Chapter Seven

Mary descended the stairs, feeling a little presumptuous in Dorothea's gown and Aunt Preston's jewels, yet enjoying the increase in her own self-regard which they occasioned. Sir Richard was just crossing in front of the stairs as Mary arrived at the landing. Seeing her, he halted.

"Why, Mary, how lovely you are this evening," he said. Mary stopped where she was and curtseyed, blushing and bowing her head, uncertain where to look.

"Come, my dear," he added, holding out his hand to her. "It does me good to see you looking so fine." Mary made her way down the remaining stairs. "I hope I have done well by my poor sister, and seeing you look such an elegant and presentable young lady makes me flatter myself that perhaps I have not entirely disappointed her."

Mary gave Sir Richard her hand as she reached the bottom of the staircase, and he took it with such a sorrowful smile she thought he might begin to weep. He did not, however, but only patted her hand with absent-minded affection as she replied, "I am sure you have done as much as could be expected of any uncle, sir, and more so, for I was not even her child. For an orphan such as myself, you have done very well indeed."

"Perhaps you are right," he replied, as he led her to the drawing room to join the others, who were already assembled, awaiting the arrival of the guests. Aunt Preston was quick to remark on her appearance.

"My dear Mary," she said. "You do look charming. Is not she lovely this evening?" she added, looking to the sisters who looked as confused as Mary, who could not recall ever hearing Aunt Preston speak such kind words to her. It may indeed have been the first time she had heard her speak her proper name.

Dorothea took in Mary's appearance.

"I always did like that gown," she said, which was the nearest to praise that she had ever spent on Mary.

"Thank-you," Mary replied with a curtsey. "And thank-you, Aunt Preston, for the loan of your jewels. It was very generous of you."

"Not at all, my dear!" Aunt Preston returned emphatically. "You do them much credit with your youth and beauty. They should be ridiculous on an old lady like myself. They are yours whenever you should wish to wear them."

Mary was as overwhelmed as she was perplexed, but before she could express herself Augusta called to her from the sofa.

"Come and sit with me, Polly," she said, an invitation Mary readily accepted. Aunt Preston began to speak to Sir Richard about the meal they were to enjoy, and the excellent price she was able to secure for the fowl. Augusta leaned in close to Mary and asked her in a whisper whether she had placed the drawing in the breakfast room, as they had discussed.

"I thought I had better wait until after dinner," replied Mary, "lest the servants might clear it away, or others might see it."

"You may not have a chance after dinner," Augusta hissed. "Go and do it now, before the guests arrive. Place it face-down if you must, but hurry."

Mary rose to follow Augusta's command, and was preceded out of the room by Aunt Preston, who was leading Sir Richard to the dining room to seek his approval of the proposed seating arrangement for the guests. Mary skipped up the stairs to her room, where she retrieved the picture and hurried back down to the breakfast

room, as careful not to be seen as she was not to tread on her ─. She placed the picture face-down, as suggested, and under a v─ the servants would know it was not left there by carelessnes─ she crept back towards the drawing room.

Slipping silently through the hall, she passed the door─ dining room, where Aunt Preston and Sir Richard were stil─ erating. The door was slightly ajar, and she stopped when sh─ her name spoken. It was Sir Richard's voice she heard.

"It is about Mary," he said gravely. "I was so very pleas─ her appearance this evening." Mary allowed herself to feel ─ of his praise, which was not long in duration, for he cont─ did not wish to say anything, for it is a delicate subject, ─ rather disappointed to see her looking so, well, to speak ─ ragged the night I arrived home. I do wish she would ta─ care of her person. She has been given every opportunity ─ not to make every effort to profit by it, I hate to say it, bu─ a little of ungratefulness."

Mary's heart began to race and her cheeks to burn. ─ Sir Richard say such a thing? She had nothing of her ow─ to improve herself. She had spent hours repairing Do─ gown to make it presentable. She had no maid to do he─ could she be expected to do any more than she already ─ achieve?

If Mary were hurt by Sir Richard's remarks, she wa─ Aunt Preston's reply, for it neither condemned her unju─ dicated her on any truthful grounds.

"You have been away many years, Sir Richard," sh─ "You do not know how fashions have changed. It is v─ for young ladies to dress as though they had spent no ─ their appearance. Girls might spend hours fixing their ─

phan could hope for. She had often dreamt of what it would be like to have the privileges that her cousins took for granted, but she did not resent the disparity of their stations. However, to be criticized for those very wants over which she had no control, and which she had always accepted gracefully as her lot, despite the constant indignation of her fellows, was more than her mind could peaceably ignore, particularly as the wound was so fresh.

She was sat next to Mr. Ingles, for which she was thankful, for his was the only company which did not press upon her, and whose wisdom and solace, as a clergyman, she felt must support her. She had previously counted Sir Richard as one of the only people who regarded her as an equal, and did not think less of her for her want of wealth or family, but now she felt Mr. Ingles alone in that count. These reflections were interrupted as she caught the end of something Mr. George Ingles was saying to Dorothea across the table.

"My brother, Mr. Ingles, shall be off to Africa before we know it."

She turned to her neighbour, asking with stilted apprehension, "Is this true, sir? Will you be leaving us, leaving the country?"

"It is possible," he replied. "My brother does enjoy a good bit of gossip, and so jumps to the most extraordinary possibility as if it were settled fact, but yes, I have written to one of our missionary societies and they may have a post for me somewhere on the African continent."

"I see," Mary replied, looking down at her plate. Her only friend in the world was to leave her company forever, and the news of it was forced upon her on an evening already full of such dejection.

"We shall all be very sorry to lose you," she said and placed a small morsel in her mouth, forcing herself to chew.

"Nothing has been settled, however, and if I do go, it shall not be for many months. There would be much to arrange." Mary nodded.

"Were I less sure of my calling, I should stay exactly where I am. It is no small sacrifice to give up my home, my family, my friends, everything familiar, but I must do what I can to bring the teachings of our Lord to all His children. I must not think of my own suffering when there are those who may not otherwise taste the sweetness of salvation and I am able to bring it to them. And you must consider matters the same way. The loss of me to this neighbourhood is nothing, but the loss of so many souls for the sake of so little cost is tremendous."

"I shall endeavour to think of it that way," declared Mary, forcing a smile.

"How interesting," Aunt Preston's voice came from down the table. "Dorothea and Augusta have just put together rather a large donation for our missionaries. They are always thinking of others, you know, and decided they could do without many of their things, for the benefit of the Church."

"That is quite true!" agreed Augusta. "I have given my boots, for example."

"You have given your new boots to the missionaries?" asked Mary in astonishment.

"Oh, not the Nankeens," she answered. "I mean the brown ones."

"I see," said Mary, "of course."

Augusta sensed that her generosity might have been called into question. "They were still in very serviceable condition," she said. "I do hope you will decide to add yours to the collection." Augusta flashed her a look of triumph and then simpered to her neighbours.

Mary would gladly have given her boots to the missionaries, if she had known anyone was collecting such donations, although she was not certain they were in respectable enough condition even to be given away.

"I am quite sure the Church will be most grateful for all this family's support to the missionary efforts abroad," said Mr. Ingles. "If only we could somehow send them some of this mutton," he added, to a round of amused and muttered agreement.

Dinner concluded more swiftly than Mary would have liked, for its end marked the drawing near of the musical entertainment of which she was expected to form a part. The party moved joyfully into the music room, where chairs were arranged to form an audience for the pianoforte. Dorothea was invited to play first, and all were in raptures with her abilities, for she played with deft artistry and sang in rich and effortless tones. Next was Augusta, who chose a more vigorous piece, which she performed with enthusiasm, particularly for the higher notes.

As Augusta rose from her seat to receive her applause, Mary's heart raced and she thought she might faint from trepidation. Indeed, she wished she would, for that would spare her the impending ordeal. Perhaps she ought to have affected a fainting spell, but she had not the clarity of thought at the time to carry out such a scheme. In silent terror, she approached the instrument, sat herself down and opened the music. Placing her fingers on the keys, she drew in a breath for courage and began. Her first chord was flat.

"Sorry," she managed to croak, then swallowed hard and began again. Her first few bars were without incident, but when it came time to sing she found she could not manage both. Her voice cracked and her fingers began to stumble. She forced her way through one verse, hitting all manner of notes along the way, after which she struck a concluding dissonant chord and left the bench, her eyes burning with restrained tears and her throat throbbing with the urge to cry.

The guests looked at each other, uncertain of how they should respond, all but one that is, for Mr. Ingles could be relied upon to act the gentleman, or at least to be ignorant enough about music to believe he had been witness to a commendable performance. He began to applaud vigorously and the others were required by politeness to join in. Mary passed them briskly as she all but ran from the room, stopping only to mutter something about a headache to a stern-looking Sir Richard as she departed.

Once in the safety of the hallway, she leaned against the wall for support, heaving a silent, pitiable sob. After a moment, she heard the sound of laughter coming from the far end of the corridor, in the direction of the breakfast room. Her curiosity overcoming her other feelings, she took a few steps towards it, only to be further mortified by the discovery that it was the laughter of Augusta and Mr. George Ingles, and the subject of their merriment was her own handiwork.

"She fancies herself quite the artiste," she heard Augusta say. "Did you ever see the like?"

Frenzied giggles ensued, united with more masculine guffaws. Mary could suffer no more. Holding up her skirts, she ran through the corridor and bounded up the stairs to her room, where she bolted the door behind her and threw herself on her bed to weep away the compounded despair of the whole wretched evening.

Chapter Eight

Morning did not bring Mary much relief, and it would be several days before her troubles would be dissipated by a most unusual occurrence. The force of her tears had brought on the headache she had falsely claimed the night before, which gave her cause at least to forego breakfast, and all the chatter that might go with it. She did not care to sit through the recounting of everyone else's joyous and charming evening, of all George Ingles' flirtations and false flattery. She might have liked hearing of Mr. Ingles, but since he was not prone to frivolity, she doubted very much that any of the family would have found anything in his conversation worth repeating. She wished she could speak to him now, if only to give him the confession of her ungenerous thoughts against everyone at Challey Hall. She had attempted to soothe her injuries with all the reasoning which had previously saved her from spite, but it was ineffectual in the face of the combined insult which had struck her in so unexpected a manner.

Mary was spared any further remonstrance regarding her performance on the pianoforte by the disingenuous succour of Aunt Preston, who responded to the rage of Sir Richard with excuses that Mary wanted for talent at music, and that Sir Richard could not expect every young lady to be as gifted and accomplished as his own daughters, whose abilities, she argued, were indeed rare. Perhaps it was cruel of them, she posited, to force such a blundering creature to display her inadequacies so publicly. Though Mary would not hear the subject raised, she could not escape the memory of her humiliation, and she was not sure whether it was worse than the feigning condescension and pity of Aunt Preston.

The matter of Mary's picture was also not to be left in peace. Augusta visited her room later that day and Mary was forced to hear from her lips how Mr. George Ingles had mocked her.

Augusta handed the picture to Mary saying, "I am afraid he did not express the same admiration for your skill that you had hoped for."

"That *I* had hoped for?" repeated Mary.

"Yes. He said it was quite amateur. Practically scoffed at it, he did."

"And did you laugh with him?" asked Mary, knowing the answer but hoping at least for some satisfaction in hearing an admission from Augusta.

Augusta shrugged. "I may have. He is so sure he knows everything there is to know about art. There is no point arguing with him, and it would hardly be polite to ask someone's opinion and then disagree with it. All the same, I do not think he shall be advancing your dream of artistic renown."

"*My* dream?" Mary challenged, for it had been Augusta's dream that she had pushed on Mary, who objected to the idea from the start. And now it was Augusta who ridiculed the ambition which she had only consented to at Augusta's own urging. "I should never have shown this picture to anyone had not you persuaded me. I should not have shown it even to you, only you insisted so."

"I was only trying to help," huffed Augusta, who had never heard anything like anger from her cousin, and who subsequently left the room in abrupt and haughty confusion.

A strained and quiet peace remained in the house for several days following, until one morning Mr. George Ingles appeared in the drawing room with an invitation to a day of revelry in honour of one Mr. Claude Belmont, an artist and a close friend of Mr. Ingles, who was visiting from Paris. Augusta leapt to her feet.

"How delightful!" she cried. "I think we should all be very happy to join you. Should we not, Dorothea?"

Dorothea smiled at their guest. "Of course we shall come. I know Papa would very much enjoy seeing you all again."

As if summoned by the mention of his name, Sir Richard strode into the room at that moment, carrying a letter and removing the spectacles that he wore occasionally for reading. "What is all this that I am to enjoy?" he asked.

"A day at Westley Park, Father," answered Augusta before anyone could draw breath to speak.

"Yes, sir," confirmed Mr. Ingles. "The weather has been so fine, we thought we might have a chance of spending a little time out of doors, perhaps get up a game of ringtoss or some such. The point is just to show my friend, Mr. Belmont, a little of English country life, and introduce him to some good company, which is why I have come to invite all of you."

"It is very good of you to think of us, Mr. Ingles," came the voice of Miss Preston. "But I do not expect to be included. I am sure you do not require the company of a dull old maid such as myself. I should only spoil your fun."

"Not at all, Miss Preston," returned Mr. Ingles. "I mean to invite all of you–you, Sir Richard, Miss Hargreaves, Miss Augusta, and Miss Green." Mary did not look up from her needlework, with which she had been silently occupying herself throughout. Mr. Ingles looked directly at her as he repeated solemnly, "All of you."

"This sounds very kind, Mr. Ingles," said Sir Richard. "And I should be very pleased to see everyone accept your invitation, but I am afraid I shall not be here to be one of the party."

"Whatever do you mean, Papa?" Augusta demanded. "You have not yet heard the date. It is only Wednesday next, and you are not to leave for another threemonth."

"I wish it were so, my dear," answered Sir Richard with a sad smile. Holding up the note in his hand, he added, "I have just had word that I am needed in London. I must leave tomorrow."

"What? But you shall be back," insisted Augusta.

"I shall, but not so soon as I would like," replied Sir Richard. "From London, I go to Scotland. I do not know how long I am to stay there, but I promise I shall return before I leave again for the Indies, though it may not be until the summer is quite concluded."

Even Augusta was momentarily speechless with disappointment. The cost of Sir Richard's knighthood was his constant and lamented absence. He had left to assume his post shortly after his wife had died twelve years earlier, and rarely returned to England. It was years since he was last home, and it seemed he had only just arrived. To have him taken away again so soon was a blow for which she was not prepared, all the more so for having the news delivered in company.

"I feel I ought to take my leave now," said Mr. Ingles. "I am sorry you must go so soon, Sir, though perhaps we may meet in London, as we will be taking Mr. Belmont there in a few weeks."

"I expect I shall miss you, as I do not plan to stay more than a week," responded Sir Richard.

"Well then, I wish you safe travels," said George, shaking hands with Sir Richard in farewell. "As for the rest of you," he said gesturing to the room. "I look forward to seeing you next week."

Dorothea, Augusta and Aunt Preston all confirmed their anticipation of a lovely day at Westley Park and thanked him again for thinking of them.

"And what about you, Miss Green?" Mr. Ingles asked, turning to Mary. "You have not answered. Will you be joining your cousins?"

"Of course she will!" interjected Miss Preston. "She is honoured to be invited, are not you, Mary?"

Mary looked up for the first time since Mr. Ingles' arrival and saw such earnest entreaty on his face as made her wish his character as becoming as his manners. "Will your brother be there?" she asked.

"I expect you mean my brother William," answered Mr. Ingles. "He is in London at the present time, and will be for another month or two. He has meetings with various missionary societies. But I would be very glad to give him your regards when I see him in town. In fact," he added with a pause and a look about the room that spoke of a hatching scheme, "if you intend to come to London for the season, you might see him yourself. I shall be leaving in a fortnight and it would be very convenient for us all to travel together, that is, if Sir Richard approves."

"Oh, please, Papa!" Augusta pleaded before Sir Richard had a moment to consider the proposal. "We have not been to London in an age."

"Well, I had not thought of it, but if your Aunt is willing to chaperone you, I can see no objection, especially if Lord and Lady Rosborough are to be in your traveling party, as well as Mr. Ingles here. I shall be gone before you arrive, but I expect I would not add much to a London season in any event. What say you, Miss Preston?"

"I think it absolutely essential for young ladies to pass as many seasons as possible either in London or Bath, and that it would be greatly in their interest to travel with such company as you have mentioned. In short, I wholly support the idea, and only wonder what we all shall wear."

"One does not buy clothes to go to London," said Dorothea. "One goes to London to buy clothes."

"I fear you shall leave today with a promise of far more of my girls' company than you came here seeking," said Sir Richard to Mr. Ingles.

"Of some things, one can never have too much," said Mr. Ingles, bowing "goodbye" and departing to the sound of feminine raptures and laughter which delighted him so well.

Chapter Nine

It was a sorrowful farewell that saw Sir Richard away from his home after barely a month's residence. Augusta wept openly. Dorothea was more restrained and only gave him a doleful look and a watery smile. Aunt Preston put on a great show of regret, though Mary sensed it was only relief the spinster felt on seeing him go. For herself, Mary was not sure of her own feelings on his departure. She had been so glad to see him when he arrived. He had always had kind words for her, and was the nearest to a parent she had ever known. Yet she could not forget the injustice of his disapproval. She longed to explain away his remarks with some kind of misunderstanding, but she could not surmise any circumstance that might do so.

Sir Richard kissed both his daughters then took Mary's hand tenderly. "I am sorry not to be here for your birthday," he said. It was the first time anyone had mentioned the subject. Mary was certain it had been quite forgot by everyone. "I have missed so many of my own girls', I thought I might at least be here for one of yours. But no matter, I shall send you something pretty to mark the occasion. And there is a very good chance I shall be back in time for Augusta's in the autumn." Taking a last look at his house and his family, he climbed into the carriage, bidding farewell from the window as it rolled off down the drive.

The following days were much as they had been prior to Sir Richard's arrival. Aunt Preston abandoned any of the tender concern for Mary that she had been quick to display for her brother-in-law. Augusta fretted over what to pack for London, and which dances to practice, while Dorothea continued her languid ridicule of her sister.

The morning of Mary's birthday was a bright one, at least as far as the weather was concerned. Mary had been unable to find any cheer in her life since the night of Sir Richard's dinner. She felt she could not remain at Challey Hall the rest of her life. She had no prospect of marriage, for the only society to which she was exposed was far above her expectations. She had thought it over during the past few days and was determined to seek a position as a governess. She had been collecting advertisements from the paper, and planned to reply to a few of them. Her education was not so complete that she could expect to find a position in a very wealthy home, but perhaps there might be a respectable, kind family willing to take her on. Perhaps in some remote corner of the kingdom she might even meet with her humble curate. She did not ask much, only her own sustenance and, if not equality, then at least civilized respect from those around her.

She came down for breakfast, aged one-and-twenty, and wearing a simple house dress.

"You are not wearing *that* to Westley Park!" exclaimed Aunt Preston. Mary did not reply but sat down to table and took a piece of toast. "It is not at all suitable. Do you insist on shaming us all?" Aunt Preston continued.

"No, I do not," replied Mary calmly.

"I am sure I can help you find something after breakfast," offered Augusta. "We shall have a little time, I think."

"Thank-you, Augusta," said Mary. "That is very kind, but it will not be necessary. I am not coming."

"Whatever do you mean?" demanded Augusta. "It is such a fine day, and we shall enjoy ourselves so very much, and you *must* meet

Mr. Belmont. You may not be introduced to his like again. He is from Paris, you know, and a great artist. How can you pass on such an opportunity?"

Mary was not at all convinced, and even less keen to make the acquaintance of yet another gentleman even more qualified than George Ingles to laugh at her.

"You are so good to consider the benefit to me, Augusta," said Mary, "but I do not think the invitation was intended to include me, and besides, I have many things to do today."

"Of course it included you!" Augusta retorted. "Mr. Ingles said he meant to invite us all, and he even asked you particularly whether you would be coming."

"He was forced by politeness to include me because I was in the room, but I do not believe he really intended that I come. I have no wish to impose myself on a party where I am not welcome. It would be awkward, and only ruin everyone's enjoyment."

"It would be infinitely more awkward for us all if you so rudely refuse such a generous invitation which you do not deserve," Aunt Preston's voice was rising, and were she not across the table, Mary might have feared of being struck. "Go and change at once. I will not hear of your being otherwise engaged. What could you possibly have to do that cannot wait until tomorrow?"

"I have some letters to write," answered Mary. She did not rise from her chair, though a flush did rise in her cheeks.

"Letters? What letters? Who could possibly be expecting a letter from you? You have no family, no friends, no acquaintances outside this neighbourhood. There is nobody who should miss hearing from you. There is nobody in the world who should miss you at all."

Mary pushed her chair back from the table. Raising her eyes to Aunt Preston's, she said hoarsely, "Then nobody shall miss me today."

As she rose and turned to go, Augusta pleaded, "Oh, do please come. I shall be lost without you."

Mary looked back at Augusta, her hand still resting on the door knob. She knew her cousin spoke true, that she would be lost without her. Mary always took care of her, but how had Augusta returned her kindness? The memory of her taunting laughter stuck in Mary's throat and she could not quite choke out a reply.

"Is not today your birthday?" remarked Dorothea. Mary could restrain her tears no more, and she pulled the door open, swinging around to leave. Her way was blocked, however, by the figure of a servant, carrying a card in a tray. She tried to step past him.

"Miss Green," he said. She stopped and looked at him as he held the tray out to her. "A Mr. Clark to see you, madam. He is in the drawing room."

"I beg your pardon," she said, all tears and confusion. Had she been looking in the direction of the breakfast room she would have seen Aunt Preston turn quite pale and begin ushering the Hargreaves girls out of their seats.

"A Mr. Clark has just arrived at the door asking to see you, Madam," repeated the servant, gesturing again to the card on the tray. "He waits on your leisure." Mary took the card and the servant departed. It read:

Horace Clark
Barnaby and Cruik
Solicitors

As Mary stood bemused in the doorway, staring at the words on the card, her cousins were pushed past her by Aunt Preston, who shoved them forth saying–

"Come along, girls. We do not wish to be late for the picnic. It would not do to keep Lord and Lady Rosborough waiting. Never mind your cousin. Leave her to her solitude and her glum reflections."

"But *I* would like her to *come*," objected Augusta as they passed through the hall. "And who is Mr. Clark? Do you know, Aunt? Ought not we to stay and find out? I am desperate to know. Polly never has visitors. Does she have a secret lover? I simply must know. What a sensation that would be!"

"I hardly think a scandal a desirable thing," responded Dorothea as they were hustled out the door, a servant rushing out after them carrying their bonnets and pelisses.

Mary stood in the silent hall, composing herself and drying her cheeks. Whatever business this gentleman had with her, he must be quick with it. After the scene that had just transpired in the breakfast room, she was more anxious than ever to find a position away from that place, no matter the terms. Yet she could not deny the mixture of curiosity, hope and dread which took hold of her as she crossed the hall to the drawing room door, pushed it open and stepped into the room.

A neatly dressed gentleman with a sallow face turned to greet her. "Miss Green," he bowed. "How very pleased I am to make your acquaintance."

Chapter Ten

The sallow-faced gentleman did not offer anything further, but stood in comfortable oblivion to Mary's confusion and awaited some instruction.

"You are Mr. Clark," she said, indicating the card in her hand.

"Yes."

"Of Barnaby and Cruik."

"Yes."

"You are a solicitor?"

"I am a clerk."

"To be clear," she said, "your name is Clark and you are a clerk."

The gentleman smiled feebly. "Yes, madam."

"And what is your business with me, Mr. Clark?"

"Why, I am here about your estate," he replied. "You are twenty-one today, are not you?"

"I am."

"As such, it is today that your estate devolves upon you, and therefore, our file is now under your direction."

"I am sorry," said Mary. "I do not understand. I have no estate."

"I do apologize, madam," said Mr. Clark, seeing that his host had not anticipated his visit as he had presumed. "I did send a letter last week to advise you of my coming. It was addressed to Sir Richard, but I expected he would have told you of it."

"Sir Richard is in London," Mary stuttered. "His mail has been forwarded to him there. I am sorry. I know nothing of anything of which you speak. What devolves?"

"Of course, Miss Green. Allow me to explain. Upon reaching the age of maturity, your inheritance comes into your own authority rather than that of your guardians. Until now, your many properties and other funds have been managed by our office, under the direction of your guardians. Now that you are of age, we require your consent to continue to act on your behalf." Noting her continued puzzlement, he directed her attention to a dossier at his feet. "I have brought with me a summary of your accounts for your review. I hope you will find them satisfactory."

Mary determined that the poor gentleman had travelled rather far for no purpose, and was sorry for her shortness with him. "Do sit down," she offered, and he obliged readily. Mary followed suit. "I believe there must be some mistake," she said. "I have no guardians and certainly no estate. My parentage is entirely unknown, you see, so it is impossible that I should have any sort of inheritance. You must be confusing me with Miss Augusta Hargreaves. Her twenty-first birthday is in the autumn, and I do not doubt she might receive something at that time, as her sister did. I am sorry you have come so far for nothing. Did you travel from London today?"

"No, yesterday. I stayed in Wycombe" responded Mr. Clark, more confused than Mary. "But madam," he fumbled on, "there is no mistake. Barnaby and Cruik are the trustees of the estate of Miss Mary Green. We do not, *could* not act for any member of the Hargreaves family. It would be a conflict of interest." Mary struggled to comprehend the significance of what he said. "I confess I am surprised, madam, that you should be so ignorant of your own affairs," he continued. "There is no such thing as a minor person of fortune who has not a guardian–without parents perhaps, but not without guardian. And you have had two. Sir Richard and Miss Preston were appointed by the Court. At first it was only Sir Richard, but when he left England, Miss Preston was appointed also, as someone had to be readily available while Sir Richard was abroad. Did they really never tell you any of this?"

"I have never heard anything of the sort," answered Mary hoarsely, barely able to speak as the implications of all Mr. Clark had said flooded in on her.

"And did they neither tell you of your many material assets?" continued Mr. Clark in evident disbelief.

"Material assets?" repeated Mary. "Do you mean to say that, forgive my vulgarity, that I am in fact rich?"

"You have over eight thousand a year."

Mary thought she would faint.

Mr. Clark calmly took the liberty of ordering tea. In his time as a clerk, he had never had such a delightful task as the one he had been given that day. The unforeseen pleasure of telling a penniless orphan that she was wealthier than half the gentry was as much joy as a man in his position could hope to have in the course of his duties.

He served her a cup of tea, made syrupy with an excessive helping of sugar. He took nothing himself, but watched with unabashed enjoyment as the news of her new station settled upon her. How could this possibly be true? Her head spun so rapidly that she barely held on to consciousness. Speech was out of the question.

When her tea had gone quite cold–for she was too distracted to drink it–he changed it for a fresh cup. After a silence of at least ten minutes' duration, which was as light as air to the two persons observing it, she turned to Mr. Clark. Through all the fog of her hurried thoughts, one clear notion penetrated. She was free.

"You say I am very rich." It was more a statement than a question.

"Yes, madam."

"And I own several properties."

"Yes madam, one rather large one, Norchester, in Gloucestershire, and one in town, as well as a few others."

"I own a house in town!" she repeated with incredulity.

"Yes, madam, in Portman Square."

"Is it vacant? Does it have staff?"

"It was vacated last month in the expectation that you may wish to make use of it for the season, madam. It does not have staff, but Lady Day shall soon be upon us, and you should have your choice of servants then."

"But until then, how might I manage?"

"Do you wish to travel to London before then?" asked Mr. Clark. "I had thought perhaps next month…"

"I wish to leave today," declared Mary, putting down her untouched tea cup and rising from her seat. "You have taken care of my affairs thus far, yes?"

"We have indeed madam, and I hope you will find our work satisfactory." He took up his dossier.

"Then pray, take care of my departure. I have no love for anyone in this house. I will collect a few of my belongings from upstairs and be down in thirty minutes. I wish to give to the poor everything I do not bring with me. The gowns may be a little worn, but many of them were very fine, and would no doubt be received with gratitude by the less fortunate, as they were by me. I may purchase new things in town, may not I?"

"Of course, madam."

"Excellent," said Mary. "I leave everything to you. I shall be ready to depart this cursed place in half an hour."

Mr. Clark took to his assignment with alacrity and set about giving instructions to the servants and ordering a carriage while Mary ascended the stairs. Reaching the top, she paused and heaved a great sigh, then another, which led to a sob, followed by many more. She wept for the lamentable, pathetic life that she left that day. She wept for all that she had endured at the hands of Miss Preston, who had been charged with her welfare, and for all the love she had never known in that place. She wept with a mixture of relief, joy, regret, and all the sorrow she had felt in the past days.

Soon, the questions that began to pose themselves to her mind overpowered her feelings. Who had left her all this property? Was it her parents? Did Mr. Clark know who they were? Could he tell her who she was, where she came from? Would she be permitted to know, or was this to be an anonymous bequest? Why had knowledge of all this been kept from her?

She dried her tears and hurried towards her room. There was so much she wished to ask Mr. Clark, and the whole long journey to London in which to learn the answers to so many mysteries, some of which were already growing clear.

Sir Richard had left Miss Preston with the responsibility of her care and well-being. Was it any wonder then, that Miss Preston would be so concerned that Mary not have any complaints about her treatment, for were she to relay the truth of the matter, what might Miss Preston expect to pay for her malfeasance? She would wish to appear as Mary's champion, to pay Mary every compliment and attention before the gaze of Sir Richard, and keep Mary in fear of his wrath to defend her own interest.

Mary's other feelings gave way to anger as she looked about the nursery which she had never left. Miss Preston had never allowed her to move into one of the bedrooms, nor to refurbish the nursery to make it more suitable to a young lady. When Sir Richard had questioned this on one occasion, Miss Preston had lead him to believe that Mary preferred to stay where she was, that it was a comfort to Mary to remain in the room in which she had stayed when first she came to them, that Mary was sentimental and would not permit any alteration in her situation. Miss Preston would not hear any challenge to this assertion, and repeated in private her threats that Sir Richard would not take kindly to her ungratefulness if she were to contradict her.

Sorting through her things, Mary came upon both her old pair of boots, deemed too decrepit even for charity, and her new Nankeen ones. It was the work of an instant for Mary to choose the old boots. She regretted a little her disregard for Sir Richard's generosity, and thanked him in her heart for having thought of her, but neither he nor anyone else would ever know, and she wished to do now what she had not thought to do in the woods. She slipped on Dorothea's old, cracked discards and added the new Nankeen boots to the charity pile. She could purchase a new pair in London. Completing quickly the balance of her packing, she was instructing a servant as to the disposal of her belongings within the prophesied thirty minutes. On returning to the ground floor, she was greeted by Mr. Clark and a lady whom she had never before seen.

"Are we quite ready, Mr. Clark?" she asked, looking with hesitation between him and the lady.

"Indeed we are, madam," he replied. "Miss Green, I hope you will forgive me the liberty," he added, "I have brought here with me today my sister, Mrs. Burrows." Like a conjurer revealing his feat, he gestured to the lady who curtseyed gracefully. "I did not know whether a companion would have been provided for you, and I thought you might consider allowing me to introduce her as a candidate, and now it seems, well, if you are to return to London with me today, her presence is as providential as it is indispensable. I expect you would not have had time to arrange for some other lady to accompany you."

"Mr. Clark, I asked you to take care of everything, and it seems you anticipated me. I am most grateful. I confess I had considered pilfering Ellie. If I am so very flush, I am sure I could afford a sum that would induce her to join me. I thought I might do it just to spite my cousins, but you have saved me from myself."

"That is a relief," sighed Mr. Clark. "I should not have liked being party to such interference with contractual relations in any event." Turning to the lady beside him he added, "Allow me to present to you my sister, Mrs. Burrows. Her late husband was also a clerk in our firm."

"How do you do, Mrs. Burrows," Mary curtseyed. "Shall we be away then? I should very much like to be hours gone and miles off when Miss Preston and her charges return."

She left a message for Miss Preston with the butler as to what had transpired and did not cast a backward glance as she left the house and climbed into the carriage, riding away from everything she had ever known and on to a life of absolute novelty.

Chapter Eleven

Mrs. Burrows was a kindly woman, but of that breed of caring which best expresses itself in determining for others what is most in their interest. In this way, she was perhaps uniquely suited as the companion to Mary Green, who had in her life barely been required to navigate a half hour's conversation much less the gauntlet that is the world. As he and his sister were in a sense now in the employ of their fellow passenger, Mr. Clark, with a stern look, prevented the otherwise forward and solicitous Mrs. Burrows from entering into any conversation unless spoken to by Miss Green. Being unaccustomed to this station of deference, Mary was unaware of the tedium she was causing her companions by the silence which her much occupied mind occasioned, and not a word was spoken in the carriage until the company were arrived at Wycombe.

At Mary's request, they did not remain, but stopped only to collect their belongings and were off again. The day was yet young for traveling and she was anxious to put as many miles as she could between herself and Challey Hall. As they arrived in that town, however, Mary thought of little Mary Potts, and wondered if they had arrived and settled as they had hoped. She wished more than ever that she had found it in herself to have given the girl's mother her new boots. Mary could buy a dozen more pairs now, and she had given hers to the poor, but she would forever be deprived of helping that particular family, or of making such a grand and noble sacrifice.

Having had a little time for her thoughts to settle, Mary began to awaken to her surroundings and felt now a growing need to know all. She began with the smaller, less daunting inquiries.

"Is it a long journey to London?" she asked. "I have never been there myself."

"Barring any delay, we should arrive tomorrow afternoon," replied Mr. Clark.

"And shall we go directly to my house? What part of the city did you say it was in? Do you think I shall like it?"

Mrs. Burrows, desperate to speak now that she had been spoken to, and increasingly curious at this meek little creature who was yet so decisive and bold as to quit her home in an instant, did not permit her brother the chance to answer.

"Portman Square is a very fashionable place, and we shall go there as soon as we are able. But tell me, is there nothing you shall regret leaving in Oxfordshire?" It was impertinent perhaps, but Mary did not mind. She was not one easily to take offence.

"I only regret that I shall not see the shock on their faces when they hear what has come to pass," replied Mary, allowing herself a small, cautious laugh.

Mrs. Burrows smiled broadly and took Mary's hand in hers. "You shall not miss out entirely," she said. "I waited downstairs while my brother met with you, and I became quite friendly with one of the footmen. He told me everything–how nobody knew you were such an heiress and how differently you had been treated. I asked if he might send word of how the family reacted to the news, and he assured me he would. If I am not mistaken, he was rather pleased to have reason to write, even if it is through my brother's firm."

Mary was stunned by her bold and friendly manner, and yet felt instantly more at ease and more intimate with this stranger than she ever had with the ladies with whom she had lived in such proximity these sixteen years.

Mr. Clark looked earnestly at Mary. "I cannot tell you, madam," he said, "how sorry I am to hear that you were not well treated by your guardians. Our firm has acted as trustee of your estate only, and I hope you will find that we have been diligent in our work. We were not involved in the selection or supervision of your guardianship. However, if indeed they were very cruel towards you, you may have a writ against them, and our firm could assist you in its prosecution. I am only a clerk but I could give you my opinion, if you wish–that is, if you do not mind discussing such things before Mrs. Burrows."

He paused for her reply.

"Certainly," she answered. "I have many questions, which I think shall take us all the way to London, so we might as well start there."

"Well then, let me hear the details of your mistreatment. Were you beaten, or threatened with beating?"

"No, no, nothing like that," answered Mary shaking her head, a little surprised at the suggestion.

"I see. Were you ever refused food or drink? Did they starve you?"

"No."

"Did they fail to provide shelter or clothing? Were you made to sleep outside of the house, in the stables or in the servants' quarters?"

"Goodness, no!" exclaimed Mary. "I slept in the nursery. My clothing, however, was never my own, that is to say never new. I had sufficient clothing, but it was always previously used by Dorothea."

"In the nursery, you say?" Mr. Clark arched his eyebrows. "There may be something in that. Did you have a child's bed, one that was too small for your person?"

"No, I had a full-sized bed, with regular bedding, albeit older bedding, that had been formerly used by the family."

"Was it cold in your room at night? Did you have a fire?"

"Yes, I always had a fire. It would be cold indeed without a fire, especially in winter. It was not that sort of mistreatment, Mr. Clark. It was more of a verbal nature, an attitude, that I was not the equal of the Hargreaves girls, that I did not deserve to stay there, that I was a burden."

"Did any of your guardians ever publicize to another, that is ever say or write to anyone, anything that was untrue of you? If they referred to you as poor, for example, that would not be accurate."

Mary thought for a moment. "I was called an orphan, most certainly, but that is not untrue, as far as anyone knows. I am an orphan, or at least a foundling. My poverty was forever implied, by my dress and by their disdain of me, but I could not say positively that I know of either Aunt Preston or Sir Richard ever stating as much directly to anyone but myself. It would have been vulgar of them, and Aunt Preston does mind her reputation in that sort of thing. But they did deliberately mislead me, at least Aunt Preston. Sir Richard did not tell me anything, but it may be assumed he thought Aunt Preston would have. He did not say anything directly on the subject that I can recall. Was there no wrong in her deceit?"

"Oh, certainly," replied Mr. Clark. "There is everything morally wrong in it, but that does not give rise to a legal remedy in every case. Lying is not itself actionable, unless it forms the basis of some other tort. The same is true for any emotional suffering, I am afraid."

"Well, that does not seem fair or just, but perhaps it is for the best," said Mary. "I do not know that I should wish to drag the matter through the Court in any event. Better I should enjoy my good fortune and forget them all. They shall make their own misery in the end, I expect."

"If I were in your place, I would seek to bring them all down in disgrace and ruin, I shouldn't wonder," remarked Mrs. Burrows. "To think they taunted you so, and made you so unhappy, when you were their superior in every way. I have only known you five minutes and already I can see that."

Mary smiled. She looked forward to keeping company with this lady, who spoke so plainly and was so immediately fond of herself.

"Nevertheless," interjected Mr. Clark, "we shall conduct a full inquiry into how your allowance has been spent. Your guardians were paid no small sum for your keeping, and though it was within their discretion how to spend it for your providing, we must yet determine if there was any wrongdoing."

"They were paid to keep me?" Mary was astonished.

"Of course they were paid!" answered Mr. Clark. "Did you think you trespassed on their hospitality for so many years?"

"I did." Mary reeled from the news. "I was told as much many times. It was always the excuse for my not having new things, not having lessons in music or art, or anything. I cannot believe it. I was begrudged even paper and stubs of charcoal. They were paid real money?"

"Quite a lot of money," replied Mr. Clark. "As I said, we will be doing a full inquiry."

"That is very reassuring, but I should like to see the books myself if I may. It is my money, and I should like to see what is done with it."

"Certainly," said Mr. Clark, taking out his dossier. "It may be a bit awkward in the carriage, but I can show you…"

"Put that away, Horace," said Mrs. Burrows. "She does not need to see it this instant. She has had quite a shock this morning, and continues to have more with every word you say. There shall be plenty of time for figures and the like when we get to London. We shall visit you at your office once we are settled."

"But you have not told me the most important piece of information," Mary resumed, "which is my first and most burning question. Who is it has left me this fortune? You must tell me that now if you know the answer. Is it my parents? Do you know who they were? Can you tell me anything about them? You might imagine for a foundling how pressing this subject might be."

Mr. Clark sighed. "I am afraid I have no knowledge of your parentage, madam," he said. "The bequest comes not from them. I thought you would have known its source. It comes from the Markhams."

"The Markhams left me their fortune?" Such generosity was, to Mary, who had known so little affection in her life, inconceivable. How could they have bestowed so much on someone of so little worth, and of no real connection to them? She had always known, in her heart, that Mrs. Markham had cared for her. In fact it was the memory of her tenderness that supported Mary through the cruelty of the Hargreaves sisters or of Aunt Preston. But she had never pretended to have been so treasured by her as to be designated her sole heir.

"Who are the Markhams?" asked Mrs. Burrows.

"They wanted to be my parents," answered Mary in a stupor. "They took me in from the orphanage, but then they died. That is why I went to live with Sir Richard, because Mrs. Markham was dead. She was his sister. They barely knew me. I was nobody. How could they have left me all their money?" To think that someone had loved her that much, had thought of her welfare in the face of such personal tragedy, was more than she could contain.

"We had been engaged to invest their fortune when Captain

Markham returned from the war." Mary's question did not demand an answer, but Mr. Clark was gratified to supply the facts. Supplying facts was, in effect, one of his most cherished practices. "The Markhams considered you as a daughter quite from the beginning, and wished to ensure you were treated in every way as if you had been their own child. We made arrangements regarding your inheritance, in case of the worst, which was fortuitous indeed, for the worst did, in fact, come to pass. When Mrs. Markham died, her fortune passed to her husband. When he died, it all became yours. You are indebted to their foresight, Miss Green. Had they tarried in this matter, their entire fortunes would have gone to Captain Markham's family and you back to the orphanage."

By now, Mary's countenance was moist and flushed with the heat of tears publicly shed. She could not prevent them. Mrs. Burrows placed her arm around Mary and passed her a handkerchief, signalling to her brother to say no more. The remainder of the journey was thus spent in a compassionate and obliging silence.

Chapter Twelve

By evening they had made it as far as Uxbridge. The night was a restless one for Mary. It did occur to her that she had entrusted her person entirely to these two, who might, for all she knew, be confidence people. What proof had she that they had not invented the entire story as a ruse to steal her away for some sordid purpose of their own? Having never been to London, she could not say with absolute certainty that they traveled towards it now. She comforted herself with the notion that even if they were bandits of a sort, they had at least fed her well, and given her a very cosy room. Perhaps she would join in their scheme, whatever it was, though it was unlikely that anyone should take the trouble of forming such an elaborate design on her if all they said of her were not, in fact, true.

Satisfied that her safety was not, for the present, under any threat, she rose the next morning with exuberance for her newfound position. They departed early, and Mary was almost as keen to hear as Mrs. Burrows was to tell about everything she could purchase and every amusement she could find within the confines of a London season. Mr. Clark, ever alarmed at how ladies could occupy themselves with a single subject for the length of so many hours, kept himself busy running calculations in his head as to what it might cost to outfit a young lady and her companion in a Portman Square house and everything associated with such an address.

The party arrived in town before dinner. Mary could smell the city even before she could see it, and the sound of so many voices, wheels, and horses was immense to a girl who had never known a crowd. She peered into Kensington Gardens as they entered the city. "Wait until you see it on a Sunday," said Mrs. Burrows. "We must get you a proper gown if you are to go strolling about in there."

At Mr. Clark's bidding, the carriage drove around Portman Square, just to give Mary a taste of it, but Mrs. Burrows convinced her new friend that there would be time enough the following day to begin on her new life. She ought, for now, to take some rest and stay with her and her brother at their far less prestigious home on the more easterly side of London. Feeling a little weary and overwhelmed at confronting the size and the bustle of the city, Mary was only too happy to be told what to do, and retired early to a sweet though modest room where she lay the length of the night wondering if she would ever grow accustomed to more grand surroundings.

She was soon to find out, for Mrs. Burrows was possibly more eager than Mary to begin the great undertaking of establishing her in London society. Having spent her own life surrounded by it, yet never really permitted to partake of it due to her relative poverty and insignificance, she delighted in the prospect of presiding over Bond Street, ordering whatever struck her fancy. It made little difference that the purchases were not for herself. It was the thrill of the spending itself that tantalized her. And she had taken quite a liking to her little charge. Mary had a sweetness about her that one did not, as a rule, encounter in London. Mrs. Burrows saw in her an uncommon innocence, and a strength that just might preserve it. She looked forward to sharing with her a lifetime's trove of observation and discernment, to be her guide through the world, of which Mary was so ignorant.

The party was off early the next morning to inspect the house in Portman Square. In fact, it was not quite on the square, but just up from it on Upper Seymour Street. Mary gasped at the size and the beauty of the rooms as they passed through its airy and elegant halls. The house was furnished, though sparsely, and at every turn Mrs. Burrows pointed out to Mary, how the draperies and the furnishings might be augmented to advantage.

"Is this really my house?" asked Mary in breathless disbelief. "Whoever would have dreamt such a thing?"

"It belonged to Mrs. Markham's mother," said Mr. Clark, "who passed it on to her daughter upon her marriage to Captain Markham. We have been able to let it at a very good rate while it awaited your residency."

"And we two ladies are to occupy all this space? I know not how I shall fill it."

"But it is nothing like so large as Challey Hall, and you have lived there all your life, more or less," remarked Mrs. Burrows.

"Yes, but only the nursery was my own. Aunt Preston and the Hargreaves took care of inhabiting the rest of the house. My presence claimed very little of it."

"Well, here shall be entirely bursting with you and no one else," said Mrs. Burrows. "Tell me, what do you love?"

"What do I love?" repeated Mary, discovering that she had never turned her mind to such a question.

"Yes; what colours, what ideas, what sentiments? Who are you Miss Green, that we might find fabrics and ornaments to match?"

"Oh, my, I cannot really say. I have only ever learned to enjoy what was given me, not to seek out what I might prefer. But I do like nature. When I was at Challey Hall, my favourite pastime was to walk in the woods behind the house. I suppose it was in part because I knew I would not be discovered there. None of the family would risk their shoes or their petticoats by seeking me out in the wilderness."

"That is an excellent foundation," declared Mrs. Burrows. "We shall begin with that notion, and see what the shopkeepers can do for us. There is such excellent shopping so very near here. I fear we shall be at great risk of spending all your fortune living in such proximity."

"Oh, I hope so," replied Mary. "I have never spent so much as a penny in all my life. I should be so happy to be poor if I had at one time known the joy of spending an entire fortune in the shops of London."

"With the greatest respect, madam," interjected Mr. Clark, "I very much doubt that."

"Then you have never known the pleasure of a good day's shopping," retorted Mrs. Burrows. "Come, we must seek you out the best mantuamaker, and then away to Cornhill for your shoes. You ought to have been properly brought out years ago, but you shall not suffer for it now, not under my watch." She took Mary by the arm and led her from the house, saying over her shoulder to Mr. Clark, "You may leave us now, brother. You may embark upon the less amusing task of seeking out some staff for this place, while we enjoy ourselves with more pleasant undertakings." Mr. Clark followed them out into the street, and before they parted ways he handed Mary a purse.

"A bit of ready money, in case you should need it," he said. "I took the liberty of withdrawing something for you before I set out to Oxfordshire."

Mary looked inside the purse and gasped. "You do take liberties!" she exclaimed. "There is near a hundred pounds here. I have never seen so much money."

"We shall guard it carefully," said Mrs. Burrows, leaning in to confirm what Mary had declared.

"There is precisely a hundred pounds," replied Mr. Clark with a shrug. "It is mere pin money to you." And with that, he turned and climbed into the waiting carriage.

Mary looked up at Mrs. Burrows, who smiled excessively, squeezed her hand and let loose a girlish giggle. "We are going to have the best day of your life, or at least of mine," she said. "Here, put this away," she added, closing up the purse and tucking it into Mary's reticule. Mary, who ought by now to have grown accustomed to being stunned, shook her head and returned Mrs. Burrows' smile.

"Yes," she said. "I think perhaps you are right." The two ladies laughed gleefully to each other and set off around the corner towards the enchanting and untested ecstasy that was New Bond Street.

Strolling the length of the busy street, the ladies surveyed its offering. In their eagerness, they had left the house quite early, and the streets were not yet infested with shoppers, as they would be in an hour or so. Mary had suggested several shops along the way, but Mrs. Burrows would only be satisfied with the best. Finally coming upon a linen-draper with the most glamorous display in its window, she ushered Mary in.

There was another pair of ladies in the shop, who were being attended to with great solicitation by the shopkeeper–a portly fellow with very little hair. Another attendant stood behind the counter, engaged in arranging the merchandise. The latter turned on hearing them come in, looked them up and down and returned to her present occupation. Mary felt suddenly awkward, standing solitary in the middle of the shop, examining the inferiority of her pelisse. She wore the same house dress she had been in when Mr. Clark called on her at Challey Hall. She had brought very few clothes with her, intending to purchase new ones in town.

Mrs. Burrows glared for a moment at the back of the man behind the counter, flushing with indignation, irate to be snubbed by the likes of these puffed up hucksters and huffing with impatience between him and the other ladies. After a few moments, even they began to feel the situation insupportable. Mrs. Burrows stepped forward. "Excuse me," she said. The man behind the counter turned around.

"May I help you with something?" he asked curtly, looking over the rim of his spectacles at Mrs. Burrows and then Mary.

"Yes," answered the former, hotly. "We would like to purchase fabric for a gown, several in fact, if we are satisfied with the quality and the price."

The other two ladies looked her and Mary up and down and covered their faces, stifling their laughter and their mockery.

"Indeed?" said the shop attendant, raising his eyebrows. Mary fumbled for her reticule.

"We, we are prepared to pay cash," she stuttered, producing the purse and taking out a few bills. The man straightened his back, his expression warming with a smile at the sight of the money. He opened his mouth to speak, but Mrs. Burrows first covered Mary's hand and purse and interrupted him.

"You know, Miss Green," she said, without taking her eyes off the attendant, "I believe we shall visit that place you first spotted. I think I preferred the *civilized* look of the place. And besides, this man is clearly occupied. Good day, sir." She kept her chin high as she turned and departed, while Mary bowed her head and curtseyed before following her out.

The door made a satisfying clang as it swung shut behind them. Without speaking, Mrs. Burrows led Mary to the first shop she had spied, a much more modest-looking frontage, just off of the main street. There they were greeted within by a very obliging and rather handsome gentleman called Graham who was most solicitous of Mary's dressmaking needs.

"I recommend something in plum," he said. "For your eyes, miss. It would be the best shade. Here," he retrieved a bolt of silk in a rich, purple hue and offered it to Mary. "I can give you an excellent price on this, and you will not find it at any other shop in London." She would never have considered choosing such a colour. She held it up to the light, and he took out a glass for her to look in. Holding the cloth to her cheek, she felt he could not have made a better choice.

"How much fabric shall I require?" she asked.

He did not reply directly, but gave her further advice about the cut of the gown. Reaching beneath his counter, he withdrew a bundle of parchments, which he rifled through until he located the one he sought. "Here," he said, passing it to Mary, "like this."

"Is this your design?" she asked, admiring his skill.

"This neckline, and these sleeves would be perfection on you, miss. And in this silk, you would be a credit even to St. James'. Do you like it?"

"I do not know what I like," she replied. "I have never had independence enough for fashionable taste."

"That is no matter," he said. "Taste is not a requirement of high society. That is why ladies have dressmakers."

"Well, that is a relief," laughed Mary. "But I do not yet have a dressmaker."

"If you would permit me, miss," he said pointing to the sheet of parchment in Mary's hand, "I could make you this gown."

"But you are a linen draper," Mrs. Burrows interrupted.

"Yes, madam, I am," he replied. "But my mother was a mantuamaker, and I learned her trade as well as any other in the city. I can give you an excellent price on the combined purchase of cloth and services, much better than if you were to have them separately. It would be such an honour for me to make something for this lady. She shall pay nothing unless she approves the finished work, so it is no risk to her." Mrs. Burrows squinted and pursed her lips. "I have many other designs, if you do not like this one," he continued, before she could voice her objections, and pleaded his case so earnestly that Mary was quickly won over, and Mrs. Burrows forced to abandon her intention of patronizing all the shops of Bond Street in a single day.

"Can you make me a pelisse as well?" asked Mary. "It would be so convenient if you could." He assured her that he could, that he would see her the finest dressed lady in London at the lowest imaginable price, and chose for her colours and fabrics such as she never knew could be so pleasing. It seemed he knew her taste better than she did herself, and she instantly made up her mind to order all her wardrobe from this gentleman, so sharp in his eye, and so eager for a bit of custom.

Mr. Graham also directed them to other craftsmen whom he considered the best in their trade, including milliners and shoemakers. None among them were located on Bond Street, nor any of the main shopping streets, but Mr. Graham insisted the workmanship would be superior and the cost less. Not everyone with advanced skill could afford the rent in Mayfair.

"Well," said Mrs. Burrows when they were back out on the street, "you are keen."

"I do not have many powers in the world," responded Mary as they hailed a cab to take them to their next destination, "but I do have a choice as to where I may lay out my money. As I am inclined to spend a good deal of it at the moment, I prefer to give it to those who need it most, provided they give me a fair price and do good work."

"And it does not hurt matters if his face be as handsome as his figure is fine."

"Nothing of the sort!" objected Mary. "If I may pay two people the same money for the same product, I should choose the one who would most benefit from it. That is all. It is a great adventure for me–to have whatever I could wish for–but it is all rather surplus to the greatest gift, which has already been given me: that of being freed from the torment of unkind company."

"I fear we are none of us ever freed from that particular affliction, whatever our circumstances," remarked Mrs. Burrows, helping Mary into the hackney coach that had pulled up in front of them. The two ladies climbed in and took their seats and the horses trotted them off to the remainder of the day's mercantile amusements.

Chapter Thirteen

Within a fortnight, the house in Portman Square was well on its way to acquiring the accoutrements of a fine home, and Mary, the beginnings of an excellent wardrobe. The little mantuamaker had proved very industrious and well-connected among his fellow artisans. With his help and the decisive guidance of Mrs. Burrows, Mary had accomplished more in the way of setting herself up as a lady of fashion than she had ever considered would be necessary in her life.

Mary knew not how, but Mrs. Burrows had procured them entry into a public ball at one of the city's more exclusive assembly rooms. As she knew no one in London, she would have to be content to come out without a private celebration. This ball would have to suffice. Davis, the new lady's maid, had worked an opus with Mary's hair, and in her new gown and cloak, Mary hardly knew herself in the glass.

"Do you think I shall survive the evening, Davis?" asked Mary. "I am all nerves. I feel myself an imposter, and I am certain I shall be found out instantly." Although only a week in her employ, Davis had already made herself indispensable to Mary, who had been disposed to like her by virtue of her endorsement from the handsome young mantuamaker. And now, having come to know Davis a little, Mary grew daily more fond of the deft and spirited young lady with her Devonshire accent and her playful smile.

"An imposter?" replied Davis, her eyebrows raised. "It is those other ones who are the imposters, with their imitation laughter and their practiced wit. You walk on your own two feet and your blush is your own, I say. Every charm of yours, every word you speak, you came by yourself, and I say that counts a whole lot more than anything those other girls were moulded into by their fancy schools and high-paid governesses."

Mary smiled. "Thank you, Davis," she said. "I am not sure that is how the rest of the world sees it, but I am glad to hear you say it."

The carriage pulled Mary and her companion away from the house as the lowering sun draped the square in a golden light that could have been the work of the faeries. "I wonder what Dorothea and Augusta would say to see me like this," she mused aloud.

"Oh," said Mrs. Burrows, starting with a sudden recollection, "I heard from my brother yesterday. He sent along a letter, which you will remember was promised me by the footman at Challey Hall when I was there. Shall I tell you what he described?"

Mary nodded eagerly. "Please do."

"Well," said Mrs. Burrows leaning closer to Mary, "apparently, when they returned from Westley Park and were told that you had gone to London, Miss Preston actually fainted. Miss Hargreaves simply said 'how nice for her' and left the room, while Miss Augusta flew into hysterics, believing her aunt had died of shock. Miss Preston was quickly revived with smelling salts and a damp cloth, but has refused to answer any of her niece's questions. Miss Hargreaves behaves as if nothing has happened, while Miss Augusta talks ceaselessly of nothing else and the footman says Miss Preston has hardly left her room. When she does, she is assaulted with questions from Miss Augusta and quickly returns to the comfort of solitude."

Mary, still unable to reconcile within herself the actions of her aunt with the station she had come to occupy, did not take from Mrs. Burrows' message all the amusement she might have expected to, and sat attempting to be entertained, yet still puzzled.

"Is not this precisely as you would have imagined?" asked Mrs. Burrows, unable to account for her friend's want of merriment.

"I suppose it is, but I am still at a loss as to my aunt's conduct," replied Mary. "If she was my guardian, and knew who I was all along, how could she be so shocked that I should discover my own wealth on my twenty-first birthday? Surely, she knew this was to come. And why would she have been so ungracious to me for so many years, knowing that I would one day be her superior? Had she been kind to me, I would be inclined to show favour to her and all her loved ones. Instead, as she has shown such contempt for me for so long, I wish to forget them all entirely. She is not without intelligence, and never acts against her own interest, so I do not comprehend her actions."

"Is it so mysterious?" responded Mrs. Burrows with a smile. "Have not you ever learned that human behaviour is rarely of so rational a turn as all that? You have not accounted for the influence of your aunt's feelings. To have shown favour to you would have been to disadvantage her own nieces, whose interests she has always sought to advance even beyond her own, by all accounts. How could her nieces have the first choice of husbands if it were known that there was an heiress in their midst? And more, as you were an orphan of unknown parentage, who had in her eyes robbed her nieces of their inheritance from Mrs. Markham, there must have been no small measure of bitterness in her heart towards you. Once you reached maturity, there would be nothing she could do to punish you for that crime. She took what chance she had while you were in her care, to cause you as much misery as she was able, to compensate for your present happiness. It may not have been wise, but wisdom is not the sole motivator of even the most intelligent people."

"But why would she have been so shocked when your brother appeared, and when she was told of what had transpired?"

"I do not believe it was shock. I believe it was fear. She believed she would have the opportunity to manage this transition. I doubt she ever expected you to leave so quickly. I also doubt she considered that my brother's firm would contact you directly, rather than through herself or Sir Richard. As Sir Richard was away, she might have believed she had time to arrange things. Did not she always find a way of controlling every circumstance?"

Mary nodded.

"Perhaps you would have been gone somewhere to a posting as a governess before you found out, and would therefore be far away and could be forgotten or ignored. To have the news brought so forcefully to bear by your departure must have left her somewhat unhinged."

"Her feelings must have been very strong to have so overpowered her reason," thought Mary aloud. "She must truly have hated me." This thought made Mary shiver, despite her warm cloak, which she wore for the first time. She stroked the fur lining with her cheek, closed her eyes and breathed in the smell of it. She would forget all the enmity that had been shown her. She would be everything gracious and forgiving. They had not so much as her, and would never be happy because their spirits were mean. She would not permit herself to be so consumed as her aunt with resentment and hatred. She was determined to enjoy every moment of her new life and to think of her past no more.

The carriage rode on in silence until it reached its crowded destination. The ladies descended, and carefully picked their way through the mud to the doors where they were admitted into a boisterous room made warm by the substantial crowd. Mary, who had hitherto been all eager anticipation for her first public ball, was suddenly seized with apprehension, for though it seemed half of London had been pressed between the walls, yet they were all of them strangers, and she without any means of introduction to any of them.

Mrs. Burrows did not appear daunted, but took Mary by the arm and led her boldly into the room. They squeezed their way through the throng to the punch, from where they attempted without success to find a seat. They had reached the far side of the room from the doors, and were just embarking on the second half of their circumambulation when Mary stopped suddenly, tugging on her companion's arm.

"What is it?" asked Mrs. Burrows.

"I see someone I know," answered Mary.

Mrs. Burrows smiled brightly. "Well, why the hesitation?" she asked. "This may be your only chance of entering into society. Who is it?" Mrs. Burrows stood high on her toes, searching the room. "Is it an unfortunate connection?"

"Not at all," replied Mary. "It is Lord Marsden."

"A lord!" exclaimed Mrs. Burrows. "You must present yourself to him, come what may!"

"But he may not know me," objected Mary. "He has not been an overly friendly neighbour, and he is ever so high above me. He has never been known for his condescension."

"But you have been introduced?"

"I have been acquainted with him since I was a child, when Mrs. Hargreaves was alive and there was always company about the house. But since that time, I have never met him above once or twice a year, many years not at all. I was not ordinarily included in invitations, you see, and was kept as invisible as possible whenever there were guests."

"Never mind any of that," said Mrs. Burrows. "If you have been introduced, you may approach him. And if he be surprised by it, let his breeding take care of that. You are a lady; therefore, you are never wrong. Now, lead me to him."

Mary gathered her courage, knowing that Mrs. Burrows spoke true, at least in that there may not be another chance all season of obtaining any sort of introduction, and that she must seize it. Her heart pounded as she approached Lord Marsden, whom she had always regarded as transcendent beyond mortal humanity, or at least immeasurably exalted above her own kind. He was conversing jovially with two other gentlemen as she stepped before him.

"Lord Marsden," she said somewhat hoarsely, curtseying and forcing herself not to choke.

"Hullo," he said, in a tone which showed he was not so fortunate as to recognize her.

"Mary Green," she said, feeling her cheeks flush, "formerly of Challey Hall."

"Ah," he sighed with recognition. "I do apologize. I have never met you in London, so it is something of a surprise to see you, though not at all unwelcome, of course." Mary was grateful for his gentlemanly manners, which were surprisingly warm. When she considered it, she realized she had never really spoken to him before, nor him to her. "Have you been in town long?" he asked.

"Not very long," she managed. "It is my first season. I am afraid you are the first acquaintance I have seen this evening. We have just arrived."

"Are not you with the Hargreaves?" he asked.

"No, no. I am no longer with them. I am in London on my own, in fact, well, with my companion, as you see." Mrs. Burrows curtseyed.

"I see," he said knowingly, without understanding at all how an orphan of no fortune could be out and looking so fine at a London ball without the support of the family that had cared for her. But then, perhaps he had misunderstood her circumstances. He would admit, he had paid very little attention to the details of that household. Perhaps she was not so impoverished as he had always assumed, if ever he had taken the time to assume anything, which in truth he really had not.

"Permit me to assist you there," he continued.

"I would be so grateful," she said.

"Well, then, allow me to begin by introducing to you my two friends here. Miss Green, this is Sir Walter Harding."

"How do you do."

"And this is The Honourable Mr. Thomas Carrington." Mr. Carrington rolled his eyes a little, while the other two gentlemen suppressed playful smiles, at the use of 'Honourable.'

"How do you do, Miss Green."

"Where are you staying while you are in town?" asked Lord Marsden.

"I have a house in Portman Square," she answered with concealed pride. "Since our arrival, we have just begun replacing the furniture, so it is still in a bit of disarray, but otherwise, it suits me very well."

"Yes, it is a charming neighbourhood," agreed Lord Marsden. "We are not far from there, in Mayfair. We must come and visit you some time."

"Yes," Mr. Carrington joined in. "And if you would permit me to introduce my sisters to you, I am sure they should be very happy to visit you also."

"That would be delightful," said Mary, with genuine enthusiasm, and a little surprised at her ready acceptance by such esteemed gentlemen.

"Fanny!" he called over the heads of those beside him. "Miss Carrington of Harptree Manor, will you come here, you boggle-headed thing!" he ordered, in mock severity. A pretty, bright-eyed girl appeared suddenly through the crowd, her countenance half engulfed in a playful smile and her auburn curls bouncing heartily.

"Yes, brother, what is it?" she said, as two other girls emerged behind her, all of similar size and equal cheerfulness.

"There is a young lady here who has just arrived in London and is in such dire need of acquaintance that I thought she might even condescend to meeting the three of you." Turning to Mary, he said, "Miss Green, please forgive me for presenting to you my sisters, Mrs. Lowell, Miss Carrington, and Miss Louisa." The young ladies did not seem to notice, or at least to mind, the derogation of their brother, so obviously meant in jest. Instead they rushed forward to greet her and practically embraced her, expressing much joy in making her acquaintance.

"You must ignore my brother," said Miss Carrington, adding over her shoulder towards him, "He was very badly brought up." The other girls erupted into laughter and they led her away from the gentlemen.

Mrs. Burrows slipped away, content to have made for her charge an entry into society. She kept her eye on Mary for the rest of the evening, and was never so pleased to watch another do so well in society, for it seemed Mary could not have received a better introduction than to the Carrington sisters. They appeared to know everyone in the place, and were keen to put their connections to good use for their new friend. Mary danced every dance, and each time

Mrs. Burrows saw her, it seemed she was talking with some new person. When it came time to leave, she had accumulated so many new acquaintances, so many invitations and so many promises of visitors that she was certain it would not be long before she gave offence by forgetting one.

Chapter Fourteen

Frances, Louisa, and Thomas Carrington sat at breakfast the next morning, laughing and quizzing each other over their partners at the ball. Harriet, the eldest girl, had been lately married to a Mr. Lowell, and stayed at her own house, but was expected shortly. While in town she was at least as much a sister as she was a wife, spending most of her days chaperoning her sisters and enjoying her role immensely.

"That will be Harriet," said Frances on hearing a ring at the door.

"Or Lord Marsden," said Tom. Both the girls looked at him eyes wide with surprise, and in Louisa's case, a mouth full of lemon drizzle.

"You never said," began Frances. Her brother shrugged.

"I was not aware I was required to share all my days' plans with my little sisters," he responded. Frances took up her napkin and threw it across the table into her brother's face. Louisa hurried to wash down her cake with a large swig of her tea, and a servant announced Harriet to the breakfast room.

"Good morning, Harriet," said Tom, smiling cheerfully up at his sister, who took a seat at the table and helped herself to tea.

"You are very bad!" said Frances, pointing her finger at her brother while Louisa set down her tea cup with a sigh of relief.

"Why?" asked Harriet with a grin of delightful curiosity. "What has he done now?"

"Only invited Lord Marsden to drop by without giving us a word of notice," answered Frances.

"Oh, that is a capital offence, Tom, and very unfair," said Harriet, furrowing her brow at her brother.

"Well, you need not even see him, if it is all that much to you," returned Tom. "He is not so much dropping in as stopping to pick me up. He offered last night that we might take a turn some time in his new curricle, and so I sent word this morning–it being a fine day–that we ought to take the thing down to Hyde Park for a spin."

"How very providential," said Frances, "for we are to meet our new friend Miss Green at Hyde Park this very morning. No doubt such was your design in setting out to that spot at the same time."

"Nonsense!" said Tom, his cheeks turning pink. "I had no idea of your plans."

"Yes, you did!" insisted Louisa. "I told you so in the carriage last night."

"Do you think I retain every little thing you chatty hens say? I have no recollection of anything discussed in the carriage last night. I believe I may even have been asleep."

"You were no more asleep than the horses, and I do believe you would recall what was said about such a pretty young girl who caught your eye," said Frances.

"That is why you are so finely dressed this morning," added Louisa. "When you said Lord Marsden was coming, I thought it might be for his sake, but now all is made clear."

Tom finished his tea in one mouthful and stood up from the table. "If you will excuse me, I shall await my friend in the drawing room."

"Have you got a wire in your cravat?" asked Harriet as he passed. He paused and let go an impatient huff.

"It is starch," he said sternly, "only a bit of starch. Everyone uses starch." The girls laughed without restraint as he marched out of the door.

"I most certainly saw a wire," said Harriet when he was quite gone. "He must truly be smitten."

"Oh, Tom does not require so noble an excuse as true love to dress himself up like a peacock," replied Frances.

"That may be so," said Louisa, "but did you see his waistcoat?"

"I did indeed," said Harriet. "And what is more, I hope it is all for the sake of our new friend. I liked her very well."

"As did I," added Frances, "though I think she may be a bit too clever to have eyes for Tom."

"Many a clever girl has married far stupider a man than Tom," said Harriet.

The girls debated the question for some minutes before the bell was heard again, and they determined to run into Lord Marsden quite by accident in the passage. Harriet strode ahead leaving Frances to stop just short of colliding with their guest as they both arrived in the foyer.

"Why, sir," she said, "what a pleasant surprise! Our brother did not tell us to expect you. I am so sorry we cannot stay, but we have a prior engagement with a friend this morning, and it would be quite shocking if we were to be late."

"Well, if you are in such haste as all that," replied Lord Marsden, "you must allow me to take you. We were only going out for a drive. I might as well make some use of it."

"But there should only be room for one," argued Tom.

"Well, then, let it be Miss Louisa," said Frances, "for she is the smallest, as well as the most fond of driving." Louisa smiled coyly and stepped forward, head lowered to hide her flushing cheeks.

"But then she shall not have a chaperone," Tom objected. "I cannot allow that."

"Well then, you drive her," said Lord Marsden. "I could use the walk." And he led them all out of the door.

Louisa raised her dejected face to her sisters, to which Frances replied with a silently mouthed "I'm sorry" and took her by the arm as they stepped out into the morning sun. Louisa's consolation was that Lord Marsden gave her his hand and helped her up into her seat, which was no small treasure to the young lady, and she savoured it as they rode away from the party towards the park.

They drove around it once before spying their friend. "I say, is not that Miss Green, whom you were come out to meet?" said Tom, pointing her out.

"Indeed it is." Louisa waved to Mary, who was looking about the place for her friends, and quickly spotted Louisa and Tom in their high carriage, walking briskly over to them and waving in return.

"Good Morning, Louisa," she said as she approached. "I expected to see you on foot. Where are the others?"

"They are just coming, walking I mean," answered Louisa.

"This is a very fine rig," said Mrs. Burrows.

"Thank you," said Tom, before Louisa could explain its ownership. "Would you ladies care to take a turn in it?" He thought it not entirely dishonest to allow Miss Green to believe he owned such a splendid thing. And if she liked it, he could always purchase one just like it.

"Not for me, I thank you," answered Mrs. Burrows. "But do let Miss Green have a turn. I doubt she has ever ridden so high."

"But of course. Louisa," said Tom, turning to his sister and indicating that she should make way for her friend.

"But she will not have a chaperone," said Louisa. "Could you allow that?"

"Oh stuff," said Tom. "We shall be quite in plain view, and Mrs. Burrows does not object. Stop being so wet and climb down. Miss

Green is waiting."

Mrs. Burrows and Mary helped Louisa down a little awkwardly, while her brother sat idle and impatient. When Mary attempted to climb up and met with a little difficulty, Tom instantly jumped down from his seat to lend her his aid and then with alacrity returned to his seat. Without a look to the other two ladies he snapped the reins and drove off.

Mary was not entirely sure she liked riding so high. The hazard of it seemed rather disproportionate to its advantages, whatever the fashion might be, and she thought Mr. Carrington drove a good deal faster than she would have preferred. He was clearly enjoying himself, wearing a broad smile and laughing into the wind, unconscious of the fast grip with which his passenger held to the rail.

"Oh, look," she said as soon as she could find an excuse to end the tour, "there are the others. Do let us go and join them."

"Certainly, Miss Green, as you wish," said Tom, a little disappointed to have his fun curtailed. They pulled up to their friends and as Mary made to descend, Tom again leapt from his place to assist her before Lord Marsden or anyone else might offer their hand.

"How did you enjoy that?" asked Mrs. Burrows once Mary was safely back on the ground.

"It does offer a very favourable view," she said, not wishing to seem ungrateful, "but I am not sure it is really the carriage for me. I am afraid I may not be so daring as some."

"No matter," said Tom, who was a little glad that he would not be required to make such a dear purchase just to please a lady. "It is Lord Marsden's rig, and should be returned to him now." Wishing to linger a little longer with the party, he added, "Perhaps one of the others would like to join you for a turn."

"Certainly," replied Lord Marsden. "One always prefers the company of a lady, when one has a choice. Miss Louisa has already been for quite a drive. Miss Carrington, would you care to join me?"

"Of course," she said, taking his proffered hand and ascending to her seat, offering poor Louisa an apologetic shrug.

Louisa and the others watched them drive off. Harriet took her sister's arm and pressed it with understanding and sympathy. Louisa would say nothing in front of her brother, but she did feel disheartened. She had only just rejoined Lord Marsden, when he set off again with Frances, who had already walked with him all the way from the house to the park. The world seemed a cruel and unjust place just at that moment.

Beside her, Tom prattled away at Mary, telling her who everyone in the park was, as they saw them, and which of them were worth knowing and which not, paying particular attention to what kind of carriage they each drove.

When Lord Marsden returned Frances to her party, he let Tom help her down, then graciously offered to take Harriet around the park.

"I thank you, no," she replied. "It is very kind of you, but I do not think it prudent for an old married woman like myself."

"All right then–come on, Tom," he said, beckoning to his friend. "I have a mind to cover all of the Gardens before the morning is quite through."

With Louisa in mind, Harriet called up to Lord Marsden, "will you be joining us for tea when you are quite finished?"

"It is very good of you to think of me, Mrs. Lowell, but I am to meet some gentlemen at a coffee house later, and I might just persuade your brother to try a curry house I have just learned of, for he tells me he has never tasted the stuff, which I find a shocking flaw in need of immediate rectification. I hope you have a very pleasant morning."

The gentlemen drove away, leaving the ladies to pine for them, or at least one of the ladies for one of the gentlemen. Frances, wishing to make amends to her sister for having unwittingly kept her from that gentleman, suggested they seek out some indulgence.

"I know just the thing," said Harriet. "Since Mary has never been to London before, she will certainly never have tried such ices as are offered at Gunter's. It is our duty and our privilege to be the ones to introduce her to those delights."

"What a perfect thought," agreed Frances. "It is such a warm day, I can think of nothing I should enjoy better than an ice from Gunter's. And, what is more, we shall certainly be able to introduce Mary to more than mere confection if we linger a little."

And so the ladies made their way to Berkeley square where they enjoyed their cooling refreshment as much as they did the gossip and the pageantry which passed before them where they stood. Mary, to whom it was all so new, thought back to her little life in Oxfordshire, where she met no one and nothing ever happened. How incredible it was to her the difference, and how much she still had to discover, she hardly thought possible to guess.

Chapter Fifteen

The days following overflowed with visitors and visits. The sisters Carrington were in Portman Square every other day, and they had quite taken Mary in as one of their own, showing her the best shops and having her over for tea. Having never known the joys of companionship, she delighted in having such constant friends. They were all three very good natured, even if they did speak of little other than fashions, hair, and dancing partners.

"Can you imagine," remarked Louisa, one morning in Mary's drawing room, "how wonderful it would be if Mary could be made one of us–If she were really to be our sister?"

"Louisa!" scolded Frances. "You must not say such a thing. You shall make our friend very awkward."

"But you said yourself, only just this morning, what a pleasant thing it would be, and we all know how fond he is of her."

Frances was quite correct. The subject did make Mary awkward, but all would have been quite forgot if it had been quickly changed instead of aired out in this prolonged manner.

"Look how Mary blushes," added Harriett. "This is most unkind and idle chatter. It is not for us to share what Tom may or may not feel, however clear it may be to us all."

"Well, I meant no harm," said Louisa, "since it is so apparent. And we would all love to have Mary as a Carrington, even if her hair is not quite auburn. Do you forgive me, Mary?"

"There is nothing to forgive," answered Mary. "Although I do not think it so clear as you all do, about your brother, I mean. He cannot be so fond of me. We are hardly even acquainted."

"Oh, that is no matter," said Harriett. "You have smiled at him have not you, and perhaps even thrown him a compliment on his waistcoat? That is all it should take for Tom, from someone so pretty as you."

Mary's blush deepened at this praise, which reaction was quite mistaken by the others.

Louisa gasped and clapped her hands. "You love him too!" she declared. "I knew it must be. I knew you were destined to be our true sister. We shall all be so happy!"

"Is it true?" joined in Harriett, her eyes growing wide. "Do you really love him?"

Looking at their three eager faces, Mary hated to disappoint, but thought it crueller to indulge their hopes with falsehood. "I am afraid I do not," she answered, quickly adding, "though it does not diminish my love for all of you."

"Then there must be someone else!" exclaimed Louisa. "You must tell us all, Mary. Do you harbour some secret passion, so profound and so shocking that you dare not speak of it? Is it someone from the country? Is it someone we know? You must not keep it from us, Mary." Her face was suddenly grave. "Tell me, is it Lord Marsden?" she asked.

Her sisters both laughed. "You only say that because you are in love with Lord Marsden," said Harriett.

"I am not!" declared Louisa with express indignation.

"I expect half of Lord Marsden's acquaintance is in love with him," observed Frances.

"Half of Lord Marsden's acquaintance are men," responded Harriet.

"I know," said Frances. "It is the other half who are in love with him." At this, the room filled with ruptures of excited laughter.

"Well, if I were to marry Lord Marsden, I should invite you all to stay with us forever at our estate," said Louisa when the noise had died down. "I have heard Westley Park is the most elegant house."

"I wonder if it is as handsome as he is," said Frances.

"I have been to Westley Park," said Mary. "I attended a ball there not long before I came to town."

"You have?" asked an incredulous Louisa. "Did Lord Marsden invite you? If so, then we have our answer, and it is indeed him whom you love."

"No, no," replied Mary, "nothing of the kind. I was included in the invitation to the Hargreaves family, and then only because one of Lord Marsden's brothers insisted on it."

"And did you dance with Lord Marsden?" asked Louisa.

"No," answered Mary. "He certainly would not have thought of me in those days. In fact, I do not recall if I saw him at all that night. It was rather crowded."

"There you have it," said Frances. "She cannot love him after all, else she would certainly remember whether she saw him or no."

"So it must be some other gentleman!" exclaimed Louisa. "Someone she has left behind, perhaps."

"No, no, no," objected Mary, waving her hands and laughing gently. "There is no such gentleman, not even in Oxfordshire, I'm afraid. My life would have been a great deal more tolerable if there had been. The truth is, I have lately been introduced to so many charming gentlemen, I am sure I have fallen in and out of love with each of them by turns every five minutes since I came to London. What is more, I am not at all as convinced as you three that your brother harbours any such feelings for me either."

"Well, I accept what you say about your own feelings," said Frances. "But you must trust to us to know our brother's heart. We should all be so pleased if you could bring yourself to return his feelings, but I suspect he may not ever be quite serious enough for you. He is a good sort, our Tom, but he is not a great thinker."

"Is that what you like, then?" asked Louisa, "a great thinker? I am not terribly fond of men who make great speeches all the time, and never laugh. I should be quite happy with someone who could keep time in a quadrille and looked well in a saddle."

"Those are very admirable qualities in a husband," said Mary, "but I do think I shall require a bit of conversation in the person I marry, and to last through so many years, there ought to be an active mind behind it, or I should grow rather bored."

"Oh, I almost forgot," said Frances suddenly. "You are to come to dinner tomorrow night. I had meant to ask you so many times, only I kept forgetting. There was always so much else to say. Do say you will come. It shall not be a large affair, but Lord Marsden will be there, and my brother, though that brings you so little joy, and of course, Mr. Lowell."

"I should be happy to come, though I may perhaps be a little uncomfortable with your brother, in light of all you have said today."

"Nonsense," said Frances. "We shall all be there, and we may even convince the gentlemen to get up a dance, if we fill them with enough port. You are always gay and easy when you are dancing."

In the end, it was conceded that three gentlemen would not suffice to make a set for dancing, and as someone would have to play the pianoforte, they could not even spare a lady to stand in for a fourth.

At the Carringtons', Mary was sat beside the illustrious Lord Marsden himself. She had always thought he most resembled his youngest brother George, but on this occasion, seated so close, she detected in his eyes as he smiled, something which very much called to mind his brother Mr. Ingles, which thought made her feel a little easier in his company.

"I am sorry our table is so out of balance," he said, turning to Mary, as if reading her thoughts. "I had rather hoped my brother Mr. Ingles might have joined us, but he could not be convinced."

"I had not realized he was still in town," said Mary, whose heart was warmed even at the mention of the name of her old friend. "I would have asked after him earlier. Where is he tonight then?"

"He has some meeting or other with one of his missionary committees. I thought he might have excused himself for your sake, but he would not be dissuaded. Urgent business, he said. Dashed inconsiderate of him I say, for a gentleman to eschew society so thoroughly, but he would not hear it."

Mary felt suddenly guilty for the elegance of her surroundings and the rich food on her plate, when her friend had forgone it for so much more noble a purpose.

"It is kind of you to have thought of me," said Mary. "I hope I shall see him while he is in town, but you must not be concerned for any offence he might give me by his absence. I think it very commendable of him to be so steadfast in his calling."

"It is true that one could never justly accuse my brother of being fickle."

After dinner, a game of whist was got up in place of a dance, and Mary was forced to play despite having no knowledge of the game. She had never been permitted to join in at cards at Challey Hall, as it not only required that she have something to gamble, which she did not, but also involved more contact with society than Aunt Preston was prepared to permit.

Tom insisted that she partner with him, and Frances attempted to guide her through the game, at which they lost terribly. Nobody would accept her money however, as it was her first time at play, and it was not fair since Frances was such a dreadful tutor. Tom suggested that Mary partner instead with Harriett, and that he himself should sit beside Mary and advise her as to the best order in which to play her cards. When she then triumphed, Tom congratulated her on her quick skill, and contended that she keep all her winnings, all with as much fervour as he had prohibited her from being parted from her losses on the previous game.

He stood always too close to her, spoke too loudly, laughed at what was not amusing and generally made a fool of himself all evening. What greater proof could Mary look for of a true and consuming affection? Her passions were not so stirred, but she was very fond of his family. She was young. He was not actually disagreeable. Perhaps she could imagine herself in love with him, if she made an effort.

"What do you think of Mr. Carrington?" she asked Mrs. Burrows on the ride home.

"I think it a very dangerous thing to take one's impression of a man when he is so clearly in love," she answered. "It can do neither party justice, for there never was a man who was not altered beyond judgment by strong emotion. You must always love a man before he loves you. It is the only way to be sure that it is the man that you love and not merely the effects of his affection, which is sure to wane in time."

"That does not seem very wise advice," objected Mary. "Would not it put me at risk of disappointed love, to confine my heart only to gentlemen who do not love me?"

"Of course it does," replied Mrs. Burrows. "That is why women are so often unlucky in romance. It takes a great deal of skill and no small part of cunning and charm not only to convince a man to love you, but also to make him believe that it was he who loved you first and had the ordeal of winning your heart."

Mary doubted whether she had anything like the requisite skill, cunning, and charm. She knew nothing of such arts, and to her it seemed all rather a matter of chance as to whether two people might happen each to prefer the other. Still, it would be rather a pleasant thing to be a Carrington, and if Tom turned out to be a bore, there would always be the consolation of the company of his sisters.

Chapter Sixteen

As she fell to sleep that night, and in the following days, Mary was determined to think of Tom Carrington. Whenever her mind would wander onto some other subject, she would chastise herself for forgetting him. There were so many reasons for her to set her affections on him, and she presented these to herself repeatedly. But love will not be born of arguments, however forceful, and as she replayed her encounters with him over in her mind, it became increasingly difficult for her to remain convinced that she could love him. There was not a single moment or gesture which captured her heart or which her imagination could work up into something she could revere.

At a public ball one evening, some time after giving up hope of loving her friends' brother, she was simply enjoying the music and quite content to watch others dance. She had not come with any company but Mrs. Burrows and was feeling far less anxious than she had at her first ball in London. In fact, she felt quite at ease. She was more plainly attired and her hair more simply dressed than might have been expected of her, if anyone had thought to expect anything. She had come with spectatorial intent only and wished for nothing. Mrs. Burrows approached with tea and sat beside Mary who smiled at her.

"Could you have imagined," Mary began, taking a cup from Mrs. Burrows, "that I should be so happy?"

"Of course I did," replied Mrs. Burrows. "Who could have doubted it? Whereas before you had nothing, now you have everything."

"I have so many friends now," said Mary. "I think, if I had been so fortunate in my friendships at Challey Hall, I should have been quite satisfied to have remained poor. Do not you think I am very fortunate?"

"I think you are indeed, and all the more so for knowing which among your many blessings most highly to prize."

"I am so glad I met Frances and her sisters so early in my stay here. They take such good care of me, you know. They are so generous, always sharing with me all that they know and I do not, such as when to return a call, and how to phrase an invitation. Harriet has even given me some instruction on deportment, and they have promised to teach me some new dances next week. I have discovered just how much I did not know. I think I should be quite lost without them, and without you, of course."

Mrs. Burrows looked with admiration at her friend, with her sincere and unaffected smile, her genuine gratitude and effortless enthusiasm. Was it any wonder Mr. Carrington was so enraptured? Mrs. Burrows doubted he would be the only one, if there were not others already.

"I take no credit for your happiness," she said. "And I do not credit Frances or her sisters either, though they have been very kind to you. An amiable disposition can be enhanced, but not created, by education."

The dance was coming to a close, and Mary turned to watch the couples take their final turns. "I do so love a Cotillion," she said. "I sometimes feel it is even more pleasant to watch and to listen to than it is to dance. I thought that tall couple particularly graceful." She gestured toward a gentleman in a grey coat. She was surprised when, after returning his partner to her party, the same grey-coated gentleman began to walk in her direction, and she discovered him to be none other than Lord Marsden on his way to take some refreshment. On seeing her, he smiled broadly and approached their table.

"Miss Green," he said cheerfully. "What a pleasure to see you here, and you, Mrs. Burrows. I hope you are both well."

"We are very well, thank you," said Mary.

"Mr. Carrington and his sisters shall be sorry to have missed you. They had another engagement this evening."

"Yes," said Mary, suddenly unsure where to look or how to hide her embarrassment at the mention of Mr. Carrington. She wondered if Lord Marsden was privy to his friend's feelings. "But I shall be seeing them very soon. Tell me, how is your brother, Mr. Ingles? Is he still in town?"

"Has he not come to see you at all?" returned Lord Marsden. "I have told him he ought to. I even gave him your address. I do apologize for him. He has the most atrocious manners, to neglect you so on your first visit to London."

"Well, you may rest easy on that account, for I never objected to his manners. I have always found him to be very considerate."

"You must allow me to compensate for his neglect and dance the next with me. I shall just go and fetch some punch and return to collect you in a moment."

Mary had barely nodded her head in acquiescence before he was off.

"I hope you are feeling lively," said Mrs. Burrows. "If I am not mistaken, it is the Spaniard next."

The dance was announced and Lord Marsden came into view with a glass held out for Mary. "I have never known myself to denounce a dance for being too lively," she replied, taking the punch, drinking half of it hastily and setting the glass down on the table. "The Spaniard is my favourite."

With that, she took her partner's arm, smiled at Mrs. Burrows and skipped off towards the set.

If Mary had noticed Lord Marsden's dancing from a distance, she was even more impressed as his partner. His movements were both graceful and strong, and the force of his full attention had an unexpected, captivating power. Had he always looked at her that way? Was this how he looked at other ladies? He appeared always to be smiling a little to himself, and perhaps a little at her, as though they shared some secret, some joke on the rest of the world. She found herself smiling in return, though more openly. Her heart raced from more than the vigour of the dance.

"What is it?" he said to her as they reached the bottom of the set.

"What do you mean?" she returned.

"You look as though you harbour some mystery."

Mary laughed. "There is no mystery to me, sir," she said. "I simply love to dance."

"Well, you put me to shame with your relentless delight."

"I hope not!" she laughed again as they rejoined the dance.

She was sorry when the music came to an end. She thought she could have carried on all evening with such a partner. He led her back to her table. "Your friend has quite worn me out, madam," he said to Mrs. Burrows, with a wink at Mary, to whom he added, "I thank you very kindly for the dance, Miss Green. If you will excuse me, my friends await me at the card tables. I wish you a good evening, and hope we shall meet again soon."

"Oh," said Mary, looking about for a chair to offer him, that she might induce him to tarry a little, but found none. "I see. Good evening then," she said and he turned away.

As he crossed the room, Mary distractedly took up her half-finished punch and, without sitting down, watched silently as his back grew smaller and disappeared through a doorway. Her humour was now entirely altered. Her peace had been supplanted by agitation and uncertainty. Had she said anything to embarrass herself? Had she been too keen? He had asked her to dance of his own volition; she had done nothing to ensnare him. Surely, he had wished to dance with her. If so, why did he leave so suddenly? And why had she not taken pains to dress more fittingly, or to make some effort with her hair? She would not repeat that error.

Entirely gone was any thought of poor Mr. Carrington. Now it was the handsome face, the warm manners, and the elegant person of Lord Marsden on which Mary exclusively dwelt. He was confirmed, in the estimation of the young lady, as the very essence of everything agreeable. She thought he combined all that was best about each of his brothers–William's kindness and George's taste – and a finer person than either of them. Her friends' remarks on the ubiquity of his admirers were no defence against the allure which had worked, by Frances' estimation, on half of London.

In truth, she had been doomed from the first by the fascination that had always accompanied the mention of his name in Oxfordshire. How was she to defend herself against such a force as his exalted reputation? He was rarely at Westley Park, and whenever he was mentioned at Challey Hall, it was with the sort of reverence that one associates with gods or monarchy, or at the very least, highly accomplished poets.

Mrs. Burrows had been in the world long enough to recognize the cause of her friend's alteration. She encouraged Mary to accept the next offer of a dance, which was not long in coming, and another, which soon followed after that, but when the young lady still spoke of nothing but how superior Lord Marsden was to any other partner, Mrs. Burrows decided they ought to be going home. It was a hopeless business.

Chapter Seventeen

Mary sat in her drawing room with Mrs. Burrows one morning when a servant entered carrying the post. With most of her acquaintance being in town and able to deliver any message in person, Mary did not often receive letters, and it was thus a moment of significance. There was but one item on the tray, and Mary took it with both curiosity and apprehension. The script was very fine, and the seal marked with a family crest which, after a moment of confusion, she gleefully recognized.

"It is from the house of Rosborough," she squealed to an impatient Mrs. Burrows, who sat at the edge of her seat, straining to see the envelope. "That is Lord Marsden's family."

With tender eagerness she sliced open the seal and unfolded the contents.

"It is an invitation to a ball!" she cried, leaping to her feet, followed instantly by Mrs. Burrows, who rushed forward to read over her friend's shoulder. "Lord and Lady Rosborough are hosting a ball and they have thought to invite me," she said, fighting to catch her breath. "Do you see what cause for celebration this is?" she said, her eyes wide as she looked up to her companion.

"But of course," said Mrs. Burrows. "Lord Marsden is sure to be there if it is at his own house."

"But so much more than that!" insisted Mary. "Lady Rosborough would never have remembered someone as insignificant as myself. She would not even know I was in town, nor care, for that matter. This means," she continued, holding the invitation up for her friend to see, "that Lord Marsden has thought of me, and fondly too, for this invitation can only be his doing. He must have particularly asked his mother to invite me. He so wished me to be there that he took the trouble of making it so. You must allow me to rejoice at this."

Mrs. Burrows had watched with some anxiety her young charge's growing fascination with her noble acquaintance. While he had always been amiable towards Mary, she did not detect from him any more keen an interest– certainly nothing on which Mary might hang any expectations from him–and she did not wish to see her friend's heart broken, however little she could do to prevent it. A girl infatuated is a girl lost to reason and blind to anything but signs of affection returned, and woe to anyone who seek to contradict her findings. Mrs. Burrows knew this as well as anyone, and so would not attempt to convince Mary that Lord Marsden was indifferent to her, but rather endeavoured to draw her attention to other young men who were worthy of her interest, if only to spare any embarrassment that might result if Mary's affections, and any subsequent heartbreak, became publicly apparent.

"Lord Marsden is always very generous, it is true," she said. "I hope, however, you will not disappoint Mr. Carrington so completely as to ignore him entirely. He may not be to your particular liking, but he has been very kind to you, and it would not be courteous simply to abandon him."

Mary did not dislike Mr. Carrington, but she also had no wish to further any attachment he may believe they were forming. "Tom is indeed very good, but I do not think it would do to give him encouragement. Do not you agree? I do not like the thought that he might believe I felt more than I did. Is not it cruel to allow him to think as much?"

"There is nothing you can do about Mr. Carrington's attachment. Whether he shall break his heart or no is entirely independent of your conduct," said Mrs. Burrows. "I only mean that you must not think only of Lord Marsden. There are many other gentlemen who might deserve your consideration. Lord Marsden is well bred enough not to allow it to colour his actions, but he is very high born. He may not be at liberty to think of you with any more strength of feeling than a passing fondness. There may be other eligible suitors. You may regret disregarding them in your occupation with one who is such an unlikely match. I do not mean that you should flirt with and then disappoint every gentleman who smiles agreeably at you, but what harm can there be in maintaining an appearance of neutrality?"

Mary nodded. She had learned to take the advice of Mrs. Burrows, who had always steered her well. "I think you must be right," she nodded. "It is well known that a lady who appears too keen only extinguishes any flicker of affection, rather than fanning it into flame. No doubt it would only work to increase Lord Marsden's regard if he were to see that I held the interest of other gentlemen. For do not gentlemen always require some sense of competition to engage their hearts?"

"That is not quite what I meant," said Mrs. Burrows. "But if that is how you choose to see it, there is little I can do."

"I must have a new gown made," declared Mary. "I believe there is time. Our friend Mr. Graham has proven his ability to produce something very fine with remarkable speed. Perhaps I shall go and see him today."

She folded the invitation and was about to order her pelisse when Frances and her sisters were announced.

"Oh," said Mary. "Tell them to wait at the door. I shall be right there. I am going out, but perhaps they should like to join me."

The ladies all left together to visit Mr. Graham's shop, the Carringtons excessively pleased to discover this new talent on which to spend their father's money, or their husband's, in the case of Harriett.

"I cannot justly say that he is the best at his trade, or even better than any other," said Mary as they hustled along the street. "I have never known any other, and so cannot, in faith, compare his work, but I will say that he is awfully amiable, and so quick. My first order from him was ready in one week, and it included several gowns."

"That is impressive," said Frances. "Perhaps I shall order something as well, for I have seen the gowns he has made for you, and they were all very fashionable and fine."

"If he is as good as all that, we must make it our task to spread his name throughout London and make his shop the best-reputed in town," said Harriett.

"Quite so," added Louisa. "I do believe it is in our power to send him a good deal of business, and it is such a satisfaction to bring prosperity to those who deserve it."

"Oh, and I assure you he does," stated Mary. Glancing back at Mrs. Burrows she continued, "And though the ladies of society shall certainly be drawn by his skill and his speed with a needle, it cannot hurt his cause if they are also driven by another, unspoken motive."

"Whatever do you mean?" asked Harriet. "Does he dabble in some less reputable trade?"

"I doubt that very much," laughed Frances. "I am sure Mary only meant that he is handsome."

"Is he indeed?" asked Louisa.

"Is he really very handsome?" said Harriett to Mrs. Burrows, who smiled knowingly.

"You must judge for yourself," she answered. "But I would not wonder at it if a few finer ladies were taken by surprise at their susceptibility to the charms of a humble dressmaker."

Out of a wish to avoid injuring her friends, particularly Louisa, Mary had not disclosed to them her newfound infatuation with Lord Marsden. She was on this occasion able to conceal the true cause of her exuberance over the invitation she had just received, for the sisters saw every justification for exultation at the prospect of a ball, and the thrill of ordering a new gown, not to mention the giddy enjoyment of flirtation with the dashing young man serving them.

The ladies did not hurry their decision over the style and the trim of the gown Mary ordered, but lingered in the shop some time, asking questions to which they mostly knew the answers, in order to test the dressmaker's knowledge, and to quiz Mary over her confessed opinion on his appearance and his charms.

"I think this fabric would do best justice to Miss Green's complexion," said Harriett, selecting a pink ribbon. Carrying it over to Mary she held it up to her cheek. "She has the most delicate skin. It positively glows, and I feel the pink such a subtle complement to its perfection. Do not you agree, Mr. Graham?"

"But it does nothing for her eyes!" objected Frances. "They are so enchanting. Surely she must choose the green if this gown is to show her to best advantage, for who could resist her when her eyes shine like emeralds as they do when set against the right shade of green. You cannot permit her to choose any other colour, Mr. Graham."

"You are all wrong," said Louisa, waving the others aside. "It must be the lilac. Neither the green nor the pink contrast the flecks of gold in her hair so strikingly as does the lilac. It shows her for the jewel she is. What say you, Mr. Graham? Does not her hair quite shimmer against this colour? Is not she magnificent in it?"

The gentleman unabashedly agreed with all of them as to the superior beauty of their friend, who was uncharacteristically jubilant in the face of their praise, which, though sincere, was expressed for the amusement of seeing her blush. They could not succeed however, for though usually ill at ease with such attention, she was unassailable in her rapture over Lord Marsden's invitation, as she considered it. In the end, Mrs. Burrows made the final decisions respecting the gown, in accordance with her appreciation of Mary's preferences and her own superior taste.

The ladies left more determined than ever to see Mr. Graham flourish and to be responsible for his success. As the daughters of a baron, neither Frances nor Louisa would ever think of him as a suitor, but it did not follow that they would not think of him. Mary was glad that they were so pleased with her discovery of Mr. Graham, but in her heart thought only of the ball, of how she might look in her new gown, and of what effect her complexion, her eyes, and her hair might have on the heart of Lord Marsden.

Chapter Eighteen

In a few days, Mr. Graham came by with Mary's new gown. Both she and Mrs. Burrows admired it openly.

"I think it is even more beautiful than I had imagined," said Mary, who stood before the glass in the drawing room, wearing the gown for the first time. "There is not anything even to be adjusted."

"Thank you, Miss," said Mr. Graham. "You do it great justice."

Mrs. Burrows inspected the details and nodded. "It will do very well," she said. "It was good of you to complete it so quickly."

"It is always a pleasure to make a piece that I know will look so well on its wearer," he replied.

"You are too kind," said Mary. "But I am very pleased with it, and so grateful for your having it ready in so short a time. I should like to settle the bill straight away."

"Thank you, miss," he said and retrieved a slip of parchment, which he handed to her.

"We shall return in a moment," said Mrs. Burrows, ushering Mary back up to her room to change. Having closed the door, she turned to Mary. "Let me see that," she said, holding out her hand for the bill. Mary gave it to her, and she pored over it, clicking her tongue. "You must check the price at other shops before you pay this. I am not sure this is the best available price. He will wish to keep your business, and will lower it if you ask."

"Not at all," said Mary. "I shall pay him what he asks, and I shall be very glad to do it."

"But that is not right," objected Mrs. Burrows. "You must not allow yourself to be taken advantage of. I know you are fond of Mr.

Graham, but this is London. Everyone is a crook, even hard-working and handsome tradesmen, and if you do not question your bills, you will soon be the victim of every manner of fraud and misrepresentation."

"No one may defraud me if I am complicit in the crime," returned Mary. "I shall soon learn by and by if Mr. Graham has overcharged me, though I doubt he has. He has done excellent work, and I am very grateful to him. I wish to pay him, and I do not mind paying him more than the least I could pay elsewhere. I shall pay him for his work, and a generous tip besides."

"I think you should listen to Mrs. Burrows," said Davis, who had come in to assist Mary in changing back into her day clothes. "You do not know what the tradesmen are like in this town."

"I do not care what they are like. I only care that Mr. Graham has done me a service. If I quibble over this bill, which I do not think inflated, will he leave here feeling chastened, and seek to better himself, or will he feel bitter and unfairly treated, and behave as selfishly and as peevishly as I had? I think the latter far more likely. And besides, I have the money to spare. I wish to be generous with it. It has been a hard thing to have been so poor that I had nothing to give anyone. I shall have no joy in my wealth if I cannot share some of it with those who deserve it." Mary walked over to her purse and took out two coins. "And to prove it," she said, handing a coin to each lady, "I shall give you each a guinea, to thank you for caring so vigilantly for my interests. And now you shall be prevented from further argument by fear of hypocrisy."

Mrs. Burrows attempted to give it back, but Mary would not have it. "You shall not change my mind," she said, laughing.

"Well, you will be turned out with nothing to your name before your first season is through, if you carry on like that," said Davis, stuffing the coin into her pocket without hesitation. "But I shan't say you won't have any friends."

"Well, I hope all those friends shall have bread to feed their children," said Mary as Davis took to her buttons and Mrs. Burrows departed the room with a sigh and a shake of her head.

Chapter Nineteen

Mary had worked herself into quite a fluster come the day of the ball. Her teeth all but chattered with anticipation and she could not keep hold of anything without fumbling and dropping it. She sat in silent agitation as Davis worked her hair into a torrent of ringlets, suspended with ribbon and lace.

"Do you think it is very becoming?" asked Mary, taking in her reflection in the glass. "That is, is it the sort of thing a very well-bred gentleman might admire?"

"There was never a gentleman who fell in or out of love over a hairstyle," replied Davis. "You can mark my word on that. It is always the lady who wears a certain fashion that makes it dear to a man, and not the fashion which endears the lady. But I *will* say it sets off your eyes very well."

"Well, that is something. Thank you, Davis." Mary knew her eyes were nothing worth enhancing, nothing to the clear blue of Dorothea's or even the bright quickness of Augusta's. Hers were rather plain and flat, and of somewhat indifferent colour. Did she really believe she had the powers to attach the likes of Lord Marsden to herself? She was not an ugly creature, nor entirely unintelligent, but she was not as beautiful as some girls, and wanted for the education that polishes a girl into a lady. How could she think that he could love her above all others?

Yet he had thought of her, had invited her. There could be no mistake about that, and that was enough to support her through her doubts for one evening. She felt there was some kind of fate involved in her loving him. She had known of his family so long, had always heard his name mentioned around her. She was so lowly for so long, and now she had emerged, had been presented to him in her respectable circumstance of wealth and connections. She was the girl who had always been there but whom he had never before seen. She felt the story a very romantic one and imagined how she might tell it one day, when it had become legend–the orphan and the lord, like Cendrillon and her prince.

The chill of spring had entirely gone from the air, yet the warmth of the evening could not calm the shivers of the trembling Mary Green as she arrived at the London residence of Lord and Lady Rosborough.

"Oh, Mrs. Burrows," she said, clinging to the arm of her companion, "I feel as though I shall faint."

"You shall do no such thing," Mrs. Burrows chided. "It is most unbecoming and I should be heartily disappointed to discover in you such weakness of character. Only dissemblers and ninnies faint at the prospect of a ball, and I do not consider you to be either."

Though spoken mostly in jest, Mary was chastened by these words, sensing that they were at least a little true.

Mary would endeavour to compose herself, to behave with dignity, and her resolve endured all the way up the steps and in through the doors of the house. It eroded completely, however, on the approach of Frances and her sisters, who assaulted her with their vivacity immediately she entered the ballroom.

Falling upon her, they praised the beauty of her gown, the elegance of her hair, and the charm of her person until she was so full of their admiration, she felt under very great threat of forgetting all together her humble self-possession.

The house was every bit as elegant as Westley Park, though of necessity smaller in proportions. Mrs. Burrows left the young ladies to go about the evening's business of examining and being examined, herself preferring the delights of sitting down and drinking punch.

"You must promise to dance at least one dance with our brother," said Frances. "He is not overly fond of dancing, but has expressed a keenness for it this evening which can only be for your sake, and it would be such a sting if you were to refuse him."

"Even if you do not particularly like him, one dance can do little harm," added Louisa, "and it would bring him so much pleasure."

"Of course I will dance with him," said Mary with a laugh, "if he asks me." She thought it advantageous to dance as many dances as possible, that the attentions of other gentlemen might increase her esteem in the eyes of Lord Marsden, for she knew there was nothing so distasteful to a gentleman as a lady ignored by others.

"Here comes your chance," said Harriet, looking over the shoulder of Mary, who turned to see Mr. Carrington sauntering towards them. "Do forgive him if he bumbles a little."

"Here you all are," he said.

"Yes, here we are," replied Frances.

"I have just been at the card tables. What a mess poor Sir Horace has got himself in. I thought I had better leave before he could take me down with him."

"I see," said Harriet.

"Thought I would come and see how you are all getting on."

"We are all still very well, as you see," said Louisa.

"Miss Green, I see you are arrived." He made a little awkward bow.

"Yes, only a few moments ago. I am having a charming time already. I hope you did not lose too much at cards."

"Oh, not at all!" he declared with a wave of his hand. "And I do not plan to spend much of my evening with those scoundrels. I am rather in a mood for dancing tonight."

"I think that sounds infinitely more pleasant," said Mary.

"Perhaps you might care to join me in the next?" suggested Mr. Carrington with the slightest waver of uncertainty in his voice.

"I would be honoured, sir," answered Mary, causing visible relief in the gentleman's countenance.

"Capital," he said, and stood with nothing more to say, for there were several minutes left of the dance presently taking place. He began to walk away, in no particular direction, saying, "Perhaps I shall just go and... I shall return." He had only taken a few steps when the dance came to an end. He stopped where he was and turned back. "Ah, here we are," he said, offering Mary his hand. Mary took it gracefully. She was in no humour to further anyone's embarrassment.

Mr. Carrington was not the worst of dancers, though a little heavy on his feet. His bulk did not prevent him, however, from dancing with great spirit and flourish, flushed with both the satisfaction of having Mary for a partner and with the exertion of his own merriment.

"It is rather close tonight," he offered. "Do not you think so?"

"It is always the way when there are so many people and so many candles." Thinking that he might divulge something of Lord Marsden's feelings, she asked, "Do I understand all of the family to be here tonight? I have only seen Lord and Lady Rosborough."

"Oh yes, Mr. George Ingles has lately arrived from Westley Park, and Mr. Ingles is yet in town, though set to return very shortly to the country. I believe he would have left already had his brother not convinced him to stay for tonight. He is going to be a missionary, did you know?"

"I did indeed. We were acquainted back in Oxfordshire. He is very well suited to his profession, I believe."

"Quite so," agreed Mr. Carrington. "You know, I do not think I could conceive of two people more dissimilar than Mr. Ingles and Lord Marsden. It is strange to think they could be raised in the same family."

"Really?" said Mary, who thought both to be generous, amiable and kind, though with differing tastes and manners. "I would say that Mr. George Ingles was the one less like his brothers."

"Perhaps you are right," he replied with the deferential smile of a man keen to flatter. "You have, after all, observed them in their country home, which I have not, and you are so much more clever and observant than I am. No doubt your judgment in such matters is superior to my own."

When the dance was through, he returned her to Mrs. Burrows, who had taken a seat beside, of all people, Mr. Ingles.

Mary rushed forward to greet him. "Mr. Ingles!" she exclaimed. "What a true delight it is to see you. Did you know you were seated next to my dear friend and companion, Mrs. Burrows?" The two were introduced and exchanged pleasantries before Mr. Carrington stepped forward.

"I thank you for the dance, Miss Green," he said. "May I be so bold as to claim one more before the evening is over? Perhaps the waltz?"

Although she did not wish to give him any false hope of her preference for him, she was determined that Lord Marsden should see her always engaged and so assented. Not wishing to spoil the pleasure of her acceptance, Mr. Carrington took his leave and returned to the card tables, where he could be easy with the other gentleman and drink up his self-assurance with Lord Rosborough's sherry.

"Here," said Mrs. Burrows, rising from her seat. "You sit here and talk with Mr. Ingles. You must have much to say to each other. I shall go and seek out some refreshment."

Mary did not protest, and sat with alacrity beside her friend. "I am so very pleased you decided to stay for this ball," she said, "for I had heard you were planning to be gone by now."

"I was indeed," he replied, "but my brother convinced me that it was my duty to stay. He assured me that you were to be here, and that it would be very shocking of me to leave town without having seen you."

"Well, he is absolutely correct, and I am very glad you have such good counsel in him," replied Mary. Looking distractedly over her friend's shoulder, she added, "Where *is* your brother this evening? I have not yet seen him."

"Both of them were at the card tables last I saw them."

"Oh, well I do not think I shall join them there," said Mary, keeping her gaze in that direction, perchance she might see Lord Marsden emerge into the room.

"No, nor I."

"I should rather lose my fortune, I shouldn't wonder, and I would rather give it away than lose it at gambling."

"Very well said," agreed Mr. Ingles. "Gambling is a dreadful sin."

"But I am getting better at it," she said, continuing to watch the room. "Just the other day, Mr. Carrington was teaching me some very clever manoeuvres and said I was rather a quick study. So it may not be long before they all lose their fortunes to me." Mary laughed a little at the idea of taking the gentlemen by surprise with her unsuspected proficiency. "But then, perhaps it is not very genteel for a lady to be so cunning," she added, turning to her friend.

"What say you? I have always valued your judgment. Is it unbecoming in a lady to display such skills? Can it be preferable to conceal one's abilities? To do so seems like pretence."

His reply was measured, and a little troubled. "I cannot abide artifice, but I should be more concerned for the *vice* of gambling rather than the comeliness of it."

Mary nodded her head in agreement, but hardly heard what he said, for just then she saw Lord Marsden across the room.

Attempting surreptitiously to catch his eye, she stood suddenly and turned about. "What do you think of my new gown?" she asked, without waiting for a reply. "Mrs. Burrows chose the fabric. She takes such good care of me, you know. We are determined to make the mantuamaker the most famous in London. I take all my friends to see him. And I have my own maid now. Could you ever have imagined such a thing? She is such a treasure to me. She persuaded me to wear my hair in this fashion. I should never have chosen it myself, for I am certainly not accustomed to such extravagance but as she was so convinced that it was the most fetching, I could not oppose her."

Mr. Ingles was bewildered and felt he did not recognize his old friend in this display of vanity. Before he could speak, she was accosted by a trill of laughter and her three friends came skipping up to her, all bangles and gaiety.

"There you are!" declared Frances, unaware she was interrupting any conversation. "We saw you dancing with our brother, but did not know where you had got to after that."

"You know, Mary, you must be very careful with Tom," said Louisa. "I know it was we who said you should dance with him, but you mustn't show him too much kindness or he shall mistake it for your favour and you shall break his heart."

"I think it is rather too late for caution," added Harriet. "I fear he is a hopeless case already. Shall I repeat what we heard him say to Lord Marsden just now?"

Mary longed to hear their gossip, particularly if it included Lord Marsden's response to praise of her person, but she was excessively conscious of the presence of Mr. Ingles, who had not been acknowledged by the sisters.

"Before you do," she said anxiously, "have you made the acquaintance of Mr. Ingles?" He stood to greet their suddenly silent and embarrassed curtseys.

"I am so pleased to see that London has not allowed Miss Green to be too lonely," he said in a starkly sober tone. "It is charming to see you all, but if you will excuse me, I believe I shall retire for the evening." He forced a smile and walked away. Mary suspected her friends may have given some offence, and excusing herself from them, she pursued him.

"Please do not go on my account," she urged. "I should so wish to speak with you more." He did not stop. "Will not you stay a little longer?" she said. "It is yet so early."

When they were a little concealed from the room by a large arrangement of flowers, he finally turned to her. With a disappointed frown and a lowered voice he said, "I only stayed in town for your sake, but it seems I need not have troubled myself. You are not the same Miss Green I knew in Oxfordshire, and I am sorry for it. I have never had a gift for fair speech, and apologize for my candour but I must speak as I find. I never thought less of you for your poverty, and I had hoped your change of fortune might not alter you. I pray I am much mistaken in finding that it has. Goodnight madam. I wish you every happiness, only I do not enjoy festivities such as these so much as others seem to. I should spoil your pleasure with my solemnity. Please return to your friends. You may not wish to be seen following a gentleman about. I do not think it is considered becoming."

Mary stood quite numb as she watched him go. She had longed to speak to him on matters of great weight since she had first learned of her wealth, and she had been so absorbed in her present distraction that she had repelled him with her triviality. Now she may not have another chance, as he would soon be gone, perhaps to Africa or the New World. He had once been her only friend, and though she loved her new acquaintances, she valued more highly his esteem. She wished to leave the ball. The evening's enjoyment was ruined for her, and she longed for the private counsel of Mrs. Burrows. She froze in her place, however, when she heard, from the other side of the flowers behind which she stood, the voice of Lord Marsden.

Her heart raced. Had he heard all that his brother had said to her? Surely not. Surely, if he had, he would have come to her. Whatever his precise feelings, he was, after all, a gentleman.

"I am sorry to have whipped you so thoroughly," she heard him say. "You really ought not to play the game if you are so bad at it."

"Well, I never was one for self-restraint." It was the voice of George Ingles. "Perhaps I shall have better luck with dancing."

"There is certainly no want of pretty partners, but whether you shall win any, I cannot say."

"Did I hear Tom Carrington say Miss Green was here this evening?"

Mary blushed at her own eavesdropping. George Ingles had never paid her a moment's notice in her life. He would not mention her name to Lord Marsden unless he suspected some partiality towards her.

"Yes, I am afraid poor Tom has rather lost his head over that one," the older brother replied.

"From the way he spoke, I would have said he was not the only one."

Here it is, thought Mary. He knows of Lord Marsden's feelings.

"Perhaps. I couldn't say really. She is sweet enough I suppose, and not a bad face."

"And rather flush in the pockets I gather. I shouldn't wonder if there were not a few gentlemen in London at her skirts."

So it is my money that has caught George's attention, Mary observed to herself. Surely Lord Marsden shall defend my merits as beyond that of my pocket book.

"Not any worth their salt," declared Lord Marsden with a snuff.

"That is rather hard," returned Mr. Ingles. "Are not you on friendly terms?"

"It is all well and good to be courteous to such a girl and I hope I shall never be ungenerous to her, or to any lady, but who is she? Nobody can say with any certainty. The Carringtons may associate with an orphan of unknown origins and be none the worse for it, but you shall not find me losing my head over such a creature, for all her property. We do not even know who she is–who her parents were, where she comes from. As the future Lord Rosborough, I can have no time for her."

Mary thought she might break in two at the sound of this account. Her head spun and her throat throbbed with the urge to cry. She did not wait to hear any more. She wished to be gone instantly, and crept away to find Mrs. Burrows, who could tell immediately on seeing her that all was not well.

"Whatever has happened?" she asked.

"Never mind that," Mary replied. "I wish to go. I wish to be home and never to return. Please may we go?"

"But of course," said Mrs. Burrows, taking her arm and accompanying her across the room. They were half way to the door when they were intercepted by Mr. George Ingles, who, on seeing them, had bounded over to Mary in a cheerful grin.

"Miss Green," he called to her. She turned to him, her face hot with indignation. "You are not going." It was more a question than an observation, for clearly she was indeed leaving. She did not reply, but allowed Mrs. Burrows to answer for her.

"I am afraid Miss Green is not feeling well."

"Oh dear," he said. "I am so sorry. But cannot I convince you to stay just long enough for me to introduce Mr. Belmont?"

"Mr. Belmont?" repeated Mary, recalling the name of the artist from Paris who was the guest of honour at the picnic she had forgone at Westley Park, and with the name the painful memory of Mr. George Ingles' laughter as Augusta showed him her private drawing.

"Yes," continued Mr. Ingles in smiling enthusiasm. "You did not make his acquaintance in Oxfordshire, and I understood from your friends that you may wish to retain an art instructor. It happens Mr. Belmont is taking on a few pupils, and I thought perhaps to recommend you to him."

"I see," she said, trembling. "Now that I am rich enough to benefit your friend, you consider me deserving of your attention and praise. I thank you for your condescension, but as I have never before been found worthy of your good opinion, I am afraid I must decline it now."

Pulling Mrs. Burrows along behind her, she fled the room, and, in so doing, ran headlong into Augusta Hargreaves.

"Polly!" exclaimed Augusta. "Polly, it is you!" She threw her arms around the startled Mary and embraced her like a long lost sister. "I hardly recognized you," she said. "How elegant you look! Dorothea, come and see. It is Polly, and she is quite transformed. Do not you think she is everything fashionable and charming?"

Dorothea, who had been standing behind her sister, looked placidly at Mary and said only, "Quite."

Mary was overwhelmed. The sight of the Hargreaves sisters and the sound of her old name were too distressing after all the feelings she had run through that evening. More than ever she needed to escape. Unable to speak for risk of tears, she broke free of Augusta and, without a word, hastened from the house.

Chapter Twenty

Mary hardly left her bed all the following day, leaving strict instructions that she was not receiving visitors. When she heard Mr. Ingles had called after breakfast, she regretted her injunction a little, as it seemed exceedingly kind of him and she would have liked to have made some amends before he left for Africa. She had long lived with others thinking ill of her, but his opinion was more valuable to her, and the more so for being justly formed.

Mrs. Burrows made several gentle attempts to draw from her the cause of her low spirits, but Mary would not confide in her. Although Mrs. Burrows did not usually have compassion for such brooding behaviour, especially in one so rich, she knew Mary was not generally susceptible to moods, and thus that her friend must truly be suffering. For her part, Mary never spoke harshly to Mrs. Burrows, but would simply claim a headache, or feign exhaustion. She could see that her companion had been in the right about Lord Marsden, and felt ashamed to admit that he was, after everything, responsible for at least some of her present misery.

After a day or two, however, Mrs. Burrows felt it in Mary's interest that she not languish about the house any longer, and that she must take some action.

"I was thinking," she said to Mary at breakfast, "that we might take a little stroll this morning. We are having such fine weather, and you know it shall not last. I hate to see you waste it by staying indoors all week."

Mary nodded. Mrs. Burrows always gave good counsel, and she knew she ought to do something. If only she could walk clear out of

London and away from the glaring pavement and lace bonnets. She thought of the woods around Challey Hall–her only fond memory of the place–and wished she might be there now, might happen upon that humble curate who would love her instantly and lead her away from the life of folly in which she had lately placed so many ephemeral hopes.

"Perhaps we could stop by Mr. Graham's shop," Mrs. Burrows continued, encouraged by Mary's assent. "I believe he was expecting some new ribbon this week."

"I should like that," replied Mary honestly. Mr. Graham's was perhaps the only face she thought might indeed raise her spirits. His sense and his kindliness could only do her good.

And so the ladies left the house, Mrs. Burrows holding Mary's arm in hers and smiling brightly at her friend. Mary was still not entirely cheerful, but felt a little braver than she had, and was forced to admit that the air was very sweet that morning and did indeed clear her gloomy head a little. When they arrived at Mr. Graham's shop, they found it quite full. Mary silently gave herself the credit of having brought such custom to this worthy craftsman, which made her feel a little smug, though mostly disappointed that they would not have all his attention to themselves.

"I wonder if we should come back a little later," said Mary, stopping on the pavement across from the shop. "It is rather busy, and I imagine quite cramped inside."

"Let us walk towards Mayfair then, for I have heard there is a new sweet shop there that I have been very anxious to try. This throng might have dispersed by the time we have sated our palates."

"All right," said Mary with a weak smile and little enthusiasm. She did not care for sweets just at that moment, but she could see the effort Mrs. Burrows was making. She yielded with a wish to appease her friend, as well as a respect for her superior wisdom.

The ladies entered the sweet shop, ordered a few items and some tea, and were just sitting down to enjoy their indulgence when the door swung open, ushering Harriet, Frances, and Louisa into the shop. When they spied Mary, their faces erupted into beaming smiles and they all instantly bustled over to her table.

"Mary! How pleased I am to see you," said Frances, taking a seat next to her. "You know we just came from your house. We were going to bring you to this very place, which we only learned of yesterday and which is already our favourite. But you have outwitted us and found it yourself, and here you are."

"It was Mrs. Burrows' idea," answered Mary.

"Mrs. Burrows must be the cleverest person I know," said Louisa. "She always discovers things before anyone else."

"Lua darling," said Harriet, also taking a seat at the table, "would you be so good as to seek out some tea for us? I am awfully parched after all that walking."

Louisa, uncomplaining, turned to go in search of some refreshment.

"Whatever happened to you at the ball the other night?" asked Frances. "We all looked and looked for you. Someone said you had left, but we thought that could not be right. You had been dancing only a few minutes before, and you looked so charming in your new dress. It seemed impossible you should not wish to stay."

"I am sorry," said Mary, looking down into her tea. "I am afraid I had a sudden headache."

"That is unfortunate," said Frances. "We were all very disappointed, though none of us so much as our brother."

"Quite right," concurred Harriet. "He said you had promised him a second dance, and I never saw a gentleman so sorry to be slighted."

"Oh dear," said Mary, looking between them in apology. "I had quite forgotten about that."

"Oh, never mind Tom," said Frances. "There were so many other people asking after you who are much more interesting."

"Indeed there were," continued Harriet. "We made the acquaintance of your two cousins, who were both very keen to see you–Miss Augusta especially."

Mary turned a little pale at the mention of her cousins, though the effect went unnoticed by all but Mrs. Burrows.

"And you never said what a beauty Miss Hargreaves is," said Louisa, who was just rejoining them, squeezing a chair up to the table. "I swear I never saw such a face, and such elegance! You know, I cannot even recall what she wore, except that I think it could have been anything in the world and she would still have captivated the room. We did not speak much with her, as she was asked to dance every dance."

"Yet she was never out of breath," added Harriet.

"I hope she danced with your brother," said Mary, "if only to make up for my ill treatment of him."

"She certainly did!" said Louisa.

"I know in my heart that his true affections are for you only," said Frances, "but I will say, he was distracted enough by Miss Hargreaves, if only to pass the evening tolerably."

"And he was not the only one," said Harriet, "for she also much interested Lord Marsden, or I am much mistaken. He was one of her first partners."

Mary's heart contracted at the mention of Lord Marsden. She returned her gaze to her tea, hoping her blush would go undetected. She needed not have worried, for they were all engaged in their own retelling of the evening.

"And he danced with me!" interjected Louisa. "You forget how he asked me also."

"Of course he did," said Frances. "I am sure you are his favourite, or will be by and by. No doubt he had forgotten Miss Hargreaves by morning–unless Mary has some intelligence from her time in Oxfordshire that would suggest otherwise."

"And that would have been most cruel to have kept from her friends, knowing their feelings," added Louisa, a mixture of hope and accusation.

Mary looked back at all three of them, their faces turned in expectation towards her. Lord Marsden was lost to her, indeed, was never hers to be lost. She did not wish to engage in their prattle, yet how could she deny Louisa a little comfort, when they had always been so kind to her?

"They shall be brother and sister soon enough." She watched as they took in the news. Louisa gasped suddenly.

"You do not mean he is to marry Miss Augusta!"

Mary could not help but laugh. "She would like that!" she said, "but no, not at all. Miss Hargreaves is to marry his brother, Mr. George Ingles."

"Oh, I see," Miss Louisa sighed in relief.

"We were all quite fond of Miss Augusta" said Frances. "It should be such a shame if I were forced to hate her for all eternity."

The sisters all laughed together while Mary took a quiet sip from her tea, wishing for a polite means of excusing herself from the table and from their company. She did not love them any less, only in her present state of mind, she could take no more of their chatter. She did not wish to injure their feelings, yet she longed to be gone.

Having observed Mary throughout, Mrs. Burrows determined it

was time to take her away. Rising from her seat, she said, "I am so sorry, ladies, but we have an appointment with Mr. Graham, and it would be frightful of us to keep him waiting."

Equal parts surprise and gratitude, Mary took her cue and stood up from her seat. "Thank you, Mrs. Burrows," she said. "I had almost forgotten, so caught up was I in news of the ball. But of course, Mr. Graham will be wondering what has become of us if we do not make haste." To the sisters she added, "Do give my apologies to your brother."

"But you may give them to him yourself, at dinner on Thursday. Do say you will be there," said Frances.

"Both of your cousins are invited, and they were so eager to see you. And Lord Marsden and his brother are coming, so you see, you must come," added Louisa.

At that moment, Mary realized she must leave London. She had no appetite for dinners and balls and shopping. She missed the country in summer–the solitude, the silence, the space for reflection, the companionship of nature. It would not do to make false excuses for avoiding her friends, and she did not have the strength to explain herself.

"I am dreadfully sorry," she said, "I shall be gone by Thursday." Mrs. Burrows looked at her in confusion.

"Gone?" the sisters were stunned. "Where on earth are you going and for what purpose that it cannot be put off until after Thursday?"

"Norchester," she replied, "my estate in Gloucestershire. It has all been arranged, and I have appointments there that cannot be put off. In truth, I really ought to have gone there before ever I came to London, though I am glad I did not or I may never have met all of you."

"This all sounds rather final," said Harriet. "You will not be gone the whole season."

"I cannot say for certain," said Mary. "It depends on how long everything takes. I have never even seen the place, at least not since I was four years old."

"You must permit us to call on you tomorrow, to say our proper good-byes," said Louisa.

"And you must then give us a more thorough explanation than this, which is terribly sudden and mysterious," added Frances.

As she spoke, the door opened again, and in strode Mr. George Ingles with Dorothea, Augusta and Mrs. Preston. Seeing them, Mary began to tremble with something like rage or panic and she struggled to fasten her bonnet.

"Of course," replied Mrs. Burrows, guiding Mary away from the table. "Do come by tomorrow. We shall be at home."

Mrs. Preston then caught sight of Mary and, without apology, turned from the shop and fled across the street and away, narrowly missing the wheels of a passing carriage and drawing the attention of everyone in the place. The ensuing dispute whispered between her charges as to whether or not to go in pursuit of her was quickly concluded in the negative as Mr. Ingles stepped forward to greet Mary and Mrs. Burrows.

"Miss Green!" he said cheerfully as they approached. "What splendid chance."

Mary curtseyed but did not reply, staring over his shoulder at Miss Preston's shrinking form, waddling away from them down the street.

"Polly!" Augusta rushed forward and embraced her, glancing quickly out of the window after her aunt. "You are not leaving?"

"We have an appointment with the mantuamaker," explained Mrs. Burrows.

"Well, you must permit us to accompany you," said Augusta, "for I should very much like to know the best place to order a new gown. It has been so long since we were last in London that I am certain it has all changed."

"Perhaps another time," said Mrs. Burrows, nudging Mary out of the door. "Your friends await you." She indicated the table where they had been sitting. "And besides, the shop was very crowded when we passed it on our way here, and I expect it shall hardly accommodate the two of us, much less a larger group. Miss Carrington, no doubt, would be most happy to take you there in a little while, when the multitudes have thinned."

Without waiting for a reply, Mrs. Burrows jostled her charge out onto the pavement and the pair of them set off at a pace away from the sweet shop where they had abandoned their desserts as well as their friends.

Chapter Twenty-One

"So we are going to Norchester, are we?" asked Mrs. Burrows as they turned the corner.

"Yes."

"It is all arranged is it? Appointments that cannot be broken and everything?"

"Yes."

"Excellent. Well, I am glad you have taken care of everything. I shall not concern myself with any of it."

"No."

"And we are leaving on what day?"

"Thursday."

"I see, Thursday. Have the staff been told?"

"No."

"Shall I tell them?"

"Yes."

"And the coachman, does he know?"

"No."

"I shall tell him as well then, shall I?"

"Yes."

"And the staff at Norchester, have they been told?"

"No."

"All right. Shall I have my brother get in touch with them and ensure everything will be ready for our arrival?"

"Yes."

"Very good. I am so glad you have thought of everything."

Mary stopped walking, covered her face with her hands and began to sob. "I am so sorry," she muttered through her gloves as Mrs. Burrows led her into a deserted lane to allow her to shed her tears in dignified seclusion.

Soon finding herself more ridiculous than miserable, Mary took the handkerchief offered by Mrs. Burrows and repeated her apologies.

"Now then, my dear, I think that is enough outing for one day, do not you agree?" Mary nodded and Mrs. Burrows ushered her back towards the street and into a hackney coach which soon had them home and comfortably installed in the drawing room with a little wine and water.

"Since your distress is depriving me of the balance of the London season, I think it only just that you share with me its cause," said Mrs. Burrows. "Why are we leaving for Gloucestershire?"

Mary set down her glass and let go a long sigh. She had not known it to be her wish until she had spoken the words that day, and now it seemed impossible that she could do otherwise, and absurd that she had not previously thought of it.

"I am ungrateful, I suppose," she began. "I have been blessed beyond the imagination of most ordinary people. Yet I want what even most beggars possess. I wish to know who I am. I am only Polly. That is all. And I do not even know if that is my real name. I feel I have been playing a part here in town, and I do not wish to pretend any longer. I do not belong in London society, at least not now. All this ordering gowns and chasing husbands, it has never been the object of my fancy. All I ever longed for was my own freedom, the power to do some good, and the love of true friends. I have made friends with some very good people here, but as I do not even know my own self, I feel their love cannot reach me." Mary paused and drew a deep breath. "I do not know what I expect to find at

Norchester–peace perhaps, or some purpose. It was the home of the only person ever to love me." Mary lowered her gaze as her eyes again grew hot and she began to feel the sting of fresh tears. "That is why I would like to go there, now, when I do not feel that anyone knows me, or loves me, or even wishes to know me. That is doubtless unfair to my friends who have been so kind. You must forgive me."

Having known her share of true hardship, Mrs. Burrows was composed more of good sense than sensibility, and not usually inclined to sympathy for the self-pity of rich young girls with houses in Portman Square; nevertheless, Mrs. Burrows was touched by the simple wish of this orphan who had always been as magnanimous with her wealth as she was in her disposition. Indeed, Mrs. Burrows herself possessed this one thing which Mary did not, and in this single way, could see that her own fortune was superior.

"I cannot agree that you are so unloved as you believe," she said as Mary took out her handkerchief and pressed it to her eyes, "nor that you do not belong in society. Indeed, society could profit very much from your influence, but Norchester is your home now, and if you wish to go home, far be it from me to dissuade you."

Mary nodded, folding the handkerchief, stroking its edges and releasing jagged, long breaths. She had not mentioned the heartbreak occasioned by her disappointed affection for one Lord Marsden. She was grateful for Mrs. Burrows' neglect of that subject also, though it was perhaps apparent to both ladies that only an event of such a nature could have occasioned so deep an alteration in both emotion and intent.

"There is much to do if we are to be gone by Thursday," continued Mrs. Burrows as she rose from her seat. "You may rest here a while but I shall go and speak to the housekeeper."

Mary looked up at her with a watery smile. "Thank you," she said hoarsely. Her friend gave no reply, but pressed her arm tenderly as she passed on her way out of the room.

Chapter Twenty-Two

The parties on the journey to Gloucestershire were the same as on Mary's journey into London, though the mood was not at all alike. Mrs. Burrows kept mostly to her novel, and Mr. Clark to his files.

Mary, a mixture of anxiety and quiet sadness, spoke barely a word as they departed the city. As they travelled further into the country, she began to relax and was able to enjoy a little of the passing scenery before falling asleep.

She had not disclosed to anyone what Mr. Ingles had said to her, but she thought of little else. The initial sting of Lord Marsden's rejection had at first eclipsed her hurt over his brother's condemnation but as the days had passed, and that sharper pain dulled a little, she found her friend's disapproval to be the more enduring, more profound wound.

Everything Lord Marsden had said was true, and so obvious that Mary felt ashamed for believing it could be otherwise. The flattery of others had blinded her to the reality that she was not part of that society into which she had cast herself. Although the admiration of Mr. Carrington was perhaps genuine, even *he* might not have found himself able to act upon it. How much less could she hope for from Lord Marsden, with his noble expectations and the affection of every lady in London! Such a gentleman was so far above her own station that only his courtesy and not his hand, or even his heart, could ever be engaged by her. She had been a fool to think otherwise, and her folly had lowered her in the esteem of the only person whose good opinion she had ever sought. She had therefore resolved to reject the expectations of society and to pursue instead a more pious and charitable life.

Mary had at first insisted on traveling by stage, as she had somewhat lost her appetite for luxury and wished to behave in a less indulgent way. She only relented and agreed to bring her own carriage when confronted by the calculations of Mr. Clark, making plain the extravagance of keeping a carriage in London during her absence rather than taking it with her.

As the journey progressed and the party drew nearer their destination, Mary's feelings of anticipation and eagerness overtook her other emotions and she began to grow more animated.

"Do you think Norchester shall be a large house?" she asked Mr. Clark. "My memories of it are that it was the size of a palace, but I was very small and had just come from the orphanage, so I do not trust my own recollections."

"It is certainly the largest house in the neighbourhood," replied Mr. Clark, "though not in the county. Your memory of it as a very large house is not misinformed."

Mrs. Burrows looked to see her reaction, which was a contemplative nod. Mary wondered to herself what she might possibly do with such a grand house, but her questions were eclipsed by her increasing impatience to return the place of which she had so often dreamt with such sweet reminiscence.

It was dark and very late when the carriage turned into the drive at Norchester. Mary held tightly to Mrs. Burrows' hand as they approached. Even with the brightness of the moon, they could not see much of the prospect, and Mary strained to take it in. All she could see in the darkness was the outline of the steep rooves of an ancient hall. Stepping down from the carriage, she turned about, eagerly breathing in the air of the place, and savouring the moment of her return. In silence they ascended the steps and entered the house, which, given the late hour, was not lit. As they were led to their chambers, Mary peered through every doorway and down every hall, in hopes of placing her faint but cherished memories.

As she stepped into the room that had been selected as her chamber, she gasped, for she knew it instantly as Mrs. Markham's old room. Only the linens and personal effects had been changed. She would not have been able to recall it in any detail, but she recognized it immediately. Mrs. Markham must have allowed her to enter it, and such occasions must have been so singular and so precious as to imprint the scene upon her mind. Here it was that she had felt the most loved, had most known her own worth.

Dismissing the servant, she sat lightly upon the side of the bed, as if not to disturb the lady of the house whose spirit may yet have slept there, and said a tearful prayer for that kind and gentle lady. Despite her tears and the long and weary hours of travel, Mary found herself indifferent to sleep, and sat some time at the window, contemplating the dark of the view and mindlessly partaking of the refreshment that had been set for her. At last feeling the exhaustion of the day, she undressed herself, as she had always done at Challey Hall, and slipped reverently into bed just as the sky began to lighten.

Chapter Twenty-Three

In the full light of morning, Mary rose and took some time alone, inspecting the details of the room, touching every corner of the furniture, and wondering what Mrs. Markham might have thought or felt when she had inhabited this room. She may not have been her mother, but she took the place of one in Mary's mind, and she wished to know her with all the depth of feeling of a daughter.

The next few days were spent in much the same way, going over the house and the gardens in the same pensive contemplation, imagining the life she might have led had the Markhams not fallen ill that fateful summer. These grounds, these halls, would have been the backdrop of her life, familiar and taken for granted, filled in with the love and affection of caring parents, which she might also have learned to undervalue. Would she have grown spoilt and presumptuous surrounded by all this wealth? She had always believed that the few short months with the Markhams had given her the strength to tolerate with gratitude and equanimity her years with the Hargreaves, and that more of it would only have benefitted her more. She now wondered whether it was merely the suggestion of their love, the possibility of it, without its prolongation that had given it such influence over her, and that, had she been immersed in it for longer, she might have simply become the girl Mr. Ingles found her to be in London–only much sooner and more irreparably so. She would never know, of course, and so her childhood at Norchester, and its effects upon her character, must only be imagined.

"I should like to hire a few more staff," she said to the housekeeper one morning. "I should like to provide employment for so many as I can without extravagance. I have discussed the matter with Mr. Clark and we have drawn up this list." She handed her a piece of parchment. "You may use your discretion to deviate from the details if necessary, provided you do not exceed the expenditure."

"Yes madam," replied the housekeeper, taking the list from her mistress.

"And I intend to use the smallest reception room as an artist's studio. Therefore, please have the carpets and furniture removed."

Mary had thought much about how best to use her new position for philanthropic ends. Engaging and employing others seemed to her the best form of charity, particularly in the case of skilled and accomplished individuals. And so in addition to the new staff, she hoped to find a tutor to aid her in improving her art. Perhaps she might in time convince others in the neighbourhood to do the same and so keep at least one talent from starvation. Locating that talent would have to wait, however, as Mary had other concerns which took even higher priority.

Having settled into the house, Mary's first order of business was to visit the orphanage where she had spent the first four years of her life. She dreaded it only a little, for she did not recall any mistreatment while she was there, nor had she any memories that would make it foreboding to see the place again. It was only apprehension naturally resulting from the passage of so many years, and a certain anxiety that feelings of loss may arise and threaten to overwhelm her. The presence of Mrs. Burrows was, however, a great comfort and assurance, for she trusted that lady to devise a quick departure if necessary and to take charge of any situation that might arise by Mary's fragility.

In the end, there was no cause for fear. Mary and her companion were welcomed by a servant girl into a clean and bright building where they met with one Mrs. Pringle, a lady of the middle age, who seemed genuinely glad to receive them.

"May I offer you tea?" she asked, ringing the bell before either lady could answer her. A girl of about eleven came demurely into the room. "This is Sarah. She is training to be a maid of all work," said Mrs. Pringle. "Sarah, please bring these ladies some tea." Sarah curtseyed in silence and briskly departed. "We pride ourselves on finding the best apprenticeships and positions for our children," said Mrs. Pringle. "Indeed, we receive inquiries from across the county, and often beyond, such is our reputation for educating our waifs and strays. You may have heard, we are not like so many homes for children. We are able to purchase the best situations for our boys and girls, and do very well by them. We do not blindly abandon them to cruel masters like so many others."

"I am afraid this is my first encounter with any home for children since leaving this one, as I have until very lately not seen much of the world. Is there really such difference between homes?"

"I wish I could say they were all as well provided for as we are, and, I flatter myself, run with as much care and skill. Sadly, that is not the case, and what is more, not everyone so much as shares my wish. I have received some criticism for treating the children so well. There are those who feel somehow that parents need to be discouraged from orphaning their children, or children from abandoning their parents."

"I am very glad to hear you do not heed such nonsense," said Mrs. Burrows. "If there are parents who, though alive, must yet leave their children to the parish, I do not imagine there to be any true choice in the matter."

Both ladies looked at Mary, whose parents may well have been in that class. A brief and uncomfortable silence followed, broken thankfully by the entrance of Sarah with the tea.

"And how are you able to provide so much better for the children in your home?" asked Mary, who was very pleased not to be confronted upon her arrival with starved and neglected foundlings. "Is this a particularly generous parish?"

"Not perhaps on the whole, more than any other," answered Mrs. Pringle, pouring the tea, "but we have been very fortunate in our benefactor. We are the beneficiaries of a trust which provides very amply for the numbers in our parish. The trust was established by Mrs. Markham some twenty-one years ago, and has enabled us to greatly improve our facilities and the quality of care we are able to provide."

"Twenty-one years ago you say?" said Mary, accepting a cup and taking only a little sugar. "That would have been when I came here, or thereabouts."

"Yes, madam," said Mrs. Pringle, "and very lucky you were to arrive at that time, for that is when Mrs. Markham began to take an interest in the place. Before that, we did not have nearly the funds to do what we are now able to, and you would have had a much harder time of it had you come to us before that." Mrs. Pringle took a sip of her tea before continuing, "However, it has been suggested that it was Mrs. Markham's fondness for you that inspired her to support the orphanage, so perhaps it was your coming that caused the change."

Mary blushed to consider that her mere existence could have resulted in such an improvement in the lives of so many. "Were you here at that time?" she asked.

"I am afraid not, madam. I have only heard of these things from my predecessor, from whom I took over this position five years ago."

"So you did not know Mrs. Markham yourself?"

"I did not, but her reputation has endured all these years, and I assure you she was the kindest of ladies. I understand she took you in just before her unfortunate end, and that she has left Norchester to you."

"She has, yes, and it shall be quite a task to replace her as mistress. I hope to learn all I can about her, and take instruction from her example."

"Well, all I can tell you is of her charity. Aside from her financial contribution, she was a frequent visitor here. She doted on the girls–taught them some needlework and other skills. Clearly, she took the greatest interest in you, though she assisted several of our older children to excellent positions. She also donated many items to the house, and her public charity spurred others on to contribute, as the other ladies of the area could not stand to be long outdone, and so we began to receive more and more donations as a result of her example. It is a wondrous thing to wield the pride of others for the good of the needy."

"I could not agree more," concurred Mrs. Burrows, setting down her cup and looking at Mary. "And now I believe Miss Green is most anxious to be shown the rest of the house, if that is possible."

"But of course," answered Mrs. Pringle. "Please, follow me."

The ladies were led through a series of clean but simple rooms and were presented several industrious but healthy children. As they thanked Mrs. Pringle, and were about to depart, Mary ventured one last question, which had been burning in her heart since first they arrived.

"I was wondering, Mrs. Pringle, whether you might know anything, that is, whether there is any way to discover information about my own case–about my parentage, I mean. Is it possible, for example, that someone might have some knowledge they could share with me? Or would there be any record of anything that might give me a clue? I do not wish to trouble anyone, but you might imagine the significance this matter holds for me."

"I am sorry Miss Green," replied Mrs. Pringle. "I took the liberty of reviewing our records when first you contacted us, and I can tell you that, as you were left secretly and without any identifying information, there is nothing that I am able to tell you, and if anyone in the area knows anything, they have not disclosed it to us in the last twenty-one years, and so are not like to do so now. There is no one here at the house at present who was here when you came to us, so there is not even anyone you could question, I am afraid."

Mary had expected this answer, though she could not help feeling the weight of a lifetime's disappointment at having her expectation met so finally. "That is as I thought," she said. "Thank you."

She and Mrs. Burrows said their good-byes and headed down the path towards the gate. They were just out onto the lane and about to enter their carriage when Mrs. Pringle came hastening up behind them calling out, "Wait! Miss Green!" They stopped and turned, Mary stepping forward to meet her. "I have just thought of something," explained Mrs. Pringle. Mary was all eagerness. "There was a nurse, a Miss Harper, who worked at the house and had done all her life, as far back as your time, I imagine. Around the time I came to work here, she left to accept a position as a private nurse. I cannot promise that she could tell you anything, but I have her address if you should wish to write to her."

Mary was delighted. "Thank you, please, yes, if it is no trouble. I would be most grateful," she said, tripping over her words in her enthusiasm.

Mrs. Pringle retrieved the address and gave it to Mary with an expression of hope that she might be successful, and that she might think fondly of the orphans when planning her affairs. Mary promised to keep the children in her prayers and to see if there was any way she could assist them.

As the carriage rolled away, Mary clung to the address she had been given as though it contained the whole of her history and not merely the suggestion of an unlikely source of unknown information.

"I was thinking," she said to Mrs. Burrows. "So much has been done for me in my life. I should like to do something for those not so fortunate as to be taken in and provided for by the likes of Mrs. Markham. At the orphanage they seem very well cared for, but beyond that, they must go somewhere. I cannot take in any of them myself, and I can only provide employment for some. Do you think we might train some of them for service? It is only us living in the house, and I could easily tolerate any of their blunders if it would aid them to have a reference from Norchester. Do you think that a good scheme?"

"I think the housekeeper might have something to say about it," replied Mrs. Burrows, "but it sounds an excellent idea."

Mary smiled and sat back in her seat to watch the countryside pass by. She did not say anything, but she thought to herself that Mr. Ingles would be very well pleased with her plan.

Chapter Twenty-Four

One morning, for the first time since her arrival at Norchester, Mary received a letter by post. It was from Frances Carrington, and Mary was surprised at how happy it made her that her friend would take the trouble to write. She opened it straight away.

My dear Friend,

I so hope you have been enjoying your time in Gloucestershire and that your journey was safe and comfortable. How intrepid you were to undertake it in a single day! I do not think I should survive it. I do wish you could have stayed for the remainder of the season, for our sakes as well as yours. We are all quite wretched without you and feel your absence every day. London was so much more pleasant with you this year, and poor Tom forces upon himself a cheerful countenance, but those of us who know him well know how he suffers. And so our wish to see you back here is quite a selfish one.

Yet it is not entirely for our own benefit that we wish you back. We have been vastly enjoying the company of your old companions and wish you could share in our pleasure. Our amazement increases with every encounter with the misses Hargreaves, as we can none of us understand your omission in recounting their charm and their exceptional sensibilities. We all eagerly await the formal announcement of engagement between Miss Hargreaves and Mr. George Ingles, yet she is so elegant, she shows not a moment's anxiety or impatience for it. Her calm and elevated demeanour is something to which I myself could only hope to aspire.

And what a kindred spirit we have discovered in Miss Augusta!

She has such amiable high spirit as I do not think we have any of us encountered before. If she is any less elegant than her sister, she makes up for it in the liveliness of her manners. I do not doubt she will also soon have some announcement to make, though there is no particular gentleman of which we are aware who has captured her affection.

We have taken them both to see your Mr. Graham, and how pleased they have been with his work! Miss Augusta has ordered at least three gowns already, and has the most extravagant tastes, while Miss Hargreaves has the simplest. At times it seems impossible that they should be sisters!

I do not write, however, merely to advise you of the goings on in town. I have some news which I hope will bring you as much joy as it does all of us. We have determined to visit Bath, rather than returning directly to the country. Papa had at first proposed Bath, but Tom would not hear of it, as Lord Marsden was to visit Lyme. We were quite in league with our brother in the beginning, though we could not bring ourselves to confront Papa on the subject. We thought there may be a bitter feud, or that perhaps Tom would simply go where he pleased and we would go to Bath without him. The matter was still not yet resolved when you announced your removal to Gloucestershire. It was thereafter quite an easy matter to convince Tom of the benefits of Bath, knowing that Norchester is not more than ten miles away. Therefore, we are settled on Bath. We depart in a fortnight, and shall stay at least two months. It is our dearest hope that we shall see you often while we are there. You are invited most heartily by everyone to join us in Bath. You may stay with us for as long as you wish.

I regret to say that the Hargreaves and the Ingles all go directly to Lyme, so you shall not have the pleasure of their company, but I hope we shall yet be quite merry.

I shall send you the direction when we are arrived. Do write and tell us how it is at Norchester for we all long to hear from you. My brother asks me to add that he has purchased a new carriage which he wishes to show you, and that he hopes you might permit him a tour of your grounds in it during our stay. I would share with you details of his purchase, but refrain for fear of shedding tears of boredom that might fall upon my page and blur the ink.

With great anticipation to see you again soon, I remain,

Your constant friend,

Frances.

Mary put the letter down beside her, then picked it up again, and read it through once more. She did miss her friends. She had disavowed London society and its trappings, but must it follow that she should also discard the friendship of those who had been so kind to her? Might she accept their invitation to join them in Bath? Should she invite them to stay at Norchester? Perhaps she could interest them in some of the charity work which she had begun. Her introduction of Mr. Graham to such ladies had done him much service. She might achieve the same ends with another cause.

Mr. Ingles could not reproach her for inviting them on such noble grounds, however silly he might have found them to be in London. If she could show them all she was doing for the orphans of the parish, they might be inspired to some act of their own. And there must be other interests in which she could engage them. She knew them all to have kind hearts and she believed that all that was required was for someone to show them how they could achieve some great good for another and they would do it.

Feeling that she required a little air to better consider her objectives, Mary set out from the house to walk about the wilderness of the grounds. The day was fine, and the grounds, though well kept, were not grand. She followed a path away from the house which took her over a stream and into a wood. Here she found a happy little bench, which must have been placed by someone who had often walked this path and known precisely when such one should wish to sit.

Mary looked around at the trees and thought how grateful she was to have their shade just at that moment. She recalled the woods at Challey Hall and how they had shielded her from so much more than the rays of the sun. They had been her refuge, her only true solitude, where nothing could be taken from her and no one could tell her who she was or was not. She smiled to think how she had secretly dreamt of meeting with a wandering pilgrim, a humble curate who might rescue her from her captors. Now she had no need of that sort of redemption. She was in her own home, was master of her own future, and finally was able to be the salvation of others who were more hopeless than she had ever truly been.

She had intended, on her walk, to consider her friends and her plans for their visit to Norchester, but she found herself instead preoccupied with the thought of Mr. Ingles. She longed to tell him all she was doing, and all she was planning. She yearned for him to know that she had not succumbed to the temptations of a life of pomp and promenades. If she could but write to him, explain to him the transient nature of her flirtation with society, surely he would understand. Surely he would excuse her distraction. But she could not write. There was not even anyone through whom she could send a message. And she could not return to the neighbourhood to speak to him in person unless she had some other reason for visiting, and she had none.

Shaking off these contemplations, she rose to continue to walk and her plans for the Carringtons. Remaining as she did beneath the trees she did not notice the rapid darkening of the sky and was quite shocked when, moments after emerging into a clearing, the clouds let loose their burden and all but drenched her in a moment. Turning and hastening back to the cover of the trees, she did not notice the figure across the clearing who had been walking in the opposite direction and, but for the rain, would have crossed her path in a few moments.

Standing in the wood, Mary considered what she might do. She was sheltered where she was, but it was a long walk back to the house, and most of that through open lawns. She might be a long time waiting for the rain to pass, as the clouds looked thick, and seemed of a tenacious persuasion. She thought perhaps she was not too far from the village by now and perhaps if she carried on, the woods across the clearing might take her most of the way, and from there she might procure a carriage to take her home. Looking up across the clearing to see if she could fathom the distance to the village she froze, for the figure from across the clearing was running towards her. Gasping in sudden terror, she attempted to slip behind a tree, tangled her petticoat in a shrub and fell upon the wet ground. She struggled to rise to her feet as her would-be attacker stood over her, offering his hand. When, in a moment, she realized she was in no danger, she looked up at the figure on the path and noticed that he was dressed as a man of the cloth. His face, though friendly, was pocked, and belied neither amusement nor great concern at her antics. He merely offered her his hand in silence until she accepted it, then pulled her to her feet without much effort.

"Are you all right?" he asked, without apologizing for startling her.

"Thank-you," she replied, brushing off her hands. "I believe I am, though my skirt may have its own grievance."

"I only meant to tell you that there is a little folly just across there," he said pointing to the other side of the clearing, "if you should wish to keep dry in it. It has a small seat, but nothing else."

"That is kind of you," said Mary. "I am much obliged."

He gestured that she should follow him, and they ran across the clearing and into the far wood, where indeed there was a small stone folly among the trees.

Recalling her manners, Mary asked the gentleman his name, which she learned was Hawthorne, the local rector.

"But I have not seen you in church since I arrived," said Mary. "Do you not preach to your congregation?"

"I have only just returned from Canterbury," he replied.

"Canterbury?" Mary repeated. Was he a pilgrim after all?

"Yes, there was a gentleman there giving a lecture on the birds of the new world, and I asked Mr. Thurber if he might watch over my flock while I was away. It was he you saw in church, though I shall be returning to my pulpit this Sunday."

She wished to tell him of her friend Mr. Ingles and his plans for Africa, but felt instinctively that Mr. Hawthorne would not be interested. He stood, rather stoic, watching the rain from the entrance of the folly and hummed to himself. She told him of her recent occupation of Norchester and wondered aloud how she might make her way back to the house.

Without turning around he replied that he might help her there. He did not have a carriage but he could send someone to order hers, if she wished. His house was only at the bottom of the hill and over the lane, and she might wait there quite comfortably.

Before Mary could object to the propriety of his proposal he added, "It is quite all right. My mother shall be there, and no doubt very glad of a visitor."

And so Mary agreed and followed him at a quick pace down the hill and across the lane to the rectory.

Chapter Twenty-Five

The rectory was solid and unassuming, built in the old style. Until the rain began, it had been a warm day, and inside the house the air yet held to the heat of the earlier sun. Mrs. Hawthorne must have been anxious to keep out any damp or draft, for as they entered the drawing room, Mary and Mr. Hawthorne discovered her seated beside a freshly lit fire.

"Well, this is convenient," remarked Mr. Hawthorne. "I was just about to order a fire to be lit for our guest, who was caught in the rain. May I present Miss Green, of Norchester."

Mrs. Hawthorne made to rise from her seat in honour of such a lady as mistress of Norchester, which made Mary herself feel awkward. She replied with a gesture for Mrs. Hawthorne to remain seated as Mr. Hawthorne drew her up a chair on the other side of the fire from his mother.

"I told Miss Green she might wait here while I send someone to Norchester to bring her carriage," he said and promptly left the room, presumably to do precisely as he said, though he did not state as much.

Mrs. Hawthorne did not seem at all put out and simply rang for tea. A female servant of Mrs. Hawthorne's age entered the room. "Tea please, Walters, and do be quick. Miss Green here has got herself soaked through and we must not permit her to catch cold."

On hearing the name of the guest, Walters' eyes turned towards Mary and did not leave her as she bobbed and assented, pausing a moment before turning to go. When she returned with the tea, Walters kept glancing over at Mary, as if scrutinizing her. Mary wondered what news of her might have spread within the village. Did everyone know she was an orphan? Did they begrudge her the fortune she had inherited, her rise above her station? Did the servants resent her promotion of the other orphans to better positions than they might have?

"Shall Miss Green be staying for dinner, madam?" asked Walters.

"No, thank you, Walters, she is just waiting for her carriage to take her back to Norchester."

Mary looked awkwardly away towards the fire as Walters left the room, looking back one last time to watch Mary take a sip from her tea.

"You must stand and turn about a little," said Mrs. Hawthorne, "to dry your dress all through. If you warm only one half, all the cold shall gather in the other and it shall be as though you had not dried yourself at all." Mary set down her cup and obliged her host, standing with her back to the fire and uncertain where to look. Spying a pile of books, many open, upon a table across the room, Mary ventured,

"Mr. Hawthorne must be very learned."

As is so often the case, the reticent and dull Mrs. Hawthorne came instantly to life at the mention of her son.

"He is always very much occupied with his work," she replied, "and such important work it is too. He has undertaken to record and describe every species of bird in His Majesty's Empire. Can you imagine the magnitude of such a task?"

"It is vast indeed," replied Mary, who wondered at the motive for such a plan.

"You might also imagine how difficult he finds it, not being able to travel himself to such places where he might obtain his own information rather than relying on the reports of others. You know, it is always so vexing for a scientist not to observe his subject with his own eyes, to draw his own conclusions. He is forever relying on the reports of others, whom he may not even be able to trust, and who often contradict one another so that he cannot include any of it. And it is impossible that he should travel to all these places himself. His position keeps him here, of course, from where he can do so little. I do not speak against his profession. It is a good one and allows him much time for his work, but I will say it does inhibit him from traveling a great deal."

Mary could only hope that Mrs. Hawthorne's feelings on the limitations of her son's profession were born of maternal anxiety and ambition, and not a reflection of Mr. Hawthorne's own sentiments, for to Mary, there could be no greater ingratitude than to scoff at a living which permitted comfortable accommodation, meaningful work, and ample time for other endeavours. Such a life had been Mary's own long-standing ambition, and she could hardly admire anyone who could take it so much for granted.

"One of our neighbours in Oxfordshire shall be leaving very soon on a mission to Africa," said Mary, thinking with pride on her friend Mr. Ingles and his noble sacrifice. He would not allow himself to enjoy a comfortable living and yet complain of his having to keep it.

"Is he a very upright sort of gentleman?" asked Mrs. Hawthorne.

"He is the most honest and worthy gentleman I believe I have ever met," replied Mary, quite ready to defend her friend, though uncertain why it should be required.

"Well, perhaps you might introduce them. I am sure Charles would benefit greatly from such a person, who might send him more reliable information than he has been wont to receive, if he is to go to that part of Africa that is within His Majesty's rule, which I am sure he must, being an Englishman."

Mary was glad to be facing away from the fire and from Mrs. Hawthorne at that moment, for she was certain her countenance would reveal her horror at the thought of Mr. Ingles' mission being used for the benefit of overstuffed bird-watchers with nothing better to do than quibble over the colour of a sparrow's beak. In avoiding a reply, she took up her tea cup again and awaited the arrival of her carriage.

Later, at Norchester, as she recounted the conversation to Mrs. Burrows, she laughed at the presumption of her host. "What could possibly justify me in making such an introduction?" she asked. "Mr. Ingles is not only the greater man on moral grounds, but he is the son of Lord Rosborough. To impose upon him some Gloucestershire clergyman with a penchant for birds in order that he may inform him on the details of African wildlife is absurd. Mr. Ingles goes not to Africa to serve the interests of an Englishman's hobby; he goes to save the souls of thousands."

"Well, if gentlemen were all judged by the presumptions of their mothers, I do not think we should find a humble one in all of England. If a man's pride in himself should ever match that of his mother's in him, it should be a frightful thing indeed."

Mary smiled. "Perhaps I ought to allow him more opportunity to contradict the image his mother has painted of him. It would be very seemly to invite the local rector to dine with us, I think."

"You must call on his mother in a day or two, and offer your thanks for their assistance. I do not think it would go amiss to send them something, some preserves perhaps. And, whatever other hospitality you offer, you must invite him to dinner when your friends come to visit. We will be short of gentlemen, and then you may see how he fares in company."

"Very well," said Mary. "It was very kind and thoughtful to spare me such a wet walk home, and any accompanying risks, but I cannot say that his behaviour otherwise was so gracious and amiable as to inspire me to much hope. He merely left me with his mother and spoke hardly a word."

"So, he shall not be your humble curate after all, then," said Mrs. Burrows. "You shall not run away with him to live a simple yet happy life?"

"I think not," replied Mary with a sigh. "In truth, I have nowhere to run from now. And I cannot imagine Mr. Hawthorne should wish to run anywhere either. Moreover, I do not see how I could marry a curate and live at Norchester. Does not it seem inconsistent?"

Mrs. Burrows shrugged. "I have heard of stranger things. I think it rather more likely that, for all appearances, the curate in this case be not all that humble." Cautiously she added, "At least, he is not as humble as another, who has already captured your heart, though you do not yet know it."

Mary was at first confused, and only after some insistent inquiry did she come to understand to whom Mrs. Burrows was referring. When she caught her friend's meaning, she was shocked to the point of offence on behalf of the gentleman. "Nonsense!" she objected. "I have been acquainted with Mr. Ingles all my life. He is infinitely my superior and I should never dream of such a thing. I think on him as a true friend, as a touchstone for goodness, not as a suitor, and he is not a suitor for he has never so much as hinted at making suit. No, there is not a shred of romance between us."

Mary continued her protestations, which were perhaps too vehement to be accepted by Mrs. Burrows as disposing of the matter, and so she continued to insist on the verity of her own conclusions.

Although Mary would not concede it, and in fact *because* she would not, she must be in love with Mr. Ingles on whom she looked with such esteem.

For several hours, Mary remained convinced of the error of Mrs. Burrows' suggestion. She admired Mr. Ingles very much, held his opinion in high regard, even liked his company, but was not enamoured of him. She had never blushed at the thought of him, nor lost her self-possession in his presence, nor ever suffered from a dizzy pain caused by his absence. Surely she could not be in love with him!

As night fell, however, and Mary lay in the quiet of her chamber, her conviction began to slip. Why should not her regard turn to affection? His station had always been so far above her own that she had never considered him as a lady might consider a gentleman, but they were now much more equal than they formerly had been. He was from a noble family, but unlike Lord Marsden, he did not have a future as Lord Rosborough, only the living of a clergyman. She had no family connections, but she did have a great deal of property, and to many that was almost the same thing.

In all her years in Oxfordshire, he had been the only person to show her disinterested kindness and friendship. It was he whose presence she had always sought whenever she had been in company, and whose feelings and opinions were always the most sympathetic with her own. His honest criticism held more value for her than all the accolades of a simpering society so in love with itself that it could only praise all devotion to its supremacy. The sincerity of his goodness, so apparent in his decision to forsake all comfort in favour of bringing salvation to the ignorant, was to her a mark in his favour far above the prestige and wealth of any lord or gentry in the kingdom. Mr. Ingles was humble. Mr. Ingles was a curate. By morning, Mary was only incredulous that she had been so blind not to recognize him as *her* humble curate.

Chapter Twenty-Six

Mary rose with a blush at the thought of Mr. Ingles, a dizzy pain caused by his absence, and a certainty that her self-possession would be entirely lost in his presence. The revelation of her feelings was not a pleasant discovery. She could not see him, nor was like to see him perhaps ever again. She had no means of writing to him, and no cause to expect any word from him. They had not parted on the best of terms, and Mary saw no way even of restoring his good opinion, much less of winning his affection in return of her own. If she loved him, it was to be in vain. She ought to have grown accustomed to deprivation, to the impossibility of all her wishes. She had always lived with all of life's pleasures in plain view yet beyond her reach. To live with the longing of the unattainable ought to have been easy for its being her practiced wont, yet it was not. There are things one may be trained to put aside. If we are to believe all of art and history, we must concede that love is not one of them.

With a sigh of sorrowful resignation she descended to breakfast where she was soon greeted by another letter which served to distract her from her present misery. She did not recognize the hand, but knew the return address immediately. It was from the nurse who had been at the orphanage when Mary had been there. Eagerly she tore open the seal.

Dear Miss Green,

I received your letter and send my apologies for not being able to reply sooner. My position keeps me very busy and I am afraid I have little time for writing. If I were in possession of some knowledge of your heritage, perhaps I might have been more hasty in my correspondence, but as it is I am barely less ignorant of your history than you are. What I do know, however, I shall gladly relate.

You were left with us at a few months of age. You were accompanied by a brief note stating your birthdate and your Christian name only. We gave you the name of Green because the basket in which you arrived was lined with green cloth. From the quality of that basket, as well as the clothing and the blankets, we assumed you must have been from a merchant family, for they were of a quality that precluded your parents' being extremely poor. You were also quite plump for a foundling, most of whom are quite sickly and thin by the time their parents accept that they cannot care for them. The basket, I recall, was quite sturdy, and we continued to use it for future infants even when you had grown out of it. If your parents were not destitute, the usual reason for leaving a foundling would be that you were the natural child of a gentleman who could not keep you. This, however, did not seem likely to us as such a child would usually be provided for through some anonymous arrangement and not merely abandoned on the mercy of the parish. We thought perhaps your parents had been on the wrong side of the law, thieves perhaps, who had acquired the means of purchasing a few nice things, but who, given their ways, could not keep with them a child. This explanation being both distasteful and fantastical, we did not much entertain it.

So you see, I can offer you no conclusive account as to your origins. I can tell you that Miss Hargreaves, as she then was, began visiting the house not long after you came to us. She took an instant liking to you, and I could see why. You were always very well tempered, even at such a tender age. We might have placed you easily with another family, but Miss Hargreaves insisted that she wished you to come and live with her once she was married, and for the promise of such a good home, and the patronage of such a generous benefactor, we obliged her.

It was nearly four years before such events came to pass, and immediately they returned from their honeymoon, they came to collect you. Captain Markham took to you almost as quickly as his wife, for whose sake he no doubt had agreed to take you on. I will not deny that I, at least, harboured some suspicion that you might have been Mrs. Markham's own child. It would be slander to suggest such a thing openly, and in the end I dismissed the possibility since Captain Markham had been away at the war throughout, and Mrs. Markham had always been so devoted to him such that it could not have been the child of another gentleman. In fact, if one is to entertain gossip, it seems she was so attached to him that she disobliged all her family and risked disinheritance by insisting on marrying him, for she was from a very old family and he merely a sailor with no particular family or connections. It was only when he returned from the war a rich captain that her parents consented to the match. Thus the idea that she might have had a child by anyone else seemed impossible.

We were all very distressed by the news of the sorry fate of Captain and Mrs. Markham. None of us knew what had happened to you following that tragic event, but assumed you must have been cared for since you were not returned to us. We were all rather fond of you as you remained in our care longer than most of the children we saw in those days.

I am sorry I could not assist you more. I wish you well on your search for the truth of your history, and in all of your endeavours. Yours sincerely,

E. Harper

Mary set down the letter, a mixture of vexation, grief and despair. Here had been her final chance of knowing who she was, her last hope of answering the question that had plagued her all her life. Not only had Miss Harper failed to satisfy her, the suggestions she raised were worse than Mary's uninformed assumptions. She could no longer imagine herself the legitimate though unfortunate child of loving parents, distressed and heartbroken to forsake her, but forced by poverty or illness to give her up, praying all the while that she might meet with a better fate than she would have in their own care. In Oxfordshire, she had drawn much of her strength from the thought that, in spite of the treatment she received from the Hargreaves girls, or Miss Preston, she was yet infinitely better situated than she might have been, and that her parents would have rejoiced that she should have even the advantages that she did, that she should be clothed, shod, fed, educated even. She thought of her parents as good people and she accepted her obscurity with that comfort.

Now, she felt this could not be the case. She must either be the discarded offspring of a man who could afford to care for her if he wished to, yet so heartless as not even to provide a basic stipend for her upkeep; or the daughter of denigrate thieves more inclined to pursue a life of delinquency than to grow respectable for the sake of their child; or, possibly worst of all, the bastard of a faithless Mrs. Markham. This latter was the most repugnant to Mary in that it destroyed not only the image of her parents, but that of Mrs. Markham as well, whom she had so long idealized and cherished in her heart as the essence of all things loving and good.

When Mrs. Burrows entered the room, she found a dejected looking Mary with a half-eaten breakfast and an open letter before her on the table.

"Oh, my dear girl," she said as she sat opposite Mary. "What on earth could have you looking so glum this early in the day? There has not yet been time for anything regrettable to have happened."

Mary looked up at her without expression. Mrs. Burrows nodded at the letter. "Does it contain some unhappy news?" she asked a little more gently, for it was clear her friend was indeed wretched.

"May I?" she reached over to take the letter, to which Mary nodded her consent. Having read its contents in silence, Mrs. Burrows set down the letter and looked earnestly at Mary, who heaved a sigh and said merely, "What good may I take from that?"

"I shall tell you," replied Mrs. Burrows with a firmness that startled Mary. "You do not know who your parents were. They may have been blackguards of the worst kind. If so, you may count yourself among the fortunate for not having been exposed to their iniquity. Many a person has suffered the tyranny of despicable parents and is the worse for *not* having been orphaned. I could name several who would be very happy never to have known their parents, and unlike you, they do not possess vast and unfettered wealth, nor a clear conscience and the will to do some good for their fellow creatures. Their characters, in many cases, are as bad as their fortunes, and in all likelihood, their ends. Whatever your past, it matters little. Here is where you have arrived, and this," she gestured to take in the surroundings, "is what you have been given." She held up the letter. "You ask what good can come of this. I say, it is good that you have now no hope of an answer, for every possibility set out here seems equally unlikely, and therefore you are relieved of the burden of choosing between them or of seeking any further to solve the mystery. Where there is no hope of an answer, one may live in serenity with the question. And now you will be happy." She folded the letter and tucked it away as Mary burst into tears.

Had her heart not already been tender and sore from the discovery of her hopeless attachment to Mr. Ingles, she might have withstood with equanimity both the contents of the letter and even the speech of Mrs. Burrows, but she was weakened and unable to rally herself.

"I am sorry," she said. "Everything you say is true. I shall do better, I promise. I shall be better. I shall cease to dwell on these insignificant matters."

"It is not that they are insignificant," said Mrs. Burrows. "Of course it should signify who your parents were. It is only that you have been given so many other gifts that perhaps this ignorance is a fair price to pay for it."

Mary nodded. "I shall thank Miss Harper for her assistance, and I shall turn my attention towards those less fortunate than myself. Perhaps Mr. Hawthorne might direct me in my efforts, as he is sure to know more than I about the most needy in the parish. I shall invite him to tea when I see him on Sunday."

"And perhaps I might direct your efforts in preparing for the arrival of your guests, whom you seem entirely to have forgotten will be arriving in less than a month and will be expecting some form of hospitality. It may be an admirable thing to bestow your kindness on strangers, but it is quite another to withhold it from your friends."

Though her heart was only a little lightened, Mary was able to finish her breakfast and together the two ladies began their plans for hosting their London friends with as much style and grace as an orphan and a solicitor's widow could conspire.

Chapter Twenty-Seven

The following weeks threw Mary into a flurry of activity, which, to anyone who has known the inescapable nag of an aching heart, is understood as the nearest thing to a cure. She set herself a daily regimen of visiting the poor and the elderly, with particular favour shown to the widows of war, for Mrs. Markham's sailor had come home, but many a lady had not been so fortunate. Mary relied rather heavily on Mr. Hawthorne and his mother for introductions in the beginning, and so was forced to endure many a lecture on the wonder and complexity of the avian kingdom before being able independently to mix with her neighbours.

The house and grounds at Norchester also benefitted from her rigorous attention, and with a little pruning and painting, quickly began to resume their former splendour. Mary began to think of the estate itself as her mother and father, in place of those parents she would never know. Norchester was her past and her future, and she wished to care for it as a loyal and grateful daughter ought. As she laboured, she contemplated how she might contrive either to visit her old neighbourhood in Oxfordshire, or to bring into Gloucestershire the one acquaintance of her old life who remained of interest to her. She considered that the Carringtons had grown quite close with both his family and her cousins, the Hargreaves girls, who, by all accounts, saw no barrier to a continued acquaintance and even friendship with herself. She did not like to scheme, but nor would it do to disregard the possibility of their assistance in bringing her into the company of Mr. Ingles before he departed the country, perhaps never to return. She could not endure the thought that he might go, and be forever gone, without, at the very least, a meeting, whatever might be the result.

When the hour of their arrival came, Mary was determined to tell her friends of her predicament, and to enlist their aid. She had planned a full schedule for them all, with a picnic, dancing in a nearby village and a dinner to which she had also invited Mr. Hawthorne and several other of her new neighbours.

As the carriage pulled up the drive, Mary bounded down the steps to greet her friends. The three sisters burst out of its doors and embraced her with rapturous laughter, followed by their brother and Mr. Lowell, who were a little more restrained in their greeting.

The ladies all spoke over each other, expressing their delight and enthusiasm for the park and the house, and of course for seeing Mary. Mrs. Lowell attempted, perhaps for the sake of her husband, somewhat to contain herself, though even she could hardly stop her tongue. They had had quite an eventful journey from London, with a lame horse and a broken axel, and one very foul inn, but their accommodations in Bath were very grand and they could not wait to show them to her, if she would consent to return with them at the end of their stay. And if she would come with them to Lyme at the end of the summer, they would certainly require a second carriage, for she would need to bring at least a hundred gowns if she were not to be disgraced at *all* the balls and parties, of which there were to be a great many, or so they understood. But now they were excessively relieved to be able to walk about, and most keen to see all of the house, and the gardens, and to hear all of Mary's news since they parted.

Their host was most obliging in showing them her new home, particularly her largely unused painting studio. "I do come in here most days," she said. "I am very keen, and sometimes I take out the paints and just look at them, even smell them. I love the smell of paint. But I have yet to receive any instruction, and so mostly I just continue my sketching. One cannot expect to find a tutor in this remote location, though I have asked. It seems I must wait until I return to London before I can really begin to improve."

"I am so sorry we did not do more for you when you were in town," said Frances. "Our tutor was away on the continent, or I should surely have recommended him to you."

"We ought to have done more," agreed Harriet. "We shall do better next time. We shall find someone for you, someone excellent, and everything shall be arranged even before you arrive, so that you may begin as soon as you reach London."

"Perhaps we could even find someone near here," added Louisa. "It would be a shame to have to wait so long."

"Oh, I don't think there is anyone around these parts, Louisa," said Frances. "If there were, I am sure she would have found one already.

"Yes, I have certainly made inquiries of everyone in these parts who might know of anyone, and all without any luck. But that is no matter. I have much to occupy me. Come, let me show you the grounds."

Mary continued her tour, pointing out the improvements they were making.

"And you must have patience with the staff," she said. "They are many of them in training and rather young. As it has only been myself and Mrs. Burrows here until now, it has not affected anyone much. The two of us are very able to tolerate their errors, though you may find the standards not so high as you are accustomed to, and it will be a new test for them all to have a house full of guests. But I dare say it shall be to their benefit. In a few months' time, they will all be ready to take on positions in the best houses in the country, and we shall start over again with a new lot, though I expect the housekeeper would prefer us to stagger them out a little, or she might lose her senses."

"Singular," remarked Mr. Lowell, "to entirely change out one's staff every few months."

"I think it is capital," returned Mr. Carrington, "and shows great character and true benevolence, to have a care for those beneath one."

The sisters looked at each other and at Mary, holding back knowing grins.

"Thank you, sir," said Mary. "I am told I must not publicize our efforts too much, however, or some may feign destitution to take advantage of our generosity. I am of the mind that one would hardly brave the workhouse or abandon a child to an orphanage unless one had no other choice, for that is where we find our servants."

"But are there to be any parties while we are here?" asked Louisa. "Will we have any dancing do you think?"

"We are here to see Mary," said Harriet. "We shall have plenty of dancing and entertainment in Bath."

"That is easily said by a married lady, but we who are yet young still wish to enjoy ourselves."

"There shall be dancing," answered Mary. "Do not fear. But let us have some tea now. You must be in need of refreshment after your long drive." She led them back towards the house.

"It is only ten miles from Bath, yet I confess I am rather fagged," said Frances. "Truly, I cannot see how you could have come the entire way from London in only one day. We took two days coming only as far as Bath, and there were moments when I thought I should throw myself into the hedgerows and take on the life of a vagrant just to escape another moment in the carriage."

"I should think not," remarked Mr. Carrington.

"Unless your vagrant life include servants carrying you in a bath chair," added Louisa.

"And roast mutton and a feather bed at a fine inn every night," added Harriet, with a good-natured smile.

"Oh, yes," replied Frances, "unlike all of you who would be so pleased to sleep among the thistles and the highwaymen, eating squirrels and bathing in a ditch."

"There shall be no squirrels or ditches while you are here at least," said Mary. "And as for traveling here in one day, I suppose it was a sort of madness. We left before the sun rose, and it had long since set by the time we arrived. I was just so eager to reach the house, that I did not mind the journey. I expect Mrs. Burrows would have been happier to have broken it up, but then, she is quite uncomplaining about such things. She might be the only one among us who really could tolerate sleeping among the thistles."

"Where is Mrs. Burrows, for that matter?" asked Frances as they took their seats in the drawing room.

"She is here," answered Mary, "just upstairs I believe, probably saving my life in some way that I shall never know about."

The conversation continued some time, with much recounting of events in London. Mary thought she would have been quite bored or even vexed by their prattling, but her friends were so amiable and unaffected that she did not mind their triviality. So engrossed were they in their conversation that they required the intervention of Mr. Lowell to remind them to dress for dinner, or they would have been quite out of time.

Everyone complimented Mary on the meal, which praise she passed on to Mrs. Burrows who had taken full charge of the food for the week, and who deferred again to the cook, who really was a marvel for producing such results while training three undercooks and a scullery maid.

After dinner the gentlemen remained a good long while at the table, Mrs. Burrows went early to her chamber, and Mary and her three friends gathered for tea in the front drawing room. Mary felt that the mood had changed, grown more nervous, though she suspected it might only be a reflection of her own anxiety, for she intended to confide in them about Mr. Ingles and she was a little uncertain of their secrecy. She could not bear to have it talked of by anyone else, and for all their good will and loyalty, she knew her friends to be fond of a little gossip.

She asked after the Ingles family, and was given a very favourable report of the charms of the two brothers who remained in London, but nobody had heard anything about the third brother. He was not much talked about, it seemed. Mary hesitated to share her own feelings, for the sisters seemed distracted and often looked out the window towards the drive. She was soon able to account for their behaviour when the sound of a carriage was heard pulling up to the house.

"What is this?" asked Mary, looking between her friends with great suspicion. Harriet covered her mouth; Frances bit her lip; and Louisa clapped her hands, grinning like mad. Rising and moving toward the window, Mary looked out to see the carriage pull away, with one passenger still inside. Ascending the stairs were two cloaked figures, one a good deal taller than the other, but otherwise indiscernible in the dark.

"Do you all know what is happening, who has come?" she asked the room, to a response of only muffled giggles.

The door of the room opened, and a servant entered. He crossed the room and presented to Mary two cards, set upon a tray. They were gold embossed, on very fine stock, and bore the names of Dorothea and Augusta Hargreaves.

Chapter Twenty-Eight

If it was indeed the height of discourtesy and imposition to appear at someone's doorstep, late in the evening and uninvited, bearing luggage and an air of triumph, Mary was alone in thinking it so. Harriet, Frances, and Louisa appeared to be not only informed but quite complicit in the surprise, which they thought very clever and jolly. In her wish not to augment her own resentment by speaking of it, Mary had never described to her friends the nature of her relationship with the Hargreaves girls, and the former assumed, quite naturally, that having all grown up together in the same house, she must regard the latter as her own sisters and feel their absence every minute, as they themselves would feel the absence of each other. They were therefore rather surprised not to witness the elation and delight that they had anticipated at the revelation of this scheme.

Mary picked up the cards from the tray, stared at them a moment then returned them. She did not invite the girls to be shown in, but chose to meet them in the hall, and followed the servant out without a word. What could they possibly mean by appearing like this? How dared they force themselves upon her in this way, in her own house, without any warning? She had never previously been at liberty to exclude them, to preside over her own domain, and now that she was, she did not intend to tolerate the usurpation of her peace by these two would-be cousins.

The boldness of her anger surprised her, and she strode into the hall armed with the righteous sword of her indignation. Before she could strike, Augusta threw herself upon her with eager embraces and a gleeful smile, spouting her joy at seeing Mary, her delight at her cousin's good fortune, her amazement at the grandeur of the house, and other unlikely sentiments.

Dorothea seemed at least a little sensible of the audacity of their appearance, though she insisted it was all Gussy's idea, and she had really had no choice but to join her. As to why they had come, they offered no explanation, and Mary could form no polite way of asking, so that she merely blurted, "Whatever are you doing here?" to which Augusta appeared to take great offence and displayed the most blameless broken heart.

"Are not you glad to see us?" she half-sobbed. "We came all this way just to see you, for you left us so suddenly, and never wrote a word, and would not see us in town, and yet here we are, ready to forgive you, with open arms and sisterly affection, and you reject us out of hand. I never thought you cruel until now, Polly, but I will say this is very hard. Having lived in our house for so many years, we did not expect to be so unwelcome in yours for only a fortnight, but we shall leave first thing in the morning, if it pleases you. That is, unless you should like to call a carriage round this instant to be rid of us all the sooner."

"Good Lord, Gussy!" huffed Dorothea. "She only asks what we do here, and has she not a right when she did not expect us? Once again, you have planned things ill, and so ill they have gone. There is no cause to spite Polly for it. Truly, it was a ridiculous idea."

The three ladies stood in silence in the hall for a moment, the guests awaiting the judgment of their host. In considering what she ought to do, and having been given, by the commotion of their greeting, a moment to overcome her initial shock and anger at their arrival, it struck her that it might indeed serve some purpose. Although it brought Mary no joy to set eyes on either of her cousins, they may quite unwittingly have provided her some means of reaching Mr. Ingles. It would thus be against her interest to send them away and lose their favour. What is more, she would then need explain to her other guests her reasons for doing so, and thereby render them very glum and disappointed, having gone to great effort to arrange this unannounced and poorly considered visit. For their sake, if not for her own, she thought it better simply to accept this circumstance. After all, is not it the truest test of one's character to show kindness to one who has done one wrong? She was sure Mr. Ingles would not hold such a grudge as to make everyone miserable for the sake of old injuries.

And so for his sake, she swallowed her former feelings, and with reluctant warmth, showed them in. An exuberant reunion followed, in which each was more jubilant than the next, and everyone so overjoyed that even Dorothea was moved to smile. The gentlemen were called in to greet the newly arrived guests, which caused a renewal of expression of all the feelings so recently demonstrated by the ladies. Mr. Lowell moved to leave again soon thereafter, but fortunately, Tom Carrington had the good manners to remain and make himself agreeable, thereby keeping the other gentleman from retreating.

Mary would not be revealing her most tender and confidential feelings to her friends tonight, or perhaps at all. Their assistance may not be required, and if she could achieve her ends without speaking of them, all the better.

"Miss Green," said Dorothea suddenly, interrupting the lively tale of their journey which her sister was in the midst of telling. "My father bade me tell you that he hopes you will always consider Challey Hall as your home, and that you will visit us there at some time. He said as much in his first letter to us in town, thinking of course that we would see you there, though we had not the opportunity to speak before your departure."

"Quite so!" concurred Augusta. "Such a sudden departure it was, and without any explanation as to why it must be so. Will not you tell us now, the great mystery of your leaving London in such haste? Or is there some secret in it that you dare not divulge? For if so, you need only say the word, and we shall press you no further, shall we?" She looked about at the company who all nodded in solemn assent, though Mary was hardly convinced.

"There is no secret," she replied. "It was the weather. You see I had never before been in town. Indeed, I had never been anywhere, and had never known much society. You may recall, the weather took a sudden turn for the warmer not long before I left, and with the crowds of people, and the pavements everywhere, I simply longed to be in the country." Mary was not at all sure that there had been any such increase in the summer heat, but did not anticipate being contradicted in her finding that London was hot and crowded.

As the conversation turned then to the London season and everything about it there was to love and to hate, Mary could think only of what Dorothea had conveyed–the invitation of Sir Richard to visit Challey Hall. Could there be a more perfect opportunity and excuse for traveling to Oxfordshire than to accept such an invitation? She would discuss the idea with Mrs. Burrows in the morning. She laughed to imagine the scene at breakfast as her companion was made aware of the arrival of the Hargreaves girls and was forced by their presence to keep her countenance despite her disbelief. The amusement Mary anticipated from this encounter, and the means now presented for bringing her into Oxfordshire so easily were ready compensation for any offence or ill will she had previously felt. She saw now in what strange and unexpected form fortune can bring the best of news.

She did not deny herself the sweetness, however, at the end of the evening, of advising the Hargreaves' that, due to the surprise of their coming and to the late hour, there had been no opportunity to prepare the guest rooms that would otherwise be theirs. There was only one room ready for them, which was quite comfortable and would certainly meet with their satisfaction for the night. Bidding them all good night, she then turned to the waiting servant and directed that he show their new guests to their accommodations in the nursery.

Chapter Twenty-Nine

Morning did bring quite a surprise for Mrs. Burrows, who took it in stride, satisfying herself with only a few underhanded remarks which were lost on the oblivion of their guests. The week passed pleasantly enough. Mr. Carrington's behaviour was as indicative as ever of a heart driven to distraction. Augusta played the devoted friend with all the art of an accomplished actress, which Dorothea regarded with open disdain. And Mr. Lowell could most often be found asleep in the library.

Enjoying a little tea and games on the lawn one afternoon, Harriet remarked how sad it was that the party was to break up so soon.

"Have not you invited them all to Bath?" said Tom in a tone of reproof. "I rather thought you had."

"I did invite Miss Green, but she does not seem inclined to come."

"It is not that I am not inclined," replied Mary, "only that I have so much to do here. I have begun several projects that I cannot simply abandon and which are not yet at a stage to be left in the care of another. I may be able to escape for a day or two, but then, with the journey, I should just arrive and be obliged to turn back again."

"The journey?" repeated Frances. "Concerns about the journey from one who traveled from London to Gloucestershire in a day–I will not have it! You must come."

"And what about your other friends?" asked Tom. "They must not be excluded."

"But of course," said Louisa. "I thought that much was clear." She turned to Augusta, for Dorothea was seated apart from the group, sipping small beer in the shade. "You and your sister must come with us to Bath! We shall have such a merry time, and we shall all be very dull if you refuse. Is not that right, Frances?"

It was agreed all round that nothing but boredom and iniquity would result if the party were to return to Bath without the sisters Hargreaves. Augusta delighted in accepting the invitation without the approval of her sister, who in all likelihood would be equally vexed regardless of her reply and equally elegant strolling through the green countryside of Norchester or the white pavement of Bath, or indeed along the Cobb at Lyme.

In truth, Augusta had rather relied on receiving such an invitation. Aunt Preston had refused to accompany them to Norchester, claiming that she would not add her own person to the burden of unexpected guests when Polly already had a full house, and assuring her nieces that they would be adequately chaperoned by Mrs. Burrows and Mrs. Lowell. Some arrangement would be made to bring them home when required, but Aunt Preston trusted to the girls to get themselves invited either to Bath, or to Lyme, or even to stay the summer in Norchester rather than risk an encounter with Mary, who might embarrass her with a demand for explanation of her past conduct.

It seemed Augusta miscalculated her sister's indifference as to place, for that night, when everyone else had retired, Mary was passing through the hall on her way to bed. As she neared the door to Augusta's chamber, she heard the unmistakable disdain of Dorothea's voice from within.

"So, are we to disappoint and offend the *Ingles* family in favour of the Carringtons and a few weeks in bath?"

"I do not see that we have any choice!" retorted Augusta. "How are we even to get to Lyme? And where should we stay when we arrive that would not disgrace us before the Ingles family? We are far better off going to Bath where we shall be kept in a befitting fashion. You, who are already as good as married, may not need concern yourself with such matters, but there are those of us who do!"

"And you think to find yourself a husband in Bath? I would not for the world trust that place to contain a man worth marrying. There is nothing there of fashion or of quality."

"The Carringtons are there!" exclaimed Augusta. "Are they not people of fashion or quality?"

Mary, whose curiosity had caused her to stop and listen at the door, felt suddenly ashamed at the act of eavesdropping. She took a step back, and as she did so, the floor board beneath her let out a great creak. The voices within ceased instantly.

"Hullo," came Augusta's voice. "Who goes there?"

"It is only I, Mary. I heard voices and I thought someone was distressed."

A brief, hoarsely whispered argument ensued before the door was opened by a beaming Augusta, her smile stretched unnaturally tight. "Mary!" she said, and forced a laugh. "How kind of you, but really, there is no distress. Dorothea was just complaining about, well, about nothing, really."

"Oh," said Mary. "I hope it is nothing I have done. That is, I hope you are well looked after here." She could see Dorothea behind Augusta, sitting at the dressing table and absently toying with its contents.

"But of course," droned Augusta, taking Mary's hands in hers. "You have absolutely spoiled us. I assure you it is nothing."

Dorothea looked up from the dressing table with a huff. "Oh, just tell her Gussy!" she said. "Your secrecy is wearisome."

Augusta's expression fell, her jaw setting and her eyes, suddenly stony, darted back to her sister. "*You* tell her," she barked as she flung open the door with all the force of her tiny form, then turned and threw herself on the bed, curling her body away from Mary to face the wall.

Having witnessed arguments of this nature many times between the sisters, Mary had taught herself never to take too much of an interest in the subject of any. So constant was their mutual venom that Mary often wondered how they had the resources to continue it. She closed the door and prepared to hear the cause of this fresh conflict, in which she thought she detected more than usual significance since Dorothea–customarily rather placid in her retorts–had raised her voice above her wont.

Dorothea stared dully at her sister for a moment then turned to Mary saying flatly, "Our father has lost everything."

Mary was stunned. Could she have misheard?

"It is yet a great secret," continued Dorothea, without any display of emotion, "though it cannot be concealed forever. Aunt Preston hopes we might both marry before it becomes generally known, though I think she misjudges the haste with which a marriage may take place without rousing suspicion. We were to visit Lyme, and had promised Lord Marsden and Mr. George Ingles that we would come. It was rather hoped that a formal announcement of my engagement to the latter might be made there, as Lord and Lady Rosborough were to be joining them next week. Sadly, we cannot now afford the cost of staying in Lyme in adequate fashion. If we go to Bath, we may be well kept by the Carrington family as guests and lose no dignity, but risk offending the Ingles. Our aunt rather dumped us here in the hope that some solution might be met with, no doubt implicating your fortune in some way. I am sorry to speak so plain, but there you are."

Augusta did not stir. Mary was dumbfounded. She looked between the sisters several times before addressing Dorothea, who had returned to fidgeting with Augusta's things on the dressing table. "How do you mean, lost everything?" she asked, still numb with the shock of the news.

"Oh, we shall rebuild in time," she answered. "We still have the house, and there is always a sum set aside for quarter days, so we shall be able to pay the staff at Michaelmas, but beyond that, we shall be quite destitute for several years at least. There is nothing for our dowries and certainly nothing for seaside holidays. To blame are some ill-advised investments which I suspect Aunt Preston convinced our father to make."

"Has Sir Richard returned from Scotland?" asked Mary.

"Not yet. He must conclude his business still, but will be back in Oxfordshire by the end of the summer."

"I see." Mary did not know what else to say. She would have expected to feel some triumph at learning of their downfall, but instead she found it all rather sad, and even considered whether she might assist them.

"Oh, please say you will help us," Augusta pleaded from the bed, raising her head from her pillow to reveal eyes red and cheeks damp with crying. "It is so unfair. We have done nothing wrong, and yet we are the ones who must suffer this indignity. If you are not kind to us, I know not what we shall do. There is no other friend to whom we can turn."

Countless times had Augusta come to Mary in tears, distraught over some matter of little to no import, begging her for assistance and claiming desolation, and always did Mary console and aid her, with pity and faint amusement at the exaggerated emotion of her cousin. Although her present circumstance may have justified her tears, Mary could not help but be reminded of all the times past, and to feel the same amused sense of pity at her desperation for the succour of one who was, until very lately, the indigent and helpless party.

"I am terribly sorry," said Mary. "This is most distressing, and I do not know what can be done, but I am very glad you have told me of it. You may be assured of my confidence, and perhaps in the morning we will see if we cannot find some satisfactory course, at least for the present."

Augusta returned her face to her pillow and her gaze to the wall.

"Very well," said Dorothea, rising from her seat, taking up her unlit candlestick and crossing the room. "I shall say goodnight then." Mary opened the door and let her pass. Bidding goodnight to Augusta, who did not reply, she followed Dorothea out into the dark of the hall. Leaning in towards Mary to take a light for her candle, Dorothea looked at her with an earnest intensity she had never before seen, and said a quiet but sincere, "Thank-you" before disappearing down the corridor toward her room, leaving Mary to do the same.

Chapter Thirty

"You know your sister is quite potty for Lord Marsden," said Mary to Harriet as they strolled through the garden the next morning.

"Oh, I do know!" Harriet replied. "She will never say as much directly, but her every action confirms it."

"And was not she desperate to go to Lyme this summer, where he is staying?"

"She was. So was Frances, I believe, but Papa preferred Bath, so there we are."

"I was thinking last night about you all," said Mary. "You know, you might go to Lyme if you choose."

"But what is there for me in Lyme? I should much rather be with my sisters, wherever they stay."

"Of course you should wish to be where they are, but must you be the one to go where they go? That is, if you and Mr. Lowell were to go to Lyme, could not they go also, under your care?"

Mary did not like deception or manipulation, but did not feel too much guilt at asking this of her friend. She knew that, even as a married woman, Harriet took her direction from Frances, and felt it could be no bad thing for the eldest sister to take the lead in this matter when, in truth, the youngest girl was so desirous of her doing so.

"But we have only just invited the Hargreaves girls to come with us to Bath," replied Harriet. "We cannot very well abandon our guests."

"Why not invite them to join you?" suggested Mary. "If you all prefer Lyme, do you not think they would do also?"

"Perhaps," said Harriet, taking a moment to ponder whether this was all sound. "But it seems rather unbecoming simply to alter our plans like that, or even to ask them their preference. They would feel obliged by courtesy to consent to the proposal whatever their true feelings."

"I know!" said Mary, her tone becoming conspiratorial. "Let me raise the subject in their presence, and then judge by their reaction whether they would rather follow you to Lyme than to Bath. That way, you may know their true feelings on the matter and can suggest the new scheme accordingly."

The Hargreaves girls played their parts to perfection, with Dorothea feigning diffidence and Augusta irrepressible in her enthusiasm. Nothing could suit her more than to change Bath for Lyme, and whoever proposed the idea must be commended as both a prodigy and an ambassador of every delight. Mary had never had such praise from her. All that remained was for Mr. Carrington Senior to be convinced, which they all felt would not be a great task so long as Tom was on board. This was the one possible weakness in the scheme, for Tom had wished to remain in Bath, presumably to be nearer to Mary. It seemed, however, that he had presently had his fill, for he was easily persuaded with promises of late nights at cards with Lord Marsden, as well as the ever tantalizing prospect of sea bathing, which even the Prince himself was reputed to enjoy.

A letter was dispatched that very day and it was decided that at the end of their stay at Norchester, they would all stop in Bath for a night or two and then set off for the seaside forthwith. Mary would remain behind, and at the end of their sojourn in Lyme, the Hargreaves sisters would be returned to her and together they would travel to Oxfordshire. All were vastly satisfied, including Mary who, though appearing to act purely for the sake of others, had her own interest in the scheme as well, for it would take her, quite without artifice, back into the neighbourhood of Mr. William Ingles. Were it not for the presence of his brothers, she even considered joining her friends in Lyme just to hasten the end of the summer, for she knew the days between now and her departure would be long indeed. Fortunately, there remained much for her to do in Gloucestershire and she would fill her hours with the house, her art, and her charity work to pass the time and occupy her mind.

Although Mary felt much concern for her cousins and their change of fortune, the girls themselves showed no sign of worry. Dorothea never betrayed any emotion and therefore one might suppose it was no effort for her to conceal any. Augusta always expressed a myriad feelings at once and all in the most heightened mode, which was perhaps also a manner of disguise. Whatever the case, the party remained merry enough for the remainder of the fortnight.

Two days before Mary's guests were to leave, the gentlemen determined that their host might have need of some fowl when they left, and it would be a great waste if they were not to have any sport in providing it. They set out accordingly on a shooting party, returning at dusk with an armload of birds.

"Was it a good day, then?" Harriet asked the gentlemen.

"It was capital!" Tom answered with a clap of his hands. "Your land is simply teeming with game," he said to Mary. "A blind man could have shot a brace out there."

"Well, there has not been much hunting on this land for some time, I would imagine. You must come back every year and stock the larder for the winter. And if I cannot eat them all, I am sure there are plenty in the village who would be happy for a bird or two, if there are so many to spare, as you say. Perhaps I shall send one of these over to Mrs. Hawthorne. I wonder if her son's interest in birds extends to eating them, or whether they might take offence at the offering."

"Hawthorne did you say?" asked Mr. Lowell.

"Yes, the rector's mother."

"I say, Tom, was that not the name of the gentleman we startled in the reeds?"

"You might be right there. I had almost forgotten. I think we might have invited him to dinner tomorrow, though it was such an odd encounter, I cannot say for sure."

Mary laughed. "If he was hiding in the reeds, it most likely was Mr. Hawthorne. He is an avid bird enthusiast, and he was probably watching out for some rare species. And he is already invited to dine tomorrow, so no awkwardness there."

"Well that is a relief," replied Tom. "I should feel sheepish to bring strange persons unauthorized to a house where I am a guest."

"Never mind that," said Louisa. "If you were to bring a vagabond by accident to Miss Green, she would no doubt find them something to eat, somewhere to sleep and possibly even a well-paid position in a great house."

Mr. Hawthorne was not a stray and did not require accommodation or employment, but he did arrive the following evening, quite ready to be fed. His presence was hardly sufficient to balance the table of seven ladies, but the gentlemen were glad to have him nonetheless, and shook his hand like old brothers reunited after a lengthy separation and not strangers who had only just collided in the woods the previous day.

"How long have you been the rector in this parish?" asked Frances as they sat down to the table.

"I have been in this post five years."

"And were you well acquainted with the former tenants of Norchester?"

"Not well acquainted, no. The house was empty for about two years before Miss Green took occupation of it, and before that, it had been used as a school, but it was not successful, and closed after only four years in operation."

"That is unfortunate," remarked Harriet.

"There were some who felt so," replied Mr. Hawthorne. "For myself I think it was for the best. After all, they would eventually have had either to close or move, for Miss Green's arrival. And besides, it was not really the right sort of school."

"How is that?" asked Mary, who could not see how any school could be wrong, unless it teach some dark art, which she doubted would be done in any sort of public way.

"Well, you see, it was open to everyone, regardless of means."

"And so there were not enough funds?" asked Mary. "Is that how it was not right?"

"Yes, that is what led to its close no doubt, but I mean that it was open to the lower classes. It is not right to encourage in them any kind of higher learning. What use can it be to them to teach them ideas above their station?"

"You do not think education is of benefit to everyone?" Mary pressed.

"Certainly everyone must learn the knowledge of their work, their trade or profession, but beyond that, no. Our nation requires a great number of labourers. It cannot help them to learn French, for instance. Why, the clergy would be entirely undone if *everyone* learned to read and write."

"Well said," chimed in Mr. Lowell. "You know, when I first saw you crouching in the reeds yesterday, I did not anticipate such erudition and insight, but I will say I think you are quite in the right there. I, for one, see no need for my scullery maid to take up poetry. It can only breed revolution. That was the mistake of the French, I would say."

"Yes, better to leave them all in the paradise of their ignorance," said Dorothea in a quiet, detached tone that only Mary suspected of being satirical. "They all seem so happy there."

"I confess I am surprised at your opinions, sir," said Mary to Mr. Hawthorne. "For one so dedicated to the advancement of science, I would have thought you more in favour of the spread of learning among all people." She did not think it polite to reveal how odious she found his reasoning.

"My work is quite in line with my vocation. There are some very dangerous and evil theories just beginning to circulate among particular men of science, and it is my intention to disprove them by their own methods."

"By the cataloguing of birds?" interjected Mrs. Burrows, who had succeeded in biting her tongue until now.

Mr. Hawthorne gave her a patronizing smile and continued. "It is a great undertaking, and only the beginning of the task. I expect my aim shall not be met in my lifetime, but I have always believed that it is a greater, more meritorious choice to dedicate oneself to a cause that extends beyond one's own life."

Mary was about to respond to this last remark when a servant entered the dining room with a small silver tray, which he presented to her, whispering that there was a lady at the servants' door who wished to speak to her. The lady said she would wait until it was convenient but that she must be gone before the guests departed that evening. She had insisted the note on the tray be immediately delivered, unopened, to Miss Green.

On the tray, lay a small piece of parchment, folded and sealed with unmarked wax and addressed to herself. She looked sternly at the servant. Were it not for her curiosity and discretion, she would have scolded him for the interruption. The conversation at the table was growing heated and all the guests were engaged in it sufficiently that they did not take note of this little exchange.

"She was most insistent," repeated the servant in his defence, "but I shall send her away if it be your wish."

Mary sighed. Perhaps this lady had heard of her charity and was in real need. Would it be fitting to dismiss her so quickly? She would be eternally tormented if she did not at least read the note.

Taking it up quickly and dismissing the servant, she broke the seal under the table and stole a look at its contents on her lap. The increasing volume of the voices around her turned silent in her ears. She felt suddenly cold and unsteady on her chair, as though the dining room were the coop of a ship and the seas choppy with a gale. The writing on the parchment read simply, "I know the name of your mother."

Chapter Thirty-One

Mary gripped the seat of her chair, looking about the room in agitation. Why must this long-awaited news come while she had a table full of guests? The information she had longed for all her life was sitting downstairs, and she could not reach it. The lady had said she would wait, but had to leave before the guests departed. This was very strange, but must mean that so long as the guests were in the house, she would wait. Thus Mary did not need to escape the table right at that instant. She could choose her moment. Yet it seemed to Mary absurd that she should take that risk. What if the lady changed her mind, or was taken suddenly ill, or was already ill and died waiting to tell Mary what she knew? Would Mary really risk these albeit unlikely eventualities merely to avoid offending her guests who, if they knew the truth, would surely excuse her without hesitation? She could not. She was far too distracted to play host in any event and so quietly rose from her seat. She looked at Mrs. Burrows who was in the midst of saying, "So you would prevent them from improving their minds, but would fault and punish them for failing to improve their lot?"

Seeing Mary stand, everyone ceased talking and looked towards her. "Please just excuse me for one moment," she said. The gentlemen rose.

"Are you quite well?" asked Tom, "for true you do look rather pale."

"I am quite well. Please, do sit. I shall only be a moment. It is nothing– just a matter with the servants."

Before anyone could inquire further she slipped from the room, hearing only, "How very odd," from Mr. Lowell as she did so. Lifting her skirts, she ran through the house and down the stairs. Reaching the bottom, she was suddenly confronted with the sight of Walters, the maid from the Hawthorne residence, seated by the door and sipping a cup of tea.

Walters immediately arose and set down her cup. Mary, out of breath and surprised at the identity of the lady, raised the note in her hand and managed to ask, "Did you write this?"

Curtseying deeply, she answered, "I beg your pardon, Madam, for interrupting you like this, only it is very difficult for me to get away, and it didn't seem right to put it in a letter."

"Never mind that," said Mary, pushing past her to open the door. "Let us speak outside. I feel I cannot breathe."

"Mr. Hawthorne never goes out of an evening, and the one night he does, he comes to your house."

"It is no matter. My guests have plenty of food and company. They shall hardly miss me. I forgive your intrusion, but only if you keep me in suspense no longer. Your note says you know who my mother was. I beg you would tell me straight out before anything might prevent you."

"Yes, madam," Walters curtseyed again. "Your mother was Mrs. Edward Markham, Miss Georgiana Hargreaves as was."

A wooden barrel lay just beside the door, and Mary collapsed weakly upon it, her breath growing rapid not with exercise but with emotion. "I have wanted to tell you since I first saw you at the rectory, but how could I in front of Mrs. Hawthorne?"

Mary shook her head. "Of course. How then, that is, who, who is my father? Do you know that?"

"Why Captain Markham of course!" Walters looked offended at the implication that any other answer could be possible. "You are the daughter of Captain and Mrs. Markham."

Mary lowered her head and began to rock back and forth, squeezing shut her eyes to hold back the tears. Walters crouched before her and stroked her hands. "You may cry all you wish child," she said, "if you do not mind your guests seeing your swollen cheeks and reddened eyes." Mary nodded and blew out a few deep sighs.

"So I am the natural child of my benefactors?" she said.

"Not the natural child, no," said Walters. "Their marriage legitimized your birth in any event, but you were never born out of wedlock. I am the only living creature to know the truth and I will swear it on my life."

"But they were not married until I was four years old. It is all recorded and well known. And Captain Markham was away in the navy at the time so it was not possible."

"That is as it seems, but not as it truly was. Captain Markham was in the navy, and away, though not overseas. For a time, his ship was moored in Scotland. His location was not known to your mother's family but it was to her, and so she arranged a sketching holiday in the highlands with a friend and her family. I traveled with her, and was witness to all. When they reached Scotland, Miss Hargreaves pretended to be ill so that they might stop a few days. In secret, she left the inn one night, accompanied only by me, and met Captain Markham at a church where they were lawfully married. It had to be a secret for her parents did not approve and would have disinherited her. They were very proud people. The wedding that took place nearly five years later was a sham, but what harm could be done by married people repeating their vows before God? They were able to meet several times in Scotland, with my assistance, and a month or so later, when it was time to return home, she began to be truly ill. A doctor was called and it was discovered that it was you who was making her so. How tormented she was at this news! She longed to tell the world, to show the world the happy wife and mother that she was. But her better judgment told her that it would not go well to do so at that time, that her parents would not receive her and the child with open arms, and so we made a plan. She remained in Scotland for her confinement, convincing her friends to leave her there under the care of the doctor and myself. She paid a large sum to a family to keep her and her secret, and another sum to take you down to Gloucestershire a few months after you were born. You traveled down as their child and were left at the children's home while she returned to Norchester, to await the return of her husband and the time when they could claim you and bring you home."

"And then she did," said Mary.

"Yes. She did."

"And we were a family."

"Yes, for those few months, you were the happiest family that ever lived."

"That ever lived," echoed Mary, her voice cracking.

"I believe in her death she regretted nothing so much as she did leaving you behind." Mary's tears fell fast now as she understood for the first time the whole sad story of her life, her mother's sorrow, even her father's, being separated all those years from his love, from his child, only to see them perish, and then to be taken himself? "I suspect they were planning to tell you the truth, maybe tell everyone the truth, but the hour never came, or came too late. I, the only one who knew, was sent away immediately with everyone else when illness struck. It took her parents first, and then her. I believed she had told her brother everything. He came to bring you home with him, at her request. I never imagined she would have allowed him and you to remain ignorant. I took a position with a family in Paris very soon after Mrs. Markham died, and only returned a year ago. I took the position with the Hawthornes because I grew up in this neighbourhood, and was happy to return to my home, but I do not deny that I was curious to learn what had become of you. When I found that no one in these parts knew the truth, that everyone believed Norchester had been left in trust to be operated as a school, I realized that I was the only person who knew the truth. I must have been mistaken all those years ago; your mother must not have had the chance to tell her brother or anyone. When you appeared in Mrs. Hawthorne's drawing room that day, you can imagine my feelings. I have been most anxious to find an opportunity of telling you, of unburdening myself of this secret. I have done so now. I hope it is what you would wish for."

Mary hardly heard the last of what Walters had said, so distracted was she with the flood of feelings which attended this momentous news. Mrs. Markham had been her mother all along! It was too wonderful, too tragic, too profound a discovery.

Mary did not wish to speak to or see anyone. She longed to be alone, in her mother's room, with her memories and her imagination and her grief. Walters led her back inside, stopping a passing servant to advise that Miss Green would not be rejoining her guests but would be retiring for the night. "And to whom should this information be conveyed?" she asked Mary, who managed to reply–

"Mrs. Burrows."

The servant dashed off and Mary bid a teary goodnight to Walters, with many thanks and apologies.

"Not at all, my dear," replied the older lady. "It gives me such joy to know that I have succeeded in this task. I must return now to the rectory. Mr. Hawthorne will not stay for coffee and will be home soon. He would not be happy to learn I had left his mother for so long. We shall speak again soon, and I will tell you anything you may wish to know."

Mary took the servants' stairs to her room, slipped inside and fell, in a weary heap, upon her mother's bed.

Below, Mr. Hawthorne indeed refused coffee and was away presently. The remainder of the guests speculated as to the cause of their host's sudden illness, some professing alarm for her well-being, some alarm lest they should fall ill themselves, and some alarm at the shocking impolitic of abandoning one's guests.

Chapter Thirty-Two

"Mary?" Mrs. Burrows knocked gently on the door.

"Come in!" called a cheerful voice from within. Slowly pressing open the door and stepping cautiously into the room, Mrs. Burrows found Mary at her writing desk, the morning sun shining in on her through the uncovered window. "Come in. Come in," she repeated, gesturing to her friend without looking away from the parchment on which she wrote hastily. "I shall only be a moment."

"I just stopped to ask how you were feeling," said Mrs. Burrows taking a seat on the bed. "I see you have not died in the night after all."

"Oh, I am sorry for abandoning you like that. When I finish this I shall explain all."

"May I ask to whom you write so earnestly?" asked Mrs. Burrows.

"It is to a church in Scotland," replied Mary.

"Seeking a new post for Mr. Hawthorne I hope," mused Mrs. Burrows, "for I do not think I shall any longer be able to listen to such a man presume to preach in the name of our Lord."

Mary took no heed of her jest, but answered, knowing the full weight of what she said, "It is the church where my parents were married." She smiled to herself as Mrs. Burrows floundered in her response.

"Your parents? But who, how, when? I do not understand."

"I must have confirmation from the church records," she said, almost to herself. "After all, I believe Walters, but if I am to convince anyone else, I must have some other evidence. I must also find the family who brought me here, but in my state of shock I did not get their name or address last night. I shall ask it of Walters this week, if not today, after our guests have gone."

"Whatever do you speak of?"

Mary set down her quill and turned to Mrs. Burrows, attempting to appear stern. "My parents, Mr. and Mrs. Markham, were married in secret in a church in Scotland 22 years ago. Walters told me last night. She was her lady's maid at the time. Now, may I please finish my letter, which you must understand is of the utmost urgency and importance to me, without further interruption?"

Mrs. Burrows bit her lip as Mary turned back to her desk. She was almost as surprised at her friend's bold forthrightness as she was at the incredible revelation she had just made. She held her tongue until the moment Mary had finished and sealed her letter, at which instant she began her barrage of questions, which Mary satisfied on every point, adding, "I do not wish to reveal this to anyone else until I have the proof of it, but I was thinking that I should like to be called Markham from now on, not Green. It is what I ought to have been called all along, from the day I was taken from the orphanage. Even if I was not their daughter, I would have taken their name. It is possible they gave me the name of Mary as a sort of clue, beginning as it does with the same three letters as Markham. Do you think that is possible?"

"After everything that you have told me this morning, I believe anything is possible. Now, shall we go and sit with your cousins–who are truly your cousins and whom you call cousins but who think they are not your cousins and are not yet to be undeceived–and eat breakfast together before they leave?"

"Yes, please!" said Mary, springing out of her seat, letter in hand. "I had hardly begun eating last night when I was called away, so I am quite famished." As they made their way out of Mary's chamber and down to the breakfast room, she continued, "But there is more I must tell you about my cousins, and about our traveling to Oxfordshire. You see, I intend to help them. They are family after all, and is not one obliged to assist one's family, where possible?"

"Are they in need of your assistance?" asked Mrs. Burrows, who truly did not think she could be further surprised by her meek little friend. "And though you have not asked my opinion, I will say that I do not think you have any such obligation as regards those two ladies. If you did, it would be quite satisfied by permitting them to remain in your house, uninvited, for an entire fortnight, without any complaint."

"But how could I complain? They have done me the greatest service in coming here." The ladies stopped outside the doors of the breakfast room, Mary smiling brightly.

"You are the most perplexing creature this morning," said Mrs. Burrows. "I shall be quite on tenterhooks until I have your explanation." Mary pushed open the door for Mrs. Burrows, who entered and took her seat among the guests.

All were very solicitous for Mary's health, which she assured them could not be better. In gratitude for her miraculous recovery, they were only too pleased to take up calling her Miss Markham. Nothing could be more natural.

The ladies were all excessively sorry to be leaving her that day. Only the promise of a few weeks at Lyme could console them. Louisa was the most brave, as might be expected, going as she was with every anticipation of Lord Marsden's company. Mr. Carrington concealed his true feelings of loss in going, while Dorothea showed no discernible emotion and Augusta persuaded herself to shed actual tears as she embraced the cousin she did not know she had.

When all regrets at leaving had been expressed and every promise of writing given, the company departed and Mary and her companion withdrew to the house where the latter lost no time in reviving the subject of the morning.

"Now, pray tell me everything I have not already heard, regarding your cousins, your parents, Oxfordshire–everything," said Mrs. Burrows, settling herself on the sofa.

Mary sighed. "It is rather a sorry business. It seems my uncle, whom I now know to have always been my uncle, has made some very lamentable investments on the advice of my Aunt Preston, who is not and never shall be my aunt, but cannot escape the fact of being his sister-in-law. And now the girls, my cousins that is, are penniless. They have no dowries, and they shall have to sell their house in town if they are to hold onto Challey Hall. That is the reason we are going to Oxfordshire, to meet with Sir Richard and see what might be done."

"Is that why they came here?" asked an incredulous Mrs. Burrows, "to ask you for money? I know not whether I am more disgusted with their brazenness or impressed with their levity, for they neither of them showed any sign of distress. Augusta especially was most cheerful."

"Well it is a great secret. They would not risk giving it away. And I do not know exactly if that is why they came here. Perhaps they thought they might find a way to ask me for help, or perhaps they were simply looking for society, and here were the Carringtons. On both counts they have done well by their decision, or more likely by Aunt Preston's decision I should say."

"And you do not wish to leave them with a taste of their own medicine? Thus far, you have helped them to a fortnight at Norchester, a few days in Bath and several weeks in Lyme, all at the expense of others. They do not deserve such kindness having never shown any to anyone in their life. Would not it be better to let them suffer the indignities that you have suffered?"

"There is no small part of me that concurs with all you have said. The longer I was away from them, the easier it has been to paint them in my mind as the essence of evil. When they appeared at my door uninvited, I thought I might burst from indignant rage, but what was I to do? Was I to become like them, unfeeling and vindictive? It was at first a sort of pride that made me welcome them, and a certain self-interest which I shall come to in a moment, but once I learned of their altered circumstances, they seemed to me so pathetic that I lost any trace of ill will. Not only have they lost their fortune, but they have no resources to bear the loss–not strength of character, not even sisterly love. I have escaped my poverty, but if I do not assist them, they shall never escape theirs, and they shall be worse off than ever I was, for I was accustomed to hardship from a young age. They have not been. You know, it is so odd. Everything in my life has been reversed. I was the orphan who was such a burden to the Hargreaves all those years, and now it is to me that they turn in their hour of need, for I am the wealthy relative who shall take on their burden. Always I dreamed of leaving Challey Hall, of running away in secret, and now I cannot wait to return there. What shall be next? Shall Lord Marsden seek my hand and I find myself too much his superior to accept?"

"So that *is* what happened in London!" exclaimed Mrs. Burrows. "I knew it must be. I was very good and did not pry, which is no small feat for me, but I had guessed at the truth all along."

"Well, I did not so much seek his hand, but I did hear him speak of me to his brother George, who is equally as bad, though with less cause. It was George Ingles who asked after me, or rather after my fortune, suggesting I should be a good target for a fortune hunter, which is as much praise as I ought to expect from such a dandy. Lord Marsden replied that I was not even worth the having for all my money, since I came from nowhere and had no family. I suppose these are real considerations for a future nobleman, but you might imagine my feelings on hearing as much, and all the more so for coming on the heels of an even more painful rebuke from one whose good opinion is so much more worth having." Mary looked down at her hands and then out of the window, blushing as she added, "Mr. William Ingles did not think very well of me that night either."

"Ah. I see," said Mrs. Burrows gently.

"You must not think worse of him for speaking his mind. He is not one for pretence, and he was quite right in what he said. I was so distracted by the presence of his brother, and by my own appearance, I was really not myself. So you see, I feel I must explain myself to him before he leaves the country, for I cannot bear for him to think of me that way forever. It is too painful."

"Because you love him," added Mrs. Burrows. Mary nodded, too embarrassed to meet her friend's gaze. She had never admitted such feelings to anyone, never spoken of such matters in her life, never had a confidante with whom to share such things. Fortunate she was, therefore, to have a friend in Mrs. Burrows, who would respect the gravity of her confession and not pounce upon it with girlish delight. "And that is the self-interest you spoke of, because the Hargreaves girls, they give you a reason to visit Oxfordshire." Mary nodded again. "So all that remains is to devise a plan that will make him fall irrevocably in love with you and give up his African scheme in favour of joining you forever here in Norchester. Well, that should not be too difficult. We are, after all, both rather cunning and ingenious. Or at least I am, but you are very sweet and amiable, which is more suited to your part in the business in any event."

"Sweet and amiable?" Mary smiled. "I should so like to be much more than that, though I suppose it is better than stroppy and unremarkable, which is what I thought you might say." Both ladies let go a small cough of laughter.

"My darling girl," said Mrs. Burrows, moving from her place to the seat beside Mary, reaching out to take her hand, "you may be the most remarkable and surprising person I have ever known, and I have not lived a sheltered life with few acquaintance." She squeezed the hand she held, and passed Mary a handkerchief with which to dab her moistening eyes. "Any man who would not have you is a blind fool, doomed to rot in the misery of his own impudence."

Rising from her seat, she then strode across the room and rang the bell for tea.

Chapter Thirty-Three

With some effort, Mary was able to obtain both from the church and the family in Scotland, verification of the facts conveyed to her by Walters, to whom she felt eternally grateful and indebted. She often contrived to meet her so that she might hear about her mother every facet and detail that could be recalled and for which Mary was so hungry. She had not revealed the truth of her past to anyone but Mrs. Burrows, but had let it be known throughout the village that she was to be henceforth addressed as Miss Markham. It gave her such a feeling of joy to hear that name in reference to herself, that she was continually in a state of superior contentment and the final weeks of summer began to pass with relative ease and swiftness, despite her anxiety to be in Oxfordshire.

The letters from her friends had begun to arrive only days after their departure, one of which bore the following post-script:

"Everyone asks after you and sends their greetings, particularly Mr. George Ingles, who wishes to know whether you still seek a tutor for your painting. He bids me tell you that he knows of a very gifted master staying in the vicinity of Bath whom he might persuade to tutor you, if you should wish it."

Mary's first thought was to scoff at the presumption of Mr. George Ingles for seeking to thrust upon her one of his starving artist friends, until it was aptly pointed out by Mrs. Burrows that he was among the best connected gentlemen in England when it came to painters and poets, and that, for all his flaws, his taste could not be faulted. Mary thus reluctantly replied that she would be glad to receive his recommendations.

The presumption of George Ingles was soon revealed to know no bounds, for within ten days of posting her reply, Mary was greeted by a visitor by the name of Mr. Bailey. From the style of his dress, she at first took him for a merchant, until he produced a letter of introduction from Mr. Ingles presenting him as one of the greatest painters of the age, who should be employed at the rate of no less than five pounds per week plus room and board and all expenses.

She looked up from reading the letter, baffled and stunned. What was she to do? She had not agreed to taking anyone on, only to receiving Mr. Ingles' recommendations. Could he have misunderstood her, and thought she meant she would receive into her home the person he recommended? Did he simply expect her to support his friend so generously without her advance agreement? She had never heard of such insolence. And five pounds per week? Could this really be a reasonable fee, even for the best masters? It seemed incredible. It was incredible. She herself could not believe it and *she* stood staring it in the face–a face which grew increasingly stern by the minute.

The gentleman had been equally as importuned as she had. He had come all the way from Salisbury, not Bath as had first been suggested, and had clearly been led by Mr. Ingles to believe that she had asked for him to come. It would be terribly awkward and more than a little rude to correct him and send him away after he had traveled all that way in the expectation of employment. What if it affected her reputation among all the best masters? Would she ever be able to retain anyone if she were to do such a thing? There was no cause for her turning the gentleman away besides spite for Mr. Ingles, and Mr. Ingles alone would be unaffected by such an act. And besides, there were no other offers, and she had so long wished to have a tutor. She decided she would keep him on for a week at least and see if she liked him.

She asked to see some examples of his work, which she thought exceptionally good, though she doubted her discernment on a subject of which she was really so ignorant. She might have thought any half decent attempt by a novice to be a work of skill and accomplishment. She must rely on the judgment of George Ingles, which she regretted to admit was much beyond her own. She had Mr. Bailey's luggage sent up and, at his request, showed him directly to her studio for his inspection.

"You are fortunate," Mr. Bailey said to her as she led him down the hall. "I usually hail from Norfolk, and only tutor pupils in London, but I happened to be in Salisbury this summer and was able to spare you a few weeks. I understand you will be departing the neighbourhood at the end of the summer and require some intensive instruction in the interim."

"I need all the instruction possible," she said. "I am afraid I am entirely unschooled. I have mostly undertaken only sketches, as the cost of painting was previously prohibitive for me. I was not always so fortunate as this house might suggest."

They stepped through the door into the small, bare reception room in which she had installed her easel.

"There is excellent light in here," said Mr. Bailey, taking a tour about the studio. "It shall do well for practicing your technique. We shall have lessons in the mornings, and you must spend the afternoons with a brush in your hand if we are to make any progress at all in so short a space of time. If you show any promise, I may consider continuing with you in London when you return there. Every fine day, we shall spend some time out of doors, exploring composition, which is the foundation of all art."

"I hope we shall have enough in these parts to make for interesting subjects. I am afraid we are a little short on ruined castles and the like."

Mr. Bailey laughed. "Yes, I suppose that is what young ladies do like to sketch, and I daresay that sort of thing is very popular even among our most successful painters, but I will be quite happy with more modest scenes of ordinary life–farms and ponds and such."

"Oh that is good," said Mary. "We've plenty of those around here." She was very pleased with his simple manner and direct address. He was not entirely unfriendly, but nor was he effusive and it made her feel she could trust him. He was here to teach, not to flatter. She had never known any painters, but she always imagined them to be more of a temperamental and conceited persuasion. Thus far, Mr. Bailey had neither cursed in French, nor thrown any furniture, nor cried at the wasting of his own genius, and Mary was hopeful of his being a man of sense.

He asked to see some of her sketches and praised them for their natural style. Her heart sang at this little compliment, and rejoiced more than she would say at having the opinion of the self-professed expert, George Ingles, contradicted by one so truly accomplished.

"Of course, you have everything to learn, but I am at least pleased there is nothing that must be unlearnt. I do not approve of much of what is taught by my colleagues and it would be tedious work to have to undo it all. I see that your sensibilities already align with my own, and that you have an eye for the beauty that is already there and need not be imposed with artificial exaggeration. This shall do very well."

A little nuncheon was brought in at Mary's bidding, and Mr. Bailey began sorting and arranging her brushes and paints that they might begin work forthwith. After investing the first five pounds and one week of her time, she felt it would be a great waste not to continue with Mr. Bailey. And so, from that first morning, she hardly left her easel but for the tiresome distractions of eating and sleeping, until Mr. and Mrs. Lowell returned the Hargreaves sisters to take her from her paints and from Norchester and from all the occupations that kept her mind from Oxfordshire where they were soon to be bound.

Chapter Thirty-Four

Mr. Clark had arrived the previous day, as he was to accompany them on their journey, and assist Sir Richard with his confidential advice. Mr. Bailey soon took his leave of Mary and her companions and returned to Wiltshire, but not before being subjected to the excessive praise of Augusta Hargreaves, both in regard to his own genius and to the progress of his student. Dorothea was so effusive as to say that the one painting she took the trouble of viewing was quite good.

"Mr. George Ingles did not think so highly of your skill," said Augusta over dinner. The others had all retired early, but the three younger ladies sat up a little later to enjoy a bit of chocolate. "But for all his claims at expertise, I am sure he was mistaken. I am certainly in awe. Such achievement in such a short time can only be the result of excessive talent, I would say. Do not you agree Dorothea? But then, you only looked at one picture. You can hardly have formed an opinion on the subject."

"I know John Bailey by reputation," Dorothea returned. "I do not need convincing of his abilities. As for Polly, I–unlike you–have never doubted her talent to be superior to your own."

"That is rather a sideways sort of compliment," said Augusta. "Why must you always be so miserly?"

"If Polly has the opinion of Mr. John Bailey, she can want nothing from me. I believe her work to be very good, and I have said as much. I am not qualified to say more."

Mary reflected that either sister might be tolerable on their own, and lamented that they had to be born into the same family so that they were so often in each other's presence, which did not set either to best advantage. "How is your Mr. George Ingles?" she said, breaking up the argument. "And indeed all our friends at Lyme, how did you leave them?"

"We did not leave them at all, did we?" said Augusta. "They all left us! Well, the Carringtons and the Lowells did not, but the Ingles were obliged to return home a little earlier than we all would have liked, something about his brother, whom nobody cares about anyway. I see not why everyone's holiday had to be cut short for his sake."

"Everyone was very well," Dorothea huffed.

"I am glad to hear they were all in good health," said Mary, troubled by what had been said of Mr. Ingles, "but what do you mean about their brother? Why did they all have to leave? Is he ill?"

"Nothing so interesting as that," answered Augusta. "Only it seems the Jesuits want him sooner than they had thought, and they all had to go home to see him before he left. Though I cannot see why they must go to Oxfordshire. Surely he must travel by sea, and it would be much more convenient for *him* to join *them* than the other way around."

Mr. Ingles was to leave sooner than anticipated? He must not be permitted to depart before she could see him!

"Honestly, Gussy, Jesuits? Can you really be so unimaginably ignorant? Or is that your sorry mind's excuse for wit?" Dorothea set down the tea cup she had been holding and stood in graceful indignation. "Please excuse me. I am for bed." Usually satisfied with cold superiority, Dorothy was not, of a custom, prone to open hostility, and as she quit the room, her sister began to cry.

"She only ever thinks of herself," said Augusta between her hot and angry tears. "I am never half so cruel to her, to anyone, as she is to me. Cannot she see that? Does not she know that I suffer as much as she, nay more so, for she has her George. My own prospects are nothing like as good. I am doomed to die an old maid; worse, an impoverished old maid, and still she tramples on me in her spite. I cannot bear it."

Mary sighed. Despite everything, though their relative positions were so reversed, yet still here she was, offering Augusta comfort and solace from the slings and arrows of her sister. And although she had more cause to pity her cousin than she had ever had before, her heart was less moved, for she had her own concern to distract her. What if she arrived in Oxfordshire and Mr. Ingles was already gone? She could not allow that to happen, and she could think of no means of confirming that it had not happened already. What if she were already too late?

"I think we should leave as soon as possible," she said.

"What?" said Augusta, looking up at her through bleary eyes.

"Your father should be at Challey Hall by now. Once you are reunited with him, I know everything shall seem brighter. Together we shall find a way through this trial, and I know you shall be happier. There is no cause to tarry, and as you have not fully unpacked, we can be away very quickly. I suggest we leave tomorrow, after breakfast. I shall write to your father to expect us."

"Oh," said Augusta. "Yes," she nodded. "That does sound good. Papa will put everything right."

"You go off to bed then. You must be very tired, and it shall be a long day tomorrow."

"Yes. I am rather fagged. Good night, then." Augusta said and retired to her chamber for the night, leaving Mary to worry alone in peace over a now cold and foamless cup of rather expensive chocolate.

Chapter Thirty-Five

Mrs. Burrows and Mr. Clark had not, it seems, turned in early, but had sat up half the night drinking Madeira in the library and consequently were not overjoyed to learn that they would be embarking on a full day's journey after breakfast. The Lowell's carriage sat in the drive alongside Mary's, which was loaded with all the luggage of the party. As the travellers came out from the house, they found Augusta instructing a servant in the removal of her things. She was having them loaded instead onto the Lowell's carriage.

"Good morning!" she said cheerfully, turning to greet the others with a smile as they descended the steps.

"What are you doing?" said Dorothea.

"Well, I could not sleep last night for all my being so tired. I think it must have been the chocolate. You see, Louisa very kindly invited me to return with her and Frances to Surrey when they leave Bath in a week, and after thinking on it all night, I have decided to accept her invitation after all. I only refused for Papa's sake, but he shall be home all winter, and I shall only be staying a month or two. I shall see him by and by."

"But do you not wish to be home for your birthday?" asked Mary. "Your Papa was so pleased to be home for it."

"Oh, never mind that," replied Augusta. "We may celebrate that any day, and I know he would wish me to do whatever would make me happiest. Besides, he shall be spared buying me an expensive present if I am not there for him to give it to me. I am sure nobody shall miss me."

The mind of Augusta Hargreaves was not an easy thing to turn, and in this case, none of the party had much reason to attempt it. The journey would be undoubtedly more pleasant without the constant bickering of the sisters. The expense would be less, and indeed, Augusta was quite right that Sir Richard would be spared the cost of presents, and indeed, of the sort of large affair that she would expect to be put on for the occasion. Thus, she was permitted to go with the Lowells without much more than a polite and cursory objection.

Farewells were made, with the most sincere being between Harriet and Mary, who promised to write, and expressed every anticipation of meeting again in London in the spring. After a few minutes of repeated embraces, they were off.

The delay occasioned by reloading the luggage was not long, but was enough to increase Mary's anxiety as she regarded every passing minute as diminishing her chances of ever seeing Mr. Ingles again. The very instant the cargo was secure, she was into the carriage and hastening everyone else to be away.

"We must make use of the fair weather," she said to excuse her brisk manner. "It shall be very slow going if it rains."

The sky was clear, and the air dry, but no one cared to contradict her and they all climbed inside and were quite happy to be on their way.

The carriage was quiet. Mr. Clark and his sister soon fell asleep and Dorothea and Mary were both engaged in their own thoughts. Mary calculated the distance, the rate of speed of the horses, the number of stops required and their duration. It would not be possible to reach their destination by nightfall, but if they made good time, they might arrive not too long after dark, well before midnight in any event. Once arrived, what would be her first act? How could she learn Mr. Ingles' plans? Could she inquire of Sir Richard without raising suspicion? Perhaps the servants would know. Mrs. Burrows had been friendly with the footman on that first day. She might be prevailed upon to inquire from him any local news.

And what if Mr. Ingles were already gone? They must make haste. She must arrive before that could happen. Could the horses be made to drive any faster? Could she somehow send a message ahead of her with a courier? She could, but what would it say? She could hardly write directly to Mr. Ingles. What would such a letter possibly say?

"Dear Mr. Ingles, please do not leave for Africa before I get there. I must be allowed to tell you that I am not a flibbertigibbet. I am a very sensible girl. I only send couriers to gentlemen on matters of great importance, such as this."

It would not do. Of course it would not. She would simply have to be patient. But it was not a matter of patience. It was a matter of timing, which is not the same thing at all. If she missed him, everything would be for naught.

Here she had to contradict herself. She was going to see Sir Richard, to help her family. They were her family now, and whatever their past conduct, she would see them right. Mr. Clark would find a way to mend everything. When Mary's thoughts would wander back to her anxiety over Mr. Ingles' departure, she would look towards Mr. Clark and imagine what solution he might offer to the Hargreaves. At times, the thought of Mr. Ingles had been so constant and so consuming that she began to feel slightly ill, as though she had eaten too much cake.

By the time they made their first stop, the sky had turned from clear blue to solid grey. By the time they pulled away again, the air was decidedly damp. When they pulled into an inn at Faringdon that evening, the rain had turned the baked summer earth into rivers and lakes. The party splashed their way across the threshold into the inn, where they were greeted by a warm fire and a friendly innkeeper, who advised that they had but two rooms remaining, and that they were likely to be gone soon on account of everyone's getting out of the rain.

Mary pulled Mrs. Burrows aside. "I had rather hoped to keep going," she said. "We are nearly there now; it seems a shame to spend a night in an inn when we could be at Challey Hall so quickly."

"Quickly?" returned Mrs. Burrows. "It is another twenty miles to Challey Hall. And in this rain, it shall take longer even than usual. And night is coming. I do not fancy traveling in the dark, and nor, do I imagine, does anyone else. We are fortunate to get a room. I would not press your luck."

"But, what if it is too late when we get there? What if Mr. Ingles is already gone to Africa? I cannot take that risk for the sake of a little rain. I could never forgive myself. Please Mrs. Burrows, is there nothing we can do? Truly I am so anxious to continue."

"No, Mary," was Mrs. Burrows' stern reply. "Were it up to me, we would have stopped when the rain began. In fact, were it up to me, we would have left tomorrow when we were all well rested. If we press on, even if we do arrive safe and whole, you shall be none the better for it. You cannot call on Mr. Ingles at midnight, and nor shall he be like to depart between now and morning. We may leave at first light tomorrow and be arrived by breakfast, or just after. If Mr. Ingles departs before then, I shall chase him down myself for you, but right now, I would like a hot cup of tea and a dry bed. My bones are quite rattled enough."

Mary was forced to submit, though the grip of hope and fear would not release itself from her heart. The ladies shared one room while Mr. Clark took the other. At first all three ladies had tried sharing the one bed, but finding that untenable, Mrs. Burrows begged a few extra blankets from the innkeeper and made herself a hard but warm pallet before the fire. Uninviting though it might have been, it was clearly satisfactory, for she was asleep within minutes, leaving the other two more comfortable but wakeful in the bed.

They lay in silence for nigh half an hour–Mary unable to quieten her mind from thoughts of what she might say upon seeing Mr. Ingles. When she turned over in her restlessness, she saw that Dorothea, though still, lay with her eyes quite open.

"Cannot you sleep either?" whispered Mary.

"It is a good thing for everyone that Augusta is not here," answered Dorothea staring up into the dark. "Where would she have slept, for a start?"

"I expect she would have slept here, in the middle of the bed, sprawling out and forcing both of us off the edge."

Dorothea smiled "And then in the morning, complained that she'd had no room and not slept a wink." Turning to face Mary she continued, "or more likely, she would have forced Mr. Clark to give up his room for her and sleep in the stables."

"And what would she have complained of then?" asked Mary.

"Oh, she would find something. Augusta's powers of complaint are beyond that of mere mortals. No doubt she would astonish us all."

"Is that what is keeping you awake–Augusta's plaintive disposition?"

"No," answered Dorothea. "You?"

"No," answered Mary. Both girls nodded in silence, curled their backs to each other and returned to their solitary contemplations.

Chapter Thirty-Six

For the last leg of the journey, it was Mary's turn to sleep in the carriage. A few hours into the night, she had heard Mrs. Burrows stirring on the floor and insisted that they change places. Mary, unable to sleep anyway, thought someone else might as well make use of the bed. Not long thereafter, Mary herself fell asleep in Mrs. Burrows' place, but it was a short, restless doze, as the sun rose early, and the floor was very hard.

As they turned into the drive at Challey Hall, Mary was surprised at how small it looked, how small and how snug–the familiar ivy along the east wall, the mullioned windows to the fore. It was not so charming in her memory, where it bore such oppressive associations, but today, in the morning sun, the garden fresh and fragrant from yesterday's rain, it was just a pretty country house in need of her protection.

The reunion between father and daughter was a touching one. Neither displayed much emotion, but the duration of their embrace was enough to show how much they both felt. Sir Richard then asked why Augusta was not with them. He was at first deeply disappointed not to have both his children with him, but when the virtues of her absence were laid before him, he was a little consoled.

"Mary," he said, turning towards her and embracing her. He looked at her with an expression of sincere affection and kindly sorrow. "It is such a comfort to have you home again. I do hope you think of this as your home and that you will visit us here often–that is, if we are still here to receive you. I cannot thank you enough for coming to us now, and for bringing your friends."

Mary introduced Mr. Clark and Mrs. Burrows who were both welcomed with warmth and gratitude, and all were invited in for a much anticipated breakfast.

"You have only just missed Mr. Ingles," said Sir Richard. Mary started in her seat, then coughed to cover her reaction.

Mrs. Burrows came to her rescue. "That would be Mr. George Ingles, I presume?"

"Yes, that is right," said Sir Richard, "the youngest of Lord Rosborough's three sons. Are you acquainted with him?"

"We crossed paths in London," she answered. "He was well, I trust?"

"Oh yes, very," answered Sir Richard. "I have never known him to be otherwise. He has been visiting me regularly since I returned, concerned that I might be starved for company."

"Is Aunt Preston not here?" asked Mary.

"She is," he replied.

"I think perhaps that is what he meant," remarked Dorothea, catching Mary's eye and exchanging a grin.

"Where is Aunt Preston?" asked Mary.

"She is here," answered Sir Richard. "She has not yet come down. I thought it odd she did not come out to greet you when you arrived."

The three ladies looked around the table at each other, each recalling the two occasions when Aunt Preston refused to meet Mary–once in town when she was nearly hit by a carriage as she ran from the tea shop, and once at Norchester when she delivered her nieces and departed without leaving the carriage. She could not avoid Mary forever, especially while they were actually staying in the same house.

"I hope she is not ill," said Mrs. Burrows.

"She was quite well yesterday. I shall check on her after breakfast just to be sure."

"Did Mr. Ingles relate anything of interest?" asked Mary, returning to the subject most interesting to her, certainly more so than Miss Preston's health. "Is his family well?" She could not think how to ask any less directly after his brother.

"Thank you, Mary," said Sir Richard. "I had almost forgot. He has invited us all to dine with them next week. Of course, he did not know you were coming so soon until this morning when he was here, but he seemed very keen to see you all. I hope you do not mind, but I accepted on your behalf."

"Of course we do not mind!" exclaimed Mary, who could not believe her luck that she should not need to contrive anything, and that such an opportunity had been so hastily allowed her, provided the elder Mr. Ingles was not yet gone and would not be before then. She had endured a whole summer of anticipation to see him. She need wait only a few more days now, though every hour of their separation seemed longer than the last. "Will all the family be there, at dinner, I mean?" She held her breath as Sir Richard answered.

"I am not sure. He did not say. I should think so."

"So Mr. Ingles has not gone off on his tour of Africa then?" said Dorothea. Mary wanted to leap to the gentleman's defence against this unwarranted mischaracterization of his purpose, but she wanted the answer more and so bit her tongue.

"I could not say," replied Sir Richard. "Certainly nobody has spoken to me of such things, but then I have been rather distracted of late. I may have missed it if they had."

So Mary would have to wait to have her answer. Now that his brother knew of their being in the neighbourhood, she did not believe he would depart without saying goodbye. She wondered whether it would expose her to ridicule or speculation if she were to contradict Dorothea. In the end, she did not care. She had been exposed to worse in this house before. "It is not a tour," she said, as lightly as she could manage.

"Sorry?" Sir Richard looked up from his toast.

"Mr. Ingles' trip to Africa, it is a mission, not a tour."

"Oh," said Sir Richard. "Is it? How interesting."

Dorothea showed no sign of having heard her, or at least of caring what she said. Sir Richard's acknowledgement must be vindication enough.

After breakfast, Mary took Mrs. Burrows over the house and the grounds, pointing out all her favourite places for sketching and for walking. She showed her the nursery where she had slept from the time she was four years old until that spring. And she took her around the garden paths where she had met little Mary Potts–her heart still pained with the remorse of not having given her new boots to the girl's mother.

"You did more than most people would have," said Mrs. Burrows. "You did not need to give away to total strangers such a valuable gift."

"I did not care so much for the boots themselves. It was merely that they were mine alone. They were not cast-offs. They had never belonged to anyone else. I cannot think of anything else in my possession at the time that could be so described."

"And that is why it is nothing to regret that you did not part with them so readily."

"No, Mrs. Burrows. That is why it *is* such a regret. Now I may purchase whatever I like. I may give any number of poor ladies new boots, and perhaps I shall, but gone is my chance for such nobility as would have marked such a sacrifice as that."

"Well, Miss Markham, I cannot entirely clear you of being completely mad, but I will say that you do have a very good heart and I sincerely hope you get everything you wish for." She took Mary's hand and squeezed it, then tucked her arm into her own and led her slowly back up the path towards the house. "But if you were to marry, whatever should become of me?" she asked. "Have you ever thought of *that*, in all your lofty musings?"

"Oh, Mrs. Burrows," laughed Mary, "you should fare infinitely better in the world without me than I should ever do without you. Of that I am absolutely certain."

"In that case, I suppose I must not run away with the enamoured footman after all. 'Tis a pity. He is rather handsome."

Laughing, the ladies returned to the house to drink tea and plan Mr. Ingles' long-awaited proposal to Mary.

Chapter Thirty-Seven

In the hour before dinner, Mary stood outside the door to Sir Richard's study, holding in her hand the two letters she had solicited while in Gloucestershire, and wondering how she might begin upon the subject of their contents. As she stood, she thought she heard the sound of her uncle's own footsteps, pacing on the other side of the door. He must be most anxious, thought Mary, about his circumstances. It can be no easy thing to lose all you have, to be set back so far at such a time in life. She thought that their discussions with Mr. Clark might have eased the burden somewhat, but it must still be hard for him.

Stepping forward with a deep breath, Mary held up her hand and knocked. Instantly, the door flew open and she was confronted by the flushed and blustering face of Sir Richard.

"Mary!" he exclaimed in a startled manner, the force of his presence nearly knocking her over. Instinctively she curtseyed, then immediately felt ridiculous for behaving like a servant in a house which she now practically owned. As she looked back up to him, she saw on her uncle's face a rage that she had never before witnessed in him. She was about to excuse herself, but his invitation that she come in, and sit, were not to be disobeyed. Had she done something to give offence? She could think of nothing, but in the past, her guilt had so often been unjustly presumed that she could not be sure.

Sir Richard continued pacing the room, stopping every few moments to look back at her, open his mouth to speak, then think the better of it and continue his pacing. Mary was not sure what to do.

"Sir, I…" she began, but was stopped by her uncle.

"No," he said. "Please allow me to say all that I must, though you have come upon me before I have quite collected my thoughts, and I do not know where to begin."

"Are you angry, sir?" she asked quietly.

He stopped in front of the window, and looking out answered, "Angry does not begin to describe it."

Mary looked down at her hands, half drawn back to her childhood self—fearful and contrite without cause—and half-indignant that she should be made to feel so when she had been such a friend to this family. "Have I done something?" she began to ask, when Sir Richard spun around to face her with a look of horror.

"You? Oh, my dear child!" His expression sunk into pity and remorse. "No Mary, *you* could never do *anything*." He sighed and collapsed into his chair. "While you were out walking with Mrs. Burrows, I spoke to Miss Preston. I asked her why she would not come out of her room. She would not answer me, would not speak to me at all. The housekeeper told me that she had asked that all her meals be brought to her on a tray and left outside the door, and that she would not leave her room, nor permit any of us into it. I thought perhaps there were some delicate matter, something of a feminine nature perhaps, that may require a lady, and asked Mrs. Burrows, upon your return, to speak to her. How wrong I was! Mrs. Burrows, whom I have not known a day, and who owes me no such courtesy, was the one to tell me what no one would - neither friend nor foe nor family." Here, Sir Richard was too agitated to remain sitting and rose again from his seat to pace the floor. "I have treated that woman with such trust, such deference, and this is how she repays me? She has betrayed me so offensively, betrayed my family, the memory of my sister, you, everyone. I cannot begin to think." He turned to face Mary. "Were you really never given lessons on the pianoforte?" Mary shook her head. "And I forced you to perform before all our friends and neighbours!" Mary nodded. "And that is only the beginning, the most insignificant of offences. You must think me the worst of tyrants." Mary did not speak. Sir Richard walked over to her and sat in the chair beside hers. "You must believe that I have always thought of you as one of my own. I *never* intended that you be treated any differently from my daughters. You ought to have had every advantage, everything proper for a lady, every benefit of education. You cannot think that I knew any of this."

If Mary had ever doubted Sir Richard's ignorance, the tone of his voice now fully convinced her of it. His body trembled and his words cracked. He was, evidently, on the brink of tears. In the months since she had left Challey Hall, she had often asked herself whether it were possible that Sir Richard was really so unaware, so deceived by Miss Preston. Whether it was a willful blindness or no, it was clear to Mary that he did not see it.

"When my wife died," he continued in explanation, "I was utterly lost. I had no family but my children, and I was useless to them in my state. Their aunt was so fond of them. She never had her own family, though she always longed for one, and always doted so on her nieces. I thought it was best to leave them to her raising. She would care for them better than anyone, and as I have always thought of you as just the same as my own children, I never considered that she would distinguish so grievously between you. I suppose I underestimated the covetous love of a spinster aunt. She was always jealous of her sister, my wife, but her affection for the girls was never in doubt. I thought that love would be enough to guarantee a loving home. I wished for all to be well under her care. I never inquired too deeply lest I should discover my error I suppose, and be forced to face the realities of my life–my responsibilities as a father, as a guardian." He shook his head. "I am so sorry. It has all gone so very wrong. We never told you and the girls about your inheritance in order to avoid rivalry, because *you* were so far above *them*! We felt ignorance the best ensurer of equality. I have heard how my daughters have treated you, and while I may be ashamed of them, they only behave as they are permitted to, as they are raised to. They are only children, really. It is the adults who ought most to be ashamed. In truth, I have abandoned my own children to be nurtured into conceit and contempt. I may blame Miss Preston–and she is blameworthy indeed–but it is in myself that I am the most disappointed. I have abandoned you, who were entrusted to me by my sister with such faith. What must *she* think of me, from where she sits?" He bowed his head and began to weep. "Oh Mary," he said. "Can you ever forgive us, forgive me? Can *she*? Oh, my poor, poor sister. My poor Georgiana! What have I done?"

Mary had never seen Sir Richard cry. She had never been in the presence of any tearful gentleman in her life and was not sure what she was expected to do. She had already been through all that he was presently experiencing, and it was many months since she had come to terms with it. She had succeeded in distracting herself from her anger long enough that it had, if not passed, then dulled significantly. Any chance of its resurfacing had been quelled by the alteration in the situation of the Hargreaves family, replacing any possible resentment with pity. She had survived. She now thrived. She was sorry that Sir Richard must live with the truth and that it would inevitably bring him such pain, but it no longer grieved her as it did him.

She reached out her hand and took his. "Uncle," she said softly. "Uncle, I have cried all my tears already. You may cry yours for your own sake, if you will, but shed none for me. I am well. I have suffered, yes, and needlessly. There has been injustice in all, but it has not harmed me, and now I take such joy in being *your* benefactor, in doing for someone else what was not done for me."

Sir Richard looked up at her in awe and disbelief. "Can you be in earnest?" he said. "I know you have had time to recover from your shock, but we are not even blood. You do so much for us, when we are so undeserving. How can you be so good to us?"

Mary placed into his hands the letters she still carried, which she had hoped to present to him that very hour. "What is this?" he asked. She gestured with a nod that he read them. Reading first the letter from the church confirming the date of his sister's marriage, his face turned from curiosity to confusion, then to wide-eyed amazement. He looked from the page to Mary and back again, his mouth open with the first inklings of understanding. Mary indicated that he read the next, which he opened hastily and began to peruse, letting go little sharp cries of shock and incredulity as he did so.

"Oh Mary!" he said when he was quite finished. "My own dear girl!" he threw his arms around her in a warm embrace, holding her as he sobbed further. "Oh, forgive me, forgive me," he said as he released her and took out a handkerchief to dry his eyes. "I did not think anything could have made me happy just at this moment, but you have made me so very, very happy. If you had brought my dear Georgiana back from the dead, you could hardly have cheered my heart more."

"You did not know, then?" asked Mary.

"I confess I suspected. We all did, but we knew it to be impossible. She tried to tell me once, I believe, and I would not hear her. When I came to collect you at Norchester, she asked to speak with me. She extracted from me a promise to care for you–her daughter as she called you. I knew she was very attached to you, and wished you to be treated as her daughter, but I thought her merely sentimental. She insisted you were her own child, but I always believed she was deluded by the fever. It was not only impossible but also distasteful. Captain Markham was abroad all that time, or so we thought. As it was, you were merely an orphan. As my sister's child, you would still be orphan and worse. So we all put that thought from our minds, and what is more, the doctors said your mother would not be able to have children. She had an illness when she was young which left her weak, and we were all told she would never be able to conceive a child. That is why it was not suspicious to her family that she would wish to adopt a child so quickly after marrying, without even trying for her own. But she was not weak, not in her character. I never knew anyone so strong as our Georgiana. And here you have been, her own flesh and blood, all this time." He took Mary's two hands in his and kissed them. "You are nothing short of a miracle. I am so happy," he said. "I shall never be unhappy again, not so long as you live, my dear." He stood, handing her back the letters and said soberly, "Let Miss Preston rot in the prison she has made for herself. She does not deserve even the attention of our wrath. I shall always regret having failed you so miserably, but I shall not burden you with my misgivings if you have found your own peace."

Mary rose and took her uncle's arm. Drying each other's tears, they walked out of the study, determined to dine and to live in mutual grace and joy.

Chapter Thirty-Eight

The drive from Challey Hall to Westley Park was not a long one, but to Mary the destination might have been the other end of the country. Her stomach twisted tighter with every turn of the wheels, drawing her closer either to her Mr. Ingles or to the knowledge that he was gone from her. By the time she climbed down from the carriage at their destination, she doubted her legs would carry her.

They were seen into the drawing room, where the family was assembled. The first person she saw was Lord Marsden, who wore a finely tailored coat, an enormous cravat and an unaffected, jaunty smile. Mary was not for a moment distracted by his auburn hair, glowing in a ray of evening sun, nor by the cut of his calves as he rose from his chair. She looked right past the long-fingered, buttery hand that he held out for Sir Richard, her eyes searching vainly for Mr. Ingles.

Her breath grew shallow and her vision unsteady as she struggled to greet her hosts with calm and clarity amidst her panic at his absence, until she heard a voice say, "Mr. Ingles shall be down in a moment. You must forgive him. He is forever engaged in preparing for his departure." She looked up to see that it was Mr. George Ingles who had spoken, and was looking at her as he did so. She offered him a smile and nod of acknowledgment, though was prevented from replying by the constriction of her throat and the lightness of her head.

"Has he remembered that we are coming?" asked Dorothea, whose hand yet remained in Lord Marsden's. "That is very gracious of him, at such a time."

Mr. Clark and Mrs. Burrows were introduced and welcomed graciously, though by none with such enthusiasm as Mr. Belmont, who was also among the party, and undoubtedly glad of the presence of other common folk of some intellectual capacity. He claimed the brother for his own immediately, to the evident relief of Lady Rosborough, who, despite excellent breeding and powers of conversation, yet doubted her ability to speak for any duration with a solicitor's clerk.

Mr. Ingles did not join the party until it was time to go in for dinner, and thus his entry was rather hurried and gave Mary no time to react or attempt any sort of reunion. Lord Rosborough had just suggested that they wait for him no longer, and they were on their way out of the room when he finally appeared. Some fumbling introductions were hastily made in the doorway. Mary, being at the other end of the room, failed to draw his attention and she could just see that he and Sir Richard were immediately caught up in conversation as they passed out of the door together. Her gaze distracted by the figure of the two gentlemen, she hardly noticed Mr. George Ingles offer his arm and lead her towards the dining room.

"Miss Markham," said Mr. Belmont as they approached the table. "Please, may I beg a seat beside you this evening? But we must sit near the fish pie, as I am so devoted to that dish." Mary assented. She did not much care for fish pie, but she had no cause to refuse his request, which put her at the far end of the table, next to Lord Rosborough. Sadly, she found that Mr. Ingles had taken his seat at the opposite end, next to his mother on one side and Sir Richard on the other. She was thus as far from him as was possible to be, and precluded from any natural or private conversation. The proximity of Lord Marsden, whose presence was once so desirable and who was now directly across from her, was no consolation. She made no effort to draw his attention and was in no way offended that he spoke barely a word to her all evening, preferring instead the company of his neighbour, Dorothea.

Helping himself to a large portion from the pie plate before him, Mr. Belmont said to Mary in a low voice, "I have heard, Miss Markham, an astonishing rumour which I hope to confirm."

"Oh?" said Mary.

"I have been told that for a mere five pounds per week, you have engaged Mr. John Bailey to be your painting tutor. Can this possibly be true?"

"You think five pounds per week an insignificant fee for art lessons?"

"For the full-time attention of John Bailey, I think I never heard such a bargain. How on earth did you achieve it?"

"It was Mr. Ingles who sent him to me," she said, gesturing towards George, who sat on the other side of Dorothea, talking to Sir Richard. He was clearly amusing the older gentleman with some anecdote, for Sir Richard was just at that moment laughing into his napkin in an effort not to choke on his food. "You have heard of Mr. Bailey then?"

"His paintings hang in the Royal Academy," replied Mr. Belmont. "He is not yet generally popular with the public, but in certain circles, he is regarded as one of the greatest painters of our time. When Mr. Ingles asked me if I would tutor you, I thought it rather a great favour for me to take on such a novice, and I am not half the artist Mr. Bailey is. Nor was I willing to travel into the countryside and devote all my time to your improvement."

"Perhaps, if he is not yet well known to the public, as you say, he might have been grateful for the income. Mr. Ingles is always so interested in the welfare of his artistic friends. He must have thought it a good deal for Mr. Bailey or surely he would not have asked him."

"I think you are very fortunate to have him at all," replied Mr. Belmont, "and at such a rate as five pounds per week! It is the most incredible thing I have heard all year. If ever I am in the neighbourhood, you must allow me to come and see your work. I should be most interested in how a painter such as Bailey would begin to teach his art."

"But of course," agreed Mary, who was rather surprised to learn what a master she had been sent by Mr. George Ingles. Her attention at that moment was drawn by the voice of Mrs. Burrows. She was seated across from the elder Mr. Ingles, though she addressed herself to Lord Rosborough.

"Have you heard of all the work Miss Markham has been doing down in Gloucestershire?" she called down the table. "It is most impressive." Lord Rosborough had not heard of any such thing, and shook his head. "I know not how many young ladies in her position would make such sacrifices, would turn their attention so quickly to the welfare of others as Miss Markham has. She has already made the house into a sort of training school for destitute children. There are at least half a dozen widows that she visits every week, and she is forever sending out food to families in the parish who have fallen on hard times. She lends books from Norchester library to the orphanage, and when we return, she intends to turn some of her land over to be used by workers in Bristol to grow food. I tell you, Sir, it is remarkable." Mary blushed and looked down at her plate.

"I see," said Lord Rosborough.

Mrs. Burrows looked more towards Mr. Ingles across from her as she continued. "Most young girls are so preoccupied with fashion and their own importance that they never think of those beneath them, but not Miss Markham. She is so much the opposite.

You know, I never hear her speak a word of nonsense, and I have been in her company these five months at least. We might all learn by her example. Do not you think so, Mr. Ingles?"

"Indeed," he replied. "The heads of young people are all too full of the follies of this world. For myself, I have never understood it. My brothers shall say that it is because I was born without any natural taste, and perhaps they are right, but I do feel there is some morality in it–to waste one's days on mere pretty things and throw away the chance to do some good. I do believe, however, that the dose of charity must be given with the spoon of moral teaching. Otherwise it does not endure."

"But you have all known Miss Markham for many years, no?" asked Mr. Belmont, looking around the table. "Surely you have always known her to be of superior mind and character?"

Mary cringed at this remark, which, though made by one so lately admitted to her acquaintance, could only have been formulated with her past circumstances in mind, and as an attempt to prick their consciences.

Here Sir Richard began his own exposition on his love for Mary, which the lady herself was anxious to be done with. She knew that Mrs. Burrows had begun this in an effort to repair Mr. Ingles' opinion of her. She could see her friend's smug expression even from the four seats down, but she was not accustomed to hear herself praised so loudly within her presence. Mrs. Burrows was clearly unembarrassed, and Mary, though secretly grateful for her audacity, was yet rather relieved when it was all quite finished.

Some time after the second course had been laid, Mary was in for a fresh surprise, and nearly coughed up her salad when she heard Mrs. Burrows ask Mr. Ingles whether it were common for missionaries to be unmarried. The question was directed to Mr. Ingles, but was not inaudible to the whole table. "I would have thought," she proceeded, "that the church would prefer to send married clergymen abroad, that they might set the example of matrimony among the heathens. I am sure I have heard such sentiments expressed before."

Mary had still not solved the question of Mr. Ingles–how to speak to him, prove to him that she was worthy of his good opinion if not his love. She would not have chosen Mrs. Burrows' method, but she felt the kindness in it. Of all present, it was only for Mr. Ingles' opinion that she cared, and he alone could be relied on not to take offence at the boldness of Mrs. Burrows, nor to perceive the scheme behind it.

"In general, you are probably right," he replied, "but I do not believe the Church has the luxury of being so particular. It is not easy to find men willing to leave their homes for such a life, and traveling abroad, being exposed to every nature of savagery, away from all civilization, is hardly the life for a lady. That is, I have not met with many ladies ready to eschew the luxuries of society, and so, I am afraid, I go alone."

"Well, one can never be sure," added Mrs. Burrows. "You may yet meet with one before you are due to leave."

Mr. Clark, sharing his sister's natural amusement at the obtuse but not her intention with regard to Mary, added, "Perhaps you might meet a local girl while you are there."

Dorothea smiled and added, as she raised her fork to her mouth, "Yes, you could bring us back an African bride. Our very own Dido Belle, right here at Westley Park. What would you say to that, Lord Rosborough?"

Mrs. Burrows was quick to save Lord Rosborough from awkwardness and, ignoring the comments of the others, replied to Mr.

Ingles, "Well, as you say, there are not many ladies so interested as you are in serving their fellow creatures at their own sacrifice. Such a lady would be a rare prize indeed, and not to be passed over."

In the drawing room after dinner, when the gentlemen came in, Mr. Belmont again assumed a place beside Mary, who hid her irritation at his thus precluding Mr. Ingles from joining her. She watched as her William sat instead with Sir Richard, and was only a little cheered when Mrs. Burrows took the seat at his other side. Lord Marsden insisted that Dorothea play for them, and without any pretence at modesty, she readily obliged.

Under the cover of the music, and encouraged by a few extra helpings of wine at dinner, Mr. Belmont began rather a shocking tirade against his hosts.

"I should like to tell you, Miss Markham," he said, "that I am not in the habit of dining with such people as the Ingles family. Did you see how Lady Rosborough turned up her nose at Mr. Clark just for being a clerk? I hope Mr. Ingles does choose an African wife, if only to make things interesting. They are all so infatuated with him and his older brother. I, for one, cannot see why. I should never mix with them if Mr. George Ingles were not such a treasure."

"Whatever do you mean?" asked Mary, incredulous to hear him speak with such derision of those who were showing him such hospitality. And furthermore, she had never heard anyone say a bad word about the Ingles family in her life, especially not about Mr. Ingles.

"I know not how the youngest brother could have developed such a markedly superior character to either of the others. Their parents are so proud of Marsden for being, I don't know, so tall, I suppose, and so well dressed, when any gentleman of sufficient income could be so. There is nothing admirable in being born with a handsome face, or dressing in finery. As for Mr. Ingles, everyone always goes on about his noble sacrifice, but I have never witnessed nor heard tell of him doing any simple good deed. And he has no eye for beauty, for which I suppose I am predisposed to judge him ill."

"And does Mr. George Ingles not suffer from any of these flaws?"

"Not at all. He has exceptional taste, and therefore I see only virtue in him. He lives in promotion of beauty, and there is more good in that, as far as I can see, than in the imposition of civilization on foreigners. For without art, without poetry or music, what is civilization but a set of meaningless rules that bring about no happiness? It is art that speaks directly to our souls, that engenders empathy within the heart, and it is want of empathy that is the true definition of evil. Thus it is with great art that we combat the devil among us, and not with preaching fear to unrefined, uneducated minds starched up into seeming piety." He stopped for a moment and read Mary's response in her expression. "I am sorry," he said. "I do believe I have partaken of more wine than usual this evening. I assure you I am not always so vehement in my opinions, but I do feel you to be a kindred spirit, even if you do not agree with everything I have said. I suppose always hearing such praise of you has taught me to trust you implicitly."

"I wonder that you have heard anything of me," she said. "I do not imagine we move in much the same circles. Indeed, I hardly move in any circles at all."

"Oh, but Mr. George Ingles always speaks very highly of you, and as I have said, I never doubt his opinion."

"Now I know you cannot be in earnest, or if you are then he is not, for I know he does not hold me in high regard."

"Impossible!"

"I have heard him sneer and laugh at me behind my back, and heard him speak to Lord Marsden about my being worthless except as a pecuniary interest."

"This cannot be true."

"I assure you it is. I permitted my cousin, Miss Augusta Hargreaves, to show him one of my sketches, which were most private and dear to me, and unbeknownst to either of them, I stood outside the room as she did so. With my own ears, I heard him decry my skill and mock my efforts–my presumption at pretending to some sort of talent. You see sir, you do not know how I have been regarded and treated in the past, before the nature of my fortune was revealed. It was only Mr. Ingles who showed me any kindness, and I believe that the greatest testament of one's character is their treatment of those beneath them. For this reason, I am afraid I cannot agree with your respective assessments of him and his younger brother." She looked across the room to Lord Marsden, who was enraptured by Dorothea's performance. "His elder brother is, however, a bit of a peacock I grant you, but not such a bad sort beyond your average dandy."

As the evening drew to a close, Mr. Ingles finally approached Mary.

"Miss Markham," he said, "I am so pleased you have returned to Oxfordshire, though it be for so short a time, and I leave so soon."

"It is very pleasant for me also," she replied, breathless at speaking at last to the object of all her thoughts and imaginations for so many weeks. "To see all my old friends, who have always been so dear to me, gives me the greatest pleasure. I only regret being so soon separated from them again. You must promise me you shall not go without coming to see us all again. I know you must have much to do, but surely there is time to say a proper goodbye to old friends."

"Why, of course," he said, as though she ought to have known. "I have already told Mrs. Burrows as much, or rather I have consented to speak to Miss Preston, and so I shall see you in a few days' time."

"Miss Preston?"

"Yes," he lowered his voice. "Mrs. Burrows advises me that my services as a clergyman may be of some use. I understand she has locked herself in her room, and refuses to open the door to anyone. Your friend has suggested that I might speak to her, that as a man of the church, she might find herself unequal to refusing my counsel."

Mary smiled to herself. Once again, Mrs. Burrows had taken care of everything, without being asked and without even communicating to Mary the nature of her plan. "That is certainly true," she said. "Mrs. Burrows is wise to think of asking you to come. I very much look forward to seeing you again."

"You shall be at home, then, in the mornings, next week?" he asked, with a touch of uncertainty in his voice such as Mary had never before detected from him.

"I shall."

"Very good," he nodded, looking down at his feet. "There is something I may wish to speak to you about." His words were stilted and hesitant. Mary's heart raced. What could he possibly mean? Did he intend the question she had not dared hope to hear from him? Surely it was not possible. Surely it must be something else, and her poor, anxious heart would have no rest until she knew for sure.

As they drove home that night, and in the few days of uncertainty to come, she knew not which she should doubt more, the likelihood that Mrs. Burrows had in a single evening brought about the realization of her most ambitious hopes, or the powers of her unfailing and canny friend to do so.

Chapter Thirty-Nine

The following day after breakfast, Mary decided to follow her old habit of taking her sketching book out of doors and into the woods behind Challey Hall. She had contemplated those trees and the views beyond so many times, she thought it would pass the time to apply some of Mr. Bailey's techniques to them. There was nothing could consume so many hours for Mary as absorbing herself in her art. She had set out just after breakfast, and in the shade of the trees she did not feel the heat of the afternoon sun. When she emerged, drawn back to the house only by her growing hunger, she was delighted to discover that the day was approaching its close. As she came round the side of the house and up the drive to the front, she caught sight of Lord Marsden and Mr. George Ingles about to mount their horses and ride off. Hearing her approaching footsteps, they turned to greet her.

"Good evening, Miss Markham," called George, stepping forwards, while Lord Marsden made a polite flourish from beside his horse, which he seemed most anxious to mount and ride away. Looking back up to the front doors, Mary continued towards them saying–

"Is it just the two of you?"

"I am afraid so," answered George.

"Yes," added Marsden, "Mr. Belmont was a *little* laid up this morning. Bit of a headache, I would wager."

"And Mr. Ingles had some important business to attend to."

"I see," said Mary. "Good evening, then," and she continued past them to the front steps.

"Miss Markham," George called after her. "I wonder if I might beg a word with you. Marsden, you go on ahead. I shall catch you up."

Lord Marsden tipped his hat. "Good, evening madam." Then he climbed up on his horse and set off as the other two watched him go. Mary waited for George to begin.

"We just came to see that everyone had arrived home safe and well last night," he said. "They said you were out in the woods, and would not wish to be disturbed."

"Yes, they were quite correct. Aside from Mr. Belmont's head-ache, is everyone at Westley Park well today?"

"Oh yes, quite well."

"Please do thank your good parents for their invitation, and for a delightful evening. I thought Dorothea played very skillfully."

"Yes, but then she always does."

Mary wondered what he had to say that he had detained her. He looked down to the papers bound up under her arm.

"I see you took your charcoals with you this morning."

Mary looked down at her hands, now mostly black with the mark of her implements.

"I don't suppose you would care to show them to me." His voice was low and he shifted where he stood. He did not look at her when he spoke. "That is, I am a great admirer of Mr. Bailey, and of your work as well, and I would be honoured if you would permit me to see what you have achieved under his tutelage."

A great admirer of her work? His hypocrisy was astounding. "I think not," answered Mary. "My drawing is very private, very per-sonal. I never show it to anyone without exceptional reason–not even to Mrs. Burrows, whom I would trust with my life, nor Sir Richard, nor anyone. It is that dear."

Now was his turn to flush with shame, though Mary thought he looked more hurt than embarrassed. He raised his eyes to hers with an earnest and imploring look. "I never laughed at you," he said in so near a whisper it was barely audible.

What did he mean by this? thought Mary. She wanted to leave. She was hungry. She was tired. She did not like the soft look of his mouth, nor the tender sincerity about his eyes as he continued to hold her gaze. She had never known a duplicity like his, and she did not wish to engage with it.

"Mr. Belmont related to me what you told him last night, about your picture, and Augusta. I came here this morning expressly to explain myself." Mary wondered how he might charm his way out this time. She had heard everything. There was no explanation that could satisfy her, she was certain. "I did not know the picture was yours," he continued, as if that would justify his laughing at anyone. "I think Miss Augusta intended to take the credit for it herself. She presented it to me, seeking my praise and not informing me of its author. In truth, I was quite taken by its skillful execution and expression, far better than I would have expected from her tasteless hand. I could not bring myself to gratify Miss Augusta's smug conceit with my approbation, and so I gave the only criticism I could, which was that it wanted a little refining. Only when I failed to fall into the raptures she had hoped for did she reveal that it was your work and not hers. Then did she turn on you with such contempt and seek to draw me in to her catty reflections. Had I known you were in any way affected by our discourse, I would have set her down at once, but private as I believed our exchange to be, I thought reproof would be ungentlemanly." His voice had grown louder with disgust as he recounted the events of that evening, which appeared still to anger him. "I am sorry," he added more softly, "truly sorry to have offended you. I cannot imagine what you must have thought of me, to believe me capable of such treachery towards one in your position at that time."

"I accept your apology," she said. She was not certain that he spoke the truth, but it was a pretty apology, and the more probable for its implication of Augusta, whom Mary had no trouble imagining would attempt to take credit for her work. And if George was not being forthright, he clearly felt remorseful for his actions. What is more, there was yet some chance they would be brother and sister one day, and it would not do to risk bad blood between such near relations. She curtseyed and they both turned to go, when he spun back again saying, rather abruptly–

"How did you do it?" She stopped, looking back at him over her shoulder but not turning around. "Forgive my impertinence. I have always wondered, the way they always spoke down to you, if they spoke to you at all, and you always so kind, so forgiving. How did you tolerate it, year upon year? I am sure I should have run mad, yet you never showed any sign of bitterness. It has always perplexed me."

"You forget yourself, sir," said Mary hotly, turning now to face him.

"Forgive me. I know it is not my place, but…" Mary cut him off.

"One of those ladies is to be your wife. I do not think you should speak of her in such terms."

Mr. Ingles was taken aback. "That is your concern? After everything, it is Miss Hargreaves' honour that interests you?"

"I hope I shall always defend the honour of any lady, especially against the slander of her own betrothed."

"We have never been formally engaged," he remarked.

"And that entitles you to speak ill of her? Or do you intend to throw her off?"

"Hardly!" Now it was his voice that turned hard. "I am not such a blackguard as that, particularly not in light of, well, recent developments." He lowered his voice. "Yes, she has told me about her father's circumstances, and yes, before you ask, I intend to uphold my obligations to her. And I shall not breach her trust either. It shall not be me who reveals the truth of Sir Richard's difficulties, though they cannot be concealed forever."

Mary thought he ought to have married Dorothea some years ago. It did not seem right that he would toy with her youth. He would have been rewarded with the certainty of her dowry, whereas his reluctance to commit himself had cost him dearly.

"I am very glad to hear it," she said. "Whatever her offences against me, they do not relieve you of your duty towards her." If he refused to marry her now, he would be the greatest of scoundrels, for not only had she lost much of her wealth, she was also no longer so young. Nearly twenty-four may still be young for one with a large fortune, but for one with no dowry, it is all but middle-aged.

But George Ingles was not such a scoundrel, according to his word, and she feared she had spoken rather harshly just now. Therefore, she added, in a more light-hearted tone, "I am sure you shall still be the envy of many for marrying such a lady. It is vastly preferable to being tied eternally to her sister, for example."

George laughed aloud at this. "Now who is slandering the good name of a lady?" he jested. "Oh, Miss Markham, I do not think either of them are so bad when taken on their own. It is only with each other that they are so dreadful. I have never understood why. My brothers and I have never spoken so cruelly to each other as I have heard Miss Hargreaves speak to Miss Augusta, and believe me when I say, neither of my brothers is such a delight to live with nor is without fault that could be just as easily ridiculed."

"I confess, I have often wondered the same thing. I will say that Miss Augusta does not make it easy to be kind to her. I believe Miss Hargreaves enjoys displaying her skills, and taunting her sister is a skill she possesses in abundance."

"I shall not keep you, Miss Markham," he said, "but there is one thing you must permit me to say before I go. I suspect my brother may intend, if I am not mistaken, well, perhaps it is best not to mention directly, that is, I do not lie when I say that *neither* of my brothers is such a joy to live with, and if I were good, and kind, and of independent means, I would not accept anything from them." Mary wondered if this bumbling speech were an effort to console her for what she had heard between him and Lord Marsden in London, or whether he had some suspicion of Mr. Ingles' intention towards her.

"But Mr. Ingles has always been very kind to me," she said, hoping he might clarify his meaning.

"I am certain he was, so long as you were here, and poor, and ready to be counselled on suffering hardships to which he has never been exposed. But I ask you, did he ever visit you when you were both in town, where you knew no one and were in need of a friend?"

"He was very busy when we were both in town," she said, defensive of her good friend.

"And when you did see him, at my parents' house, did he speak kindly to you there? Did he congratulate you on your rise in fortunes? Was he kind to your new friends?"

Mary thought of their exchange that night, and did not reply. It was her own conduct which had caused him to speak to her so coldly. It was not Mr. Ingles' nature to do so.

"Well, I shall bid you good evening," he said and tipped his hat. He mounted his horse, and Mary stood for a moment on the steps.

Before he rode away, she called to him.

"Mr. Ingles, I nearly forgot. Thank you for sending me Mr. Bailey."

"Do not mention it," he said. "I was merely doing him a favour in finding him some work. You know how I always use my wealthy connections to benefit my impoverished artist friends." And without looking back, he rode away, leaving Mary even more confused as to his character than she had ever been, and for the first time, doubtful of the virtues of her Mr. Ingles.

Chapter Forty

That night, Mary sat up in her room in the guest wing, thinking over what George had said. He had seemed so genuinely sorry to have caused her pain, and there was truth in what he had said about his brother. She could have used a friend those first weeks in London. He was the only person she really knew in town, and he did not so much as call on her. She recalled all the times even Lord Marsden had remarked that he had told his brother he ought to visit her. She told herself that he was very much occupied with very important business, and that her paltry wishes for attention were selfish and unimportant in comparison. She had taken no offence then, nor did she now, but she did begin to question whether such a man would always put the needs of his profession above those of his loved ones. What might that mean if they were living abroad in an unfamiliar land with no friends and no material resources? What if they were to have children? Would he rank them below his parishioners?

She was getting ahead of herself. He had not even proposed and already in her mind they were having children. A knock at the door aroused her from her reverie, and as she looked up, she saw Dorothea slip into the room and seat herself upon the bed.

"I have just come from speaking with Papa," she said. Clearly it had been a long conversation, as Mary had been in her night dress an hour at least and Dorothea was still in her dinner clothes. "I have the most extraordinary news. I know not how to take it, much less how to tell you of it."

"More extraordinary news?" repeated Mary. "I think I have had so much extraordinary news this last six months that it is impossible anything should surprise me. First, I learn that, despite what I have been told all my life, I am in fact an heiress with an enormous fortune, then I discover that my adoptive parents were my actual parents, and then I am told that the wealthy family who raised me in poverty is now in need of my financial assistance. I know not what else could possibly be revealed that could be considered extraordinary when compared with all of that."

Dorothea stared wide eyed at Mary. "Are you really my Aunt Markham's child?" she asked. "You must allow me a moment to consider that."

"Must I, Dotty?" said Mary tiredly. "You said you had something to tell me. I am all attention."

Dorothea awaited no further invitation and proceeded to tell Mary that Sir Richard had just given his consent for Augusta to marry Tom Carrington. "He has proposed. She has accepted him, and Papa has given his consent. They are to be married by Christmas."

"Well, a winter wedding is always charming," remarked Mary, who really was quite surprised, but was not in a mood for expressing it. It was unexpected, but Augusta was, though not the equal of her sister, still very pretty, and if not persuasive then at least determined.

"This does not affect you?" asked Dorothea.

"How should it affect me? Gentlemen propose to ladies every day. It is most common that they are accepted I believe, especially fashionable, good-natured gentlemen like Mr. Carrington with a title to look forward to."

"But he was always so in love with *you*!" It was the most emphatic Mary had ever heard Dorothea, which is not saying much, but was something to Mary.

"Was he?"

"It was clear to all of us in Lyme that he was, most lamentably so. He spoke of little else. We all tormented him so over it, especially Marsden, you know. He is always so droll."

"And did Augusta join in the fun? Or did she show him some sympathy for his heavy heart? Did she tell him softly why I must be blind not to see his worth? Did she say that any fool would return his affection instantly, and then turn sadly away, leaving him with a sense of pity mingled with self-importance that so naturally leads to love?"

"That is not what surprises me."

"You think it impossible that anyone could love Augusta? I know you are not the dearest of friends, but she is your own sister."

"She shall be very pleased." Dorothea did not answer the question. "She shall delight in one day being Lady Augusta and, most importantly, ranking above me. She imagines I should be very jealous, but in truth, I wish her every happiness. She shall not be an old maid and shall not fall to me when Papa is gone. No, I am very glad for her and her foolish admirer. I mean, I never thought him all that sparkling to begin with, but in choosing you to love, he showed some promise at least. In attaching himself to my sister, he has shown himself as dull as ever I suspected him to be. Imagine exchanging you for Augusta? Men really are so fickle, so blind."

Mary thought her cousin might begin to cry, but the self-possession of Dorothea Hargreaves was not to be overestimated.

"So you really are my cousin?" she said, "after all these years of calling you so."

"I am. But do not think me a bastard. My parents were married in secret five years before they were married in public."

"Excellent. I should hate to be obliged to be ashamed of you. I should be quite alone without you."

Whatever was the cause of all this? wondered Mary. Did Dorothea really fear losing her sister despite all their acrimony? Although she despised her in a sense, Augusta had always been there. Perhaps Dorothea's self-worth depended upon her in a way. Without her senseless sister to provoke her, she was newly adrift and uncertain.

Mary crossed over to sit beside her. "You shall not be alone!"

"I am not so young as I was, and now Papa cannot give me any sort of dowry. I shall be wasted."

"But you have Mr. George Ingles," protested Mary. "He was always to marry you, and marry you he shall. You need not fear of being destitute, or of dying an old maid."

"Oh, George Ingles," sighed Dorothea. "I could have done so much better than George Ingles if I had known I did not have time on my side. And, if I had known I was to marry him in the end anyway, I should not have strung him along so many years. I should have agreed to marry him right at the beginning, when I could be sure of being provided for. The Hargreaves are a very old and prestigious family, and Challey Hall is no small prize, though I cannot think how we shall afford to keep it on a thousand a year."

"You strung *him* along?" asked Mary, who naturally had assumed it had been the reverse.

"I am afraid so," conceded Dorothea. "How many times he proposed, and how many times I told him I would give him an answer by and by. It became something of a joke between us, and now it has gone on so many years that though he never had the pleasure of my acceptance, he is bound to marry me, though I suspect his love for me has long since expired. I am sure it grows tiresome to be so often rejected. And I am bound to marry him, though he be only the third son of a minor lord, and has no profession and very little income. I can do no better now, and so I must have him." Seeing Mary's expression, she added, "Do not worry, Polly. We shall rub along all right. We are at least friends, which is more than most couples can claim. And I know him to be of good character–better at least than his selfish prig of a brother."

"Who, Lord Marsden?" asked Mary, surprised to hear Dorothea disparage such a gentleman.

"No, Mr. Ingles." Mary was astonished.

"How can that be?" she said, "Mr. Ingles has always been very kind to me, to everyone surely, and I do not think you should say such things about a man of the cloth."

Dorothea clearly cared not what profession or station anyone occupied. All were equally open to her censure. "His mother is ill," she said.

"What?" Mary had never heard so much as a rumour to that effect. "But she looks so well, and she was just in London, holding parties. Are you quite sure?"

"Yes, most certainly, though she is a proud woman and does not suffer pity. She is very ill, in fact. She may not last the year. That is why they all went to Lyme. They thought it might help. It does not appear to have done much good, at least not more than the traveling has undone. She has been told to stay where she is and to rest her nerves. Any sort of shock or excess of emotion could spell the end for her. And at such a time as this, Mr. Ingles chooses to leave the country. George has begged him not to go, and Lord Rosborough, but he is deaf to them, and blind to his own callousness." She paused to recover her composure. She stood up from the bed and walked over to Mary's dressing table, picking up a trinket box and taking off the lid. "Lord Marsden is nearly as bad, always going off to London. Only George has the goodness to stay close to home, to think of others besides himself." She put the lid back on the trinket box and replaced it, turning back to Mary who had gone quite pale. Surely William was not so heartless as to abandon his dying mother. If so, she had entirely misjudged his character, whatever small kindness he had shown her. "I know not what Mr. Ingles has ever done for you, but I can assure you, George has done more. He always remembered you, you know, not like some, who only began to pay you mind once you had your money."

"How so?" she asked, incredulous.

"Well, he sent you that tutor, for a start, Mr. Bailey. Did Mr. Ingles ever offer to assist you in that way? He could have, but it was George who did so. And Mr. Bailey did not want to go. George had to pay him a good deal of his own money to convince him, because he thought you deserved the best, as redress for never having had lessons all your life. I thought it was a fool's game, but he insisted. And he always thought of you when there were parties and balls. Do you remember that night when Papa returned home unexpectedly? The ball that night, it was George made sure you came to that, were specifically included on the invitation. Mr. Ingles would never have thought to do that. It would require him turning his mind unbidden to someone outside of himself, and I doubt he has ever done such a thing in his life. And when we arrived in London this spring, and Lord and Lady Rosborough were throwing that ball, it was again George who ensured you received an invitation. He is forever doing little things like that. And he does have such nice hair." She nodded to herself in a reassuring way. "I always did like his hair."

"Yes," said Mary who was far more surprised by all that Dorothea had just said about the Ingles brothers than by Augusta's engagement, which was almost forgot amidst all the rest.

"And we shall not be so very poor," added Dorothea. "He shall have something on his marriage, and he already has a thousand pounds per annum, plus I shall have this house when Papa is gone. No, we shall rub along all right, Polly. You need not worry about me." She checked her reflection in the glass and adjusted a strand of hair. "Better than Augusta and that half-wit," she added, then departed, without a backward glance or a goodnight to her stunned and confused little cousin whom she left in her nightgown to reconsider everything she had ever thought she knew about the man she had so lately admired with all her heart.

Chapter Forty-One

When Mr. Ingles finally arrived at Challey Hall, Mary was exhausted. She was weary of having her heart battered and confused, having all her notions of everything and everyone turned on their heads and then turned back again. She had sat the whole morning in her old nursery room. It no longer held for her the sense of oppression nor the sense of familiarity that it once had, devoid now of all her possessions and of her prior circumstances. It was simply a room, bright and warm, but stark, furnished with partially broken, abandoned furniture deemed unfit for use by the family themselves. Standing up from the bed on which she sat, she walked over to the vanity and peered into it, searching in her image for the truth of her own feelings, for the face that could never have imagined anticipating a proposal from the son of Lord Rosborough, much less rejecting it.

All her features were there, looking back at her. She wondered what she might tell herself, if she could reach back into the past and speak to the Mary Green who had sat before that very glass so many times. And what would that Mary tell her to do now? That Mary would never have turned down the opportunity to leave everything behind and run away to Africa with her humble curate, but she doubted now whether that were what she really sought, or whether she only ever wanted her own freedom. She also doubted the humility of the curate in question, if everything she had heard over the last few days were true. At that moment, all she wished for was to go home, to Norchester, to her paints and to the bed where her mother had slept.

In the glass, she noticed that the door to the wardrobe was open behind her. Absently, she walked over to it and pulled open the door. There, on the floor of the wardrobe were the nankeen boots given to her by Sir Richard. Clearly the servants had not understood her message to send them away with all her other clothes to be donated to the poor. She bent down and picked them up. They were the only things that had ever really been her own. Sitting down on the bed, she slipped off her shoes and slipped on the boots, lacing them up and tying them tightly on. They were not a perfect fit, but they were still neat. She decided she would find another pair to donate to the poor. These were hers, and besides, she thought Sir Richard would be pleased to see her wear them, to be reminded that he had in fact been kind and generous to her.

William arrived some hour or so later, while she was in the drawing room working from the work basket at the window.

"So, you have come to speak to Miss Preston," she said. "It was very good of you to come."

"Not at all," he replied. "You know it is always a pleasure to see you." She did not ring for tea. Anyone else might have taken offence. Mr. Ingles did not even notice.

She set down her work for a moment and met his gaze. She had determined to say nothing about his leaving, nor to attempt to persuade him out of it. Lord Rosborough had tried. Mr. George Ingles had tried. And all was to no avail. What power or place had she to intervene, and what chance of success where those with so much more claim on his obligation had failed? It seemed to her hopeless and possibly improper. But for the sake of Lady Rosborough, for the sake of decency, she felt at that moment that she must.

She gathered her courage and with a quiver in her voice asked, "Is there really no possibility you might reconsider?"

"Reconsider what?" he asked. "Speaking with Miss Preston? Are my services no longer required?"

"No, I meant your trip, your mission. Must you really go?" She feared her entreaty might be taken as an insinuation of feelings or wishes she no longer had. "I say this not for my own sake, but for yours, for your family's. I know you wish to do good in the world, but I see so much that can be done here, without need of such dramatic steps as leaving the country. Cannot you minister to the needs of your own countrymen? Why must it be Africa?"

He looked back at her with sympathy. "Oh, Mary," he said. "I do not expect you to understand. I do not expect anyone really to understand. I know one may do good anywhere, but I wish to do something great." He stepped forward to take the seat beside her, his voice growing impassioned as he continued. "I do not wish to lay on my deathbed and think what I might have done but did not for want of courage, or for fear of offending others. I do not want to look back on my life with regret at never having left England's shores, never doing something truly heroic and important. I am a simple man. I do not feel attachment to the things that gentlemen seem to value–clothing, carriages, balls, grand houses. They do not hold me, and I feel it is my calling to cast them off, to leave them behind in pursuit of my destiny."

Mary could see by the spark in his eyes that opposition was futile.

"I do not imagine I shall see you very often in the future then," she said, returning to her sewing.

"No, I think not." He sat back in his chair. "Your friend, Mrs. Burrows, is very considerate. She has put it in my head that I ought not to go to Africa without a wife, though I leave so very soon."

"Well, Mrs. Burrows does say a lot of things," returned Mary with a short cough of a laugh. "As you so astutely pointed out the other evening at dinner, it is not likely you would find a lady in such a short time who might be willing to leave everyone and everything they care about. People have obligations, you know–family and the like. I feel there is no more important duty than to one's family, one's parents, who have given one life. As you know, I do not have parents, at least not living parents, but I hope I should always know what I owe to Sir Richard."

"Indeed," he said nodding his head in mindless agreement. "The Hargreaves have always been very good to you."

Good to me? thought Mary. Could he really be so completely obtuse? Could she so lately have regarded this man as the very pinnacle of human achievement?

"Do you recall the last time we met?" she asked, growing bolder as her indignation began to swell. "That is, before the other evening at Westley Park. Do you recall seeing me in London?"

"Did I see you in London?" he said, squinting in an effort to recollect their meeting. "Oh yes," he said, "at that party my parents held. Pardon me. I was so very busy when I was in town, I had quite forgot. Did not I go to bed early that night? I think I must have. I do not dance, as you know. I do not think it quite fitting for a clergyman, though it is no great loss for me, as I have never had any skill or enjoyment in it."

"It is no matter," she said smiling. "As I said, you may find Miss Preston in her room." She rang the bell and directed the servant to show Mr. Ingles to Miss Preston. He bowed and followed. Evidently he succeeded to some degree with her, for he did not instantly return.

Shortly after he went up, Mrs. Burrows joined Mary in the drawing room. "Well?" she said. "Am I to wish you joy?"

"I told you, I did not intend to accept him," replied Mary without looking up from her work.

"And he did not make you change your mind, with amorous addresses and promises he did not intend to keep?"

"No."

"Was he heartbroken then? Has he gone off to cry over your rejection?"

"I did not reject him."

"So I *am* to wish you joy?"

"I did not need to reject him because he never proposed. I do not think he ever intended to."

"He never proposed at all?" Mary shook her head. "After all my encouragement, did not he even attempt it, not even make a start?" Again Mary indicated no. "Well, more fool him then!" said Mrs. Burrows and rang for tea.

"It is possible I rebuffed him before he had a chance to make his proposal, but I do not think so."

"A gentleman is never dissuaded from proposing once he has made his mind up to it," said Mrs. Burrows, taking a seat and reaching out for the basket Mary passed to her. "They always have to say their piece, however much a lady begs them not to, and whatever the consequences." She took out a sock and a darning ball and the two ladies sat at the window together for nearly an hour before they heard Mr. Ingles descend the stairs. Mary anticipated he would return to take his leave. He did not, and after a moment she got up and left to pursue him out of the house. She was just in time to see him mount his horse to return home.

"You are leaving then, Mr. Ingles?" she said from the top of the steps. "Will not you stay for tea?" He may not have turned out to be the man she expected, but he was still her old friend. She would still enjoy his conversation, and the truth remained that he was going away very soon for a very long time. She also worried that she may have offended him with her manner of speaking to him. She had only wished to prevent his proposing, and her vexation at his insipidity had got the better of her. He did not appear to have been offended, but she herself did not enjoy feeling that she had been ungenerous to anyone.

"I am afraid not, madam," he said pulling his gloves tight. "There is not time."

"But Miss Preston, is she all right?"

"Oh yes, Miss Preston is quite well. You need not worry about her. My advice is to continue to leave her be. She will soon be done with this business."

"Well, thank you for coming," she said. She was most confused and a little vexed. She had expected at least some effort or insinuation at a proposal. What else could he have meant when he said that he wished to speak to her about something? Had that never been his intention? "Will we see you again before you depart for Africa?"

"I imagine so," he replied.

"Was not there something you wished to speak to me about?" If he had not intended to propose, she must know what he meant.

"Was there?" He searched his mind. "I am sorry. I have so many things to think of at present, I cannot keep them all straight. Ah yes. There was something. But it has resolved itself now so it is no matter. Thank you for your hospitality, Miss Green. It is always such a pleasure to see you."

She waved to him as he rode away. Had he not been told of the change in her name? Had he been told and failed to remark it? Had he forgotten? Or did he call her that on purpose, and if so, to what end? She was excessively confused about him. One thing she knew for sure–she did not wish to go to Africa as his bride, and at very little cost, she had managed to evade the embarrassment of telling him as much.

Chapter Forty - Two

"I shall be quite happy to return home to Norchester," said Mary to Mrs. Burrows as they walked home from church on Sunday, allowing themselves to fall behind Sir Richard and Dorothea, who were accompanied by an attentive Mr. George Ingles. "I know we have barely arrived, but I am anxious to be off again. Everything I came here for is now over, and there is so much that draws me back to Gloucestershire."

"You do not like it here, then? I would have thought that you might have enjoyed presiding over Challey Hall, in a sense, triumphing over your cousins, over Miss Preston. Is it still unpleasant, the memories that the place recalls for you?"

"It is neither," said Mary. "I feel a little sad to leave, in fact. When I left in the spring, I could not wait to be away, to escape. I felt I was breaking free, compelled by my disdain for the house and everyone in it. But now, I have no such compulsion. I am not driven by a wish to leave, but am drawn by a desire to be elsewhere. It is a very new feeling for me. There was formerly never anywhere I wished to go. I only ever wished to be gone. Everything about this place now matters so much less, and that makes it much more pleasant." She kicked the dust of the dry autumn path as they walked. "I have also come to like the people here more than I did before. Sir Richard and I are on much less strained terms, and Dorothea seems to me more sad than malicious. You know, she actually said something in my praise, or hinted at it at least, when she told me about Augusta."

"Did she?" said Mrs. Burrows with surprise. "A hint is more than I would expect Dorothea to give to anyone."

"Yes, she is quite transformed. And her sister is happy, which is also a great change. Though she is not here now, I imagine that if she were, I would only find her amusing rather than the cause of any suffering. And without Miss Preston looming about all the time, the atmosphere is so much more peaceful."

Mrs. Burrows nodded in contemplation. "And what of Mr. Ingles?" she said. "I do not think you like him better than you did before."

Mary sighed deeply. "No, I do not. In a sense I feel I have lost him already, though he is not yet gone from Westley Park. Did you know he is taking over a half dozen servants with him?" Mrs. Burrows raised her eyebrows. Mary nodded. "Dorothea told me as much. I can understand that he requires some assistance, to lift and carry things, to cook and so on, but surely he could engage the locals in some of those tasks. Half a dozen seems an awful lot for a single missionary. He also brings a stove, and quite a lot of furniture. He shall not be sleeping on the floor of a grass hut and eating termites."

"A stove?" returned Mrs. Burrows.

"Yes, apparently he wishes to make his heroic sacrifice without actually giving up the comforts of home. No, I do not think my opinion of him is quite the same as it was a month ago".

Looking up towards the party ahead, she added, "But I do feel that his brother has risen a good deal in my esteem, and that almost compensates for it."

"Is that so?" she said and they carried on down the path through the dense hedgerows–arches of bramble filtering the early autumn sun, the fields beyond full and golden. "And if the Hargreaves are all so much less distasteful to you now, does that mean you intend to help them? I know they do not deserve it, but I suppose they are your only family."

"I have decided to lend Sir Richard enough money to support himself and the girls until they are both married, and once that is achieved, he will let out Challey Hall and come to live with us at Norchester. He has decided to retire from his post in the Indies. I think he regrets being so long absent from his home and his children. It is really too late to redress any of that by remaining in England, but I at least shall be very pleased for the company. Since it is I who suffered most by his absence, perhaps it is right that I should benefit most from his return."

"I do not think you shall be in need of company for long. Surely you do not already despair of marrying. You are yet so young and so eligible."

"I may marry one day, or I may not." Mary picked a leaf as she passed and toyed with it as she carried on. "At present it all seems a sordid game and I am grown weary of all the highs and lows of love, or whatever you call it. When I think of Dorothea and Mr. George Ingles, the way they are forced to marry where there is no love, ensnared by the expectations of society and doomed to unhappiness, it seems such a waste. I think how lucky I am to have escaped unscathed, unfettered. In truth, despite everything, I am fortunate to have been an orphan all my life until now. I was not worth having designs on, not worth planning for, and all the trappings of privilege have not got hold of me. I always thought I was so imprisoned in my life, but in fact, I am the one who is free. I may do as I like. And what I like is to sit at home and drink chocolate with all the other orphans, and maybe do something useful with my life."

They emerged from the shade and into the sun. They crossed a stone bridge where Mary threw her leaf into the brook and watched as it disappeared from sight.

"Is that all you regret about George Ingles, then," said Mrs. Burrows, "that he shall be unhappy with Dorothea, and she with him?"

Mary laughed. "Oh, Mrs. Burrows, do not attempt to interpret for me the desires of my own heart. It was your promptings that led me to think of Mr. Ingles, and look how far off the mark that was."

"I relied entirely on your opinions." Mrs. Burrows defended herself with the calm assurance of one convinced of her innocence. "If you were incorrect in your own assumptions and information, I cannot be blamed for that."

"Well, I shall not be taught to think now of his brother," said Mary. "And if that is a great loss, then it is a small price to pay for my happiness. I have lived this long without love of any kind, nor any family, nor my own home, nor money. I now have all of these things. To live without romantic love is a deprivation I am willing to endure for the present."

Mrs. Burrows shrugged. She could not disagree, and she did not wish to convince Mary otherwise. After all, as she had said before, what should become of her if Mary were to marry? Her friend's celibacy was far more in her interests, and she was not of a persuasion to act against those.

The ladies walked off the bridge, talking and laughing together, and were just rounding a bend in the path when they collided with Mr. George Ingles coming at a pace in the other direction. Mary was knocked to the ground, but did not appear hurt. Only she found the humour in it; Mr. Ingles was horrified and Mrs. Burrows severe upon him. The former helped her to her feet, and as she rose, it seemed she was not so uninjured as she thought. A little bruising on her hip made her limp as she attempted to continue down the path.

"I am so sorry," said Mr. Ingles. "I had only just run back at Sir Richard's request to see that you had not been set upon by thieves or the like. We reached the house, and looking back, could not see you anywhere."

"We were just enjoying a leisurely ramble," said Mary, brushing the dust off her skirt. "Now, I fear we shall be so much longer in getting back that they will really begin to worry."

"Well, Mr. Ingles here may help you back to the house," said Mrs. Burrows. "I shall hurry ahead and let them know that everyone is well, or at least that we were so before you came to ensure as much. You take as long as you need."

She received the thanks of the other two and set off at a brisk walk. Running was not something Mrs. Burrows did unless pursued by a threat more serious than the force of her temperament could banish.

"The best thing is to walk it off," said Mr. Ingles, offering his arm. "At least, that is what I am told, and we have little choice in the matter."

"I am sure I shall be all right in a moment." She took his arm and leaned on it as she hobbled along. "I have been meaning to thank you properly, Mr. Ingles," she said, glad of a chance to unburden her thoughts, "to thank you and to apologize. I am so very grateful for your sending Mr. Bailey to me. I confess I was a little surprised, more than a little, at your boldness in foisting him on me, but I know now what a kindness it was, and I do wish you to know how much I appreciate what you have done for me. I have acquired so many things in the last few months, and everyone has been very kind, but only you gave me what I really wished for. Please accept my thanks. And please permit me to repay any expenses you might have incurred on my behalf."

"Not a bit of it," replied Mr. Ingles with a smile. "You cannot know what a joy it was for me to do. I have been accused of presumption in my life, of assuming to know what is best for others, and it delights me no end to get it right, and to pull it off. It was a bit of a risk, I admit. There was a chance you would turn him away, but I thought–I hoped–you would be too good to do that once you learned how far he had traveled."

"You must be very cunning then," laughed Mary, "for that is precisely as it was."

"I would have sent Mr. Belmont, but he would not go."

"Oh, sir!" said Mary, stopping and turning to Mr. Ingles. "That is what I wished to apologize for. I spoke so harshly to you about him in London. I believe I insulted you as well as him. I was so wretched at that moment when you approached me, I might have said anything. But that is a sorry excuse, and I've no right to be forgiven, but I ask anyway."

Mr. Ingles laughed and replied, "I would not have sent you Mr. Bailey if I had taken your rebuke to heart! As soon as you spoke, I could see that you were distressed. I never take anyone seriously when they are distressed. It causes my parents no end of bother."

Mary was feeling much better after a few minutes' walking, and felt she could probably walk quite well unaided if she wished to. But she found she rather liked the strong arm of her companion. "I did call on you in the morning," he continued, "the day after the ball, but I was told you were not well. That excused your behaviour well enough for me. I am never myself when I am not in good health."

"That was you?" she said. "I thought it was your brother come to apologize, or at least to make peace. They only said it was a gentleman named Ingles."

"No chance there, I'm afraid. I do not believe William has ever apologized for anything in his life. Did you have words with him?"

"It is more that he had words with me," she answered. "I am not sure whether I should say more."

"Please do," he answered. "I am always ready to hear what I should not be told."

She had not repeated to anyone the content of that evening's exchange, but she felt somehow that she could confide in Mr. Ingles, that he would be a friend to her. "The truth is, I was in a very silly mood that night and he chastised me for it. He said that wealth had affected me and he did not approve of the alteration."

"What an absolute pig!" exclaimed Mr. Ingles. It was a far stronger response than Mary had anticipated. "To think, he should presume to tell *you* how to behave, he who has never known a day's hardship in all his life, to judge one who has always born with grace trials which he shall never understand. What business is it of his to criticize you for making merry in your new situation? I never knew anyone so thick!"

It warmed her to hear him set his brother down so strongly in defence of herself. "I have recovered from worse," she said.

She recalled that evening in London and the conversation she had overheard between George Ingles and Lord Marsden. She wondered at the discrepancy between the former's generosity to her, his kindness which extended back to the time when she was obscure and penniless, or at least believed to be so. How could he have said, as she clearly remembered, that her money was the only virtue of hers which could interest a gentleman? She had heard him say as much, yet his every action contradicted this opinion.

Shaking his head, he mused aloud to himself, "How could I have been born to such a family?" She looked up at him and saw a look of genuine consternation. "You know, I remember that night, in London, arguing with my other brother, Marsden. He was so disparaging towards you, so unjust in his feelings. I was so angry with him that I had to walk away or I might have caused a scene."

This did not at all accord with Mary's impression of the conversation she had overheard, but then, she had run off to find Mrs. Burrows before she could hear how Mr. Ingles had responded. She tried to remember what she had heard him say that night. Was it that she was a good catch for a fortune hunter, or could he merely have been expressing a concern that she might be the object of prey to such gentlemen? It was, after all, Lord Marsden and not Mr. Ingles who had said the worst by suggesting that she was not worth having even with all her fortune. Perhaps in her unhappy state, she had construed his comments in the worst light, and the truth was quite the reverse. Considering all she now knew of him, this explanation seemed increasingly likely and she was rather ashamed for having thought otherwise.

"I am glad you did not ruin the party on my account," she said.

"You know," he said with a grin, "I was rather struck by the way you defied me. When I heard you had gone off to town so suddenly that spring, I wondered what might become of you. You were such a gentle creature, and London has destroyed many a sheltered young lady like yourself. I did not worry any more for you after that night. I knew, if you could tell me off like that, you would have no trouble with any of the city's villains. There are not many would speak so sternly to a son of Lord Rosborough."

"There was never any real danger on account of any villains," said Mary. "Mrs. Burrows is a formidable and scrupulous protector. I am very fortunate to have her on my side." She was now utterly confident in the friendship and the goodness of George Ingles, and as such, let go any final traces of resentment which she may yet have born. She could now return to Norchester harbouring naught save goodwill and contentment for her fellow creatures. It was a welcome feeling and one which she would not lightly relinquish.

On they walked, talking easily and enjoying the crisp scenes of autumn as they went, the cool breeze and the warm sun playing on their contented faces. She told him about Norchester, about her parents and about her plans to take in Sir Richard. He told her that her endeavours in Gloucestershire had inspired him to apply his connections and interests in an enterprising new way. He had decided to begin a career as an art dealer. His family's name could gain him entrance into the greatest houses in the country, and he was already well acquainted with most of the nation's painters. All he wanted was the resolve, which he had lately acquired by her example.

"For a lady who knows no one and has had almost no exposure to the world to achieve such great things rather put me to shame," he said. "My father has agreed to assist me in making a few acquisitions to begin with, and who knows what I might achieve in time. Perhaps I shall be a credit to Miss Hargreaves after all."

"I think you already are," she said honestly. "But if you are very successful in your vocation, I may, perhaps, permit you to purchase something of mine."

He threw back his head in a laugh. "Yes, and just imagine how Miss Augusta might take *that* news!"

They carried on, speaking of the old days, laughing together over old and ridiculous arguments she had heard between Dorothea and Augusta. As they approached the house, she said, "There is only one thing which has never been adequately explained about my old life."

"And what is that?" he asked.

"It is Miss Preston. I cannot comprehend her reasons for having been so cruel to me." Mr. Ingles nodded, assisting her up the steps to the door. "Mrs. Burrows says she was guarding the interests of her nieces. Sir Richard says it was perhaps motivated by her jealousy of her own sister, but neither of those reasons seems to me sufficient for so many years of malevolence and deception. And why will she not come out of her room? She has nothing to fear from me. Mr. Clark's firm completed their audit, and there is no actionable cause in the figures. I told her as much, through her chamber door, but she would not even acknowledge me. I do not understand any of it."

Helping her into the house, Mr. Ingles shrugged and gave her the simplest yet most satisfactory answer of all. "Some people are just a bit mad."

Chapter Forty-Three

The days were still warm, though the nights cooled the house enough that a fire was required to make any of its rooms habitable. It was the day before the Norchester party was to leave Challey Hall. Mary, Mrs. Burrows, and Sir Richard sat in the drawing room where they could hear Dorothea practicing the pianoforte.

A noise was heard in the drive and Mary and Mrs. Burrows looked out of the window to see a carriage pull up bearing Mr. Ingles and his personal luggage. Mrs. Burrows leaned in to say to Mary, "I told you a gentleman never foregoes a proposal once he has made up his mind to make it. I would say this gentleman has not given up on you yet."

Mary hoped her friend was wrong. She did not care to live through the rigours of rejecting Mr. Ingles. "He must not be given a chance," she whispered back. "Do not leave me alone with him. You know nothing good may come of it."

All rose as the gentleman was announced. Dorothea ceased playing on the pianoforte, but only after being directed to do so by her father. She sighed, gathered up her music and left the room without acknowledging Mr. Ingles. Unfortunately for her contemptuous purposes, the gentleman was not sensible of the offence.

"I have come to take my leave of you all," he said. "I am on my way to Dover, from which I sail in only three days' time. Can you believe it?"

"That is remarkable," said Sir Richard, eager to make up for his daughter's poor manners. "Will you take tea with us?"

"I do not think there is time," he replied. "I have a long journey ahead, and I have already called upon several houses on my way out, and drunk enough tea to last me all the way to Africa."

"It is very good of you to have stopped in," said Mary.

"Yes, shall we see you to your carriage?" said Mrs. Burrows. "We must not, for our own pleasure, detain a man from such important work."

Sir Richard was surprised at the eagerness of the ladies to see Mr. Ingles gone. He looked towards Mary, who gave no indication of disagreeing with Mrs. Burrows.

"Oh, well, yes," said Mr. Ingles and looked back to the door through which he had just come. He smiled at the ladies as they came forward to accompany him.

As they walked out onto the steps, Mary noticed a servant securing a trunk onto the carriage, and another lifting a portmanteau. "Oh dear," she said, and detached herself from the goodbyes. "Excuse me!" she called to the servant as she skipped down the steps. "Excuse me. There must be a mistake. This is Mr. Ingles' carriage. We do not depart until tomorrow." She thought to herself that even with her novice apprentice servants at Norchester, such a mistake would not be made.

"Orders of Mrs. Goodfellow, madam," replied the servant. "She was most particular that the baggage was to be loaded onto the carriage as soon as it arrived." He clearly did not think himself beholden to Mary, and was eager to complete his task. Mrs. Goodfellow, the housekeeper, was very strict with her staff, and would not countenance insubordination.

Mary therefore followed him in pursuit of Mrs. Goodfellow, whom she found directing traffic below stairs. Everyone stood to attention as she entered the passage.

"Miss Markham," said Mrs. Goodfellow coming forward in stern efficiency. "What brings you down here?"

"The servants are loading baggage onto Mr. Ingles' carriage. I think there is some confusion. Mrs. Burrows and I are not leaving until tomorrow. Could you please have our bags removed so Mr. Ingles may depart? He is anxious not to be detained."

"Oh, but they are not your bags, madam," said Mrs. Goodfellow.

"Not my bags?" repeated Mary. "Well, if what has been loaded belongs to Mrs. Burrows, it is in equal need of removal. It surely does not belong to Mr. Ingles."

"No, madam, none of it belongs to you nor to Mrs. Burrows nor to Mr. Ingles. They are Miss Preston's trunks."

"Miss Preston's trunks?" What could be meant by this? Was Miss Preston donating her belongings to the people of Africa? "Why on earth are Miss Preston's trunks being loaded onto Mr. Ingles' carriage?"

"Because she directed that they be so, madam," replied Mrs. Goodfellow. "She did not offer any explanation, and it is not my place to ask, but she was very clear. Her things were brought down this morning at her bidding, and have all been loaded onto the carriage which came precisely at the hour she said it would."

"Thank you, Mrs. Goodfellow," said Mary, who had not been so confused since the day she first met Mr. Clark. She left the housekeeper and climbed the stairs to Miss Preston's room, where she found the door open. Hastening down the main staircase, she caught sight of the older lady exiting by the front door. She pursued her, calling after her. She was joined in the foyer by Dorothea, and the two girls exited together to see Miss Preston step onto the gravel drive and make towards the carriage, where Mr. Ingles was already seated.

"Aunt?" said Dorothea, bewildered.

Miss Preston stopped and turned back to look at her niece. Her eyes darted between Dorothea and Mary beside her. Her hesitation was brief and she hastened back, taking the former's hands in hers, kissing her swiftly goodbye and turning instantly back to the carriage. As she did so, she said with a sweep of her hand, "I have done all I can for you and your sister, my dear. I hope you will not forget my kindness and the sacrifices I have made for you, but there is nothing more I can give." She hoisted herself into the carriage and closed the door behind her. From the open window she continued, "I am called away now, that the wild tribes of Africa might benefit from my care and attention, as you have. Do send my regrets to Miss Augusta that I shall not be at her wedding. She may take consolation in knowing that it is for good reason that I must miss it. My Lord has summoned me, else I should never have been absent for such a precious occasion. Goodbye, my dear. Be well and Godspeed!" She nodded to Mr. Ingles who knocked on the wall of the carriage. They pulled away as Miss Preston waved and smiled out of the window at a pack of stunned and unmoving onlookers.

When the travellers were quite gone from sight, the four observers began to regain their senses.

"Has Miss Preston gone to Africa with Mr. Ingles?" asked Sir Richard, to no one in particular.

"I believe so, sir." It was Mrs. Burrows who was next to regain the power of speech.

"Well, good riddance," he said and marched back into the house where he poured himself a large glass of brandy and took up his newspaper.

The three ladies remained outside a few moments longer. "Africa, is it?" said Dorothea. "I hope Mr. Ingles has a strong constitution and high tolerance for inanity." Returning to the piano, she resumed her playing, this time choosing to rehearse a piece of German opera, which she sang at such a volume it could be heard by Mary and Mrs. Burrows outside, where they remained for some minutes attempting to comprehend the absurdity of what they had just witnessed.

"What in the name of all things…?" began Mary over the shrill yet exquisite tones of Dorothea's singing. "Am I in a dream?" She descended the steps, looking down the drive after the route the carriage had taken. She looked back to Mrs. Burrows. "Can you explain this?"

"Certainly," she replied. Although she was surprised at the turn of events, Mrs. Burrows considered them to be most convenient—better even than she could have planned it. "It was your idea, really." She walked down to meet Mary. "Or at least, you inspired the idea, the suggestion that Mr. Ingles needed the care of a lady in his journey. Miss Preston was in need of a purpose now that her charges are to be married, and a means of escape from the consequences of her maltreatment of you. No doubt, when Mr. Ingles came to speak to her, she saw her chance. He, thinking so highly of his purpose, would see nothing but high-mindedness in her offer to accompany him. And having spent several days in contemplating the advantage of a female companion, he might even have seen it as divine intervention. In a way, it is a perfect outcome for her as well as for him."

"I simply cannot believe it. I could never have imagined it. I would have laughed at anyone suggesting such a thing—Miss Preston going to Africa as part of a mission with Mr. Ingles? It is the most unlikely scheme. I would not have thought it possible if I had not seen it with my own eyes. I suppose some people really are a bit mad."

"Come, my dear," said Mrs. Burrows taking her by the hand and leading her to the house. "You have had a shock. What you need is some tea—yes, some excessively sweet tea and a Germanic aria." They reached the drawing room just in time to hear the crescendo of Dorothea's song, following which she closed her music and came to sit beside her father and silently finish his brandy.

Chapter Forty-Four

Mary and Mrs. Burrows left the next day for Norchester. Their parting was warmer and more tender than Mary would have imagined when she set off for Challey Hall just over a month prior. Even Dorothea seemed genuinely sorry to see them go.

Mr. Clark was no longer with them on this occasion, but the footman was most willing to accompany them when asked. The few weeks between their first journey and this was the difference between the departure of summer and the arrival of autumn. The trees that had welcomed them were mostly bare and the ladies kept their hands in their muffs and their hoods up.

Mary barely had her cloak off at Norchester before she headed for her studio. She took out her paints and smelled them then ran her hands over her brushes. She spread out some of the sketches she had done with Mr. Bailey, deliberating over which to attempt in colour. She chose one of the view from the top of the hill, looking down over Norchester. Leaving her work out to continue at a later time, she followed the dictates of her hunger to the breakfast room where a simple nuncheon had been laid. Meal times, and indeed all times, would be quiet now, but she hoped they would not remain so for long. There was much to be done before winter came.

"I shall go and see Mrs. Hawthorne tomorrow," she said to Mrs. Burrows. She and Walters will, I hope, be glad to see me. I shall send them some apples from the orchard. Do you think we can trust our new cook to make us a tart? I am so fond of apple tart, and we almost never seemed to have it at Challey Hall."

"I do not know why you are so kind to Mrs. Hawthorne. She is not a very amiable sort of woman, nor even very sensible."

"You know I mostly go to see Walters. I do not think I would go if she were not there. And besides, Mrs. Hawthorne gives me my best ideas. You know that it was she who put me in mind to set aside some land for the factory workers."

"I did not. I would have thought such a kindly scheme would be distasteful to her."

"Oh, it was," said Mary. "She told me of another gentleman she had heard of doing the same thing in Leicestershire. She was complaining about it to me, saying what a waste of good land it was, how it was encouraging poverty and idleness, tempting the working class into revolt by giving them a little of what they did not have. She went so far as to suggest that the workers who were allowed to use the plots of land would collude to overthrow the master of the house, murder his family, and establish themselves as lords of their own kingdom. So I thought I had to try it."

Mrs. Burrows laughed. "I see," she said. "You must always ask Mrs. Hawthorne what she considers the worst, most dangerous and unpatriotic thing to do, and then pursue it with alacrity."

"Precisely," concurred Mary. "I cannot wait to hear what she suggests tomorrow. I wonder what she would think of our re-opening the house as a school."

"Oh, Mary, take care. Let us do one thing at a time. After your cousins are both married, and Sir Richard comes to stay, we can discuss the future of the estate. By then you shall see how things lie, and what we might do."

"Yes, of course," Mary agreed. "It is just that I feel such a rush, such a thrill to think of grand schemes, to consider what may be possible."

"Will it be possible to order a new gown in time for Augusta's wedding, for example?"

"Oh, I think not. I do not believe I could face any more travel before the new year. Let them come and see us here in the spring."

"They shall be in town in the spring, I would think. I cannot imagine she would miss the season as a new bride."

"Shall we go to town as well, then?"

"Do you wish to?"

Mary let out a long sigh. "I do not know. You must decide. No. No, I think I do not wish to go. There is nothing to be got in London but new gowns and husbands, and I have no need of either just at present."

The light was already beginning to fade, and Mary decided not to return to her studio, but to indulge her wish of drinking chocolate by the fire, and ordered some be brought up, though it was yet early. As she sat with her companion, sipping from her steaming cup and recollecting all the events of the last few months, one thought continued to occur to her–Dorothea did not deserve George Ingles. She wondered whether Augusta really deserved Tom Carrington either, but it did not disturb her so deeply. Many gentlemen did not deserve their wives, and many ladies won deserving gentlemen by artifice. It was the way of the world, she told herself. So why should she be so concerned with this particular match? Dorothea was a beauty. She was accomplished in all things required of ladies and she brought with her the estate of Challey Hall, which was no small holding. She was not gentle and humble like some ladies, but Mary no longer considered her harsh judgments so unjustified. She had only ever been dismissive and aloof towards Mary, never actually cruel. So what perturbed Mary so much about her marrying a good man with only a thousand pounds a year? Was it perhaps that Dorothea did not love him?

"Do you think Dorothea will be happy with Mr. George Ingles?" she asked.

Mrs. Burrows looked at her over the top of the book she was reading. "Is it Dorothea you are more concerned for, of the two?" she returned.

"To own the truth, I cannot really say. I only know it does not make me happy to think of them, suffering each other, learning to resent each other, growing increasingly spiteful. It does not seem right, no matter how many others before them have endured such a marriage and survived."

"I may tell you my opinion, though you will not like it."

"It is only that you have too much influence over me," said Mary. "If you tell me your opinion, it very quickly becomes truth, whether or not it previously was."

"Well, I shall restrict myself to the facts then, and omit any opinion. What I see is that you fell in love with Mr. Ingles for reasons which have turned out to be more true of Mr. George Ingles. You thought it was Mr. Ingles who always remembered you, thought of you, was kind to you. It turns out George was the one responsible for ensuring your inclusion in invitations, for giving you what you most desired in Mr. Bailey, who makes the greater sacrifice out of duty by marrying Dorothea in spite of his real feelings. It pains you to think that you cannot preserve him when he is a far better man than the one to whom you were prepared to give your whole future."

"Oh, Mrs. Burrows," Mary set down her cup put her head down into her hands. "It is all true. He is not only the better man, I believe he may be the best man, and he is to be wasted on her! What am I to do? I know very well there is nothing I can do." She let go a great sigh, dropped her hands and fell back into the sofa. "I am very fortunate for what I have. I am very grateful, I swear to you. There shall be other gentlemen, I know. And I am rich. I shall purchase the next one that crosses my path. What about Mr. Graham? He was very handsome, and clever. Perhaps I could make a fit partner of him."

"Oh, you already have, my dear."

"What?" Mary raised her head to look her inquisition at Mrs. Burrows.

"Well, his shop was doing so well, as a result of your patronage, that my brother saw fit to invest some of your capital in it. There was an opportunity to expand the business and you have bought into it. So he is already your partner, in a manner of speaking."

"Am I really profiting from Mr. Graham? I never meant to do that! How clever of me."

"My brother is also arranging to advertise your trained staff to large households in more remote regions of the country who may not find it easy to get good help, and indeed, to the Colonies. English-bred staff are such a mark of distinction among the Americans that he believes you will be able to fetch a fair commission, and they, excellent terms. He intends to charge a finders' fee of sorts, which ought to cover more than the costs of training them, and since you already save considerably on their wages, you will be a good deal richer for your charity there too."

"All the better to get me a husband then," said Mary and began to laugh. The release of her laughter unlocked the other feelings that she had been restraining, and it quickly turned to tears.

"There, there my dear," Mrs. Burrows moved across to sit beside her friend, placing her arm across her back in consolation. "It is very hard, I know. And you must cry or you shall never overcome it. But it must be only for one night. In the morning, you must make yourself forget it, as you have done so many hardships before this one. You are strong, and your heart is good. You shall be at peace before you know it. But for now, you must grieve." Mrs. Burrows held the girl close, keeping a handkerchief at hand and wondering if those two sisters would ever be sensible of the sacrifice their little cousin made for them, ever be capable of the gratitude she deserved to be shown, or ever do anything to justify her kindness.

Chapter Forty-Five

It was not easy for Mary to take Mrs. Burrows' advice, but she did. She rose with purpose the next morning, and every morning thereafter, determined to satisfy her heart with the undertakings in which she so delighted. The refurbishments both inside the house and outside gave gainful employment to local tradesmen as well as gave Mary the joy of seeing the property in the state her mother would have kept it. Mrs. Burrows insisted that Mary should allow the steward to take care of the allotments for the Bristolian workers, but Mary was equally insistent that she have personal knowledge and direction of everything taking place within her estate. In time, this effort of will began to bear fruit and she began to live in the pleasure of purposeful enterprise.

One particular morning, she had been out meeting with the farmers, to settle the best place to locate these allotments so as not to deprive the tenants of any of the commons. They would need to drain a bog on the west side of the estate, and she had been traipsing through it with the steward since sunrise. She arrived at breakfast, her hair and dress quite soaked and her boots tracking gleeful prints of mud across the polished floor. She felt revived from the rain and hungry for refreshment.

"Every day I give Mrs. Hawthorne more and more cause to admonish me," she declared to Mrs. Burrows with a sly grin.

"I ought to admonish you!" declared Mrs. Burrows. "Look at the state of your dress. I hope you do not intend to behave like this when Sir Richard arrives. But tell me what you have done this time to deserve the condemnation of that crone Hawthorne, and thus the praise of every sensible and feeling person."

Mary laughed. "I told her yesterday of my latest plan. I was thinking about the orphanage, about the families who are forced to abandon their children because they cannot care for them. It is one thing to offer care and education to the children, but would not it be greater still to enable such families to keep their children with them?"

"I imagine it would, yes. But how can you do that from Norchester, if the families work in Bristol?"

"Well, I intend to grant the allotments to those families who have the most children, so that they can feed them with the food they grow. They may even have a little extra that they might sell, to provide clothing, or other needs. I know it is not much. It can only be a few families, but it is something."

"Would not it be better simply to enclose the land, grow larger numbers of crops and then give them to the families, or give them the profits made from their sale?"

"Oh, I think not," said Mary. "I have spoken to the farmers, and they tell me it is better for the land to grow a variety of crops, in small batches, and besides, it does not feel so much like charity to the families if they control the plot themselves. They shall do the most with the land if they feel it is their own, and if they can sell the excess themselves. Who knows what might be possible."

"And what harm could Mrs. Hawthorne find that she had not done already?"

"She said that by rewarding multiplicity of offspring, I was promoting licentiousness among the poor."

Both ladies laughed at the old lady's expense and continued their breakfast. As they were about to leave, a servant came in with a letter for Mary. It was from Frances. Mary took it upstairs with her to her room, where she had ordered a fire, and where she removed her wet things and sat warming her toes.

My dearest Mary,

I hope you will forgive me for failing to write for so many weeks. You must believe me that you have been in my thoughts daily, though I have hardly had time to sit down at my desk. To own the truth, we have all felt a little awkward about our brother, and were not sure how to begin. We had not heard from you either in such a long time that we thought you must be very upset. I have decided simply to brave whatever hatred you may have saved for us, and write you this explanation.

Our brother was, indeed, most devoted to you, and none of us could believe that his heart could be so quickly possessed of love for someone else. But we were all so much together at Lyme, and even at Norchester, that it is not entirely inconceivable. And much as we would have loved having you as a sister, and as ill as it becomes me to say so as Tom's sister, I think he may not have been clever enough for you. We all feel Augusta is really a much better match, and that you are bound to attract the attention of a more suitable gentleman very soon.

We are quite taken with Augusta. If I recall correctly, you did not enjoy living with her in your youth, though I cannot account for it. I know she is a bit silly, and we all taunt her about the ferocity of her temper, but she is so little that we all just dote upon her, and if she is ever disagreeable, can hardly take her seriously. How we laugh together! The house is never dull so long as Augusta is in it.

I also wished to repeat our invitation to join us over Christmas. The wedding is to take place here, just two weeks prior, and if you are coming, I do hope you will stay with us and then you can simply stay on after for as long as you wish. It will fill the void that will be left by my brother and Augusta when they go, and more than that, it would be just lovely to have you with us again. We all do miss you so. Please say you will come and light up the whole winter for us with your presence.

I am sorry for the shortness of this note, after such a lengthy interim, but I am even now called away by my sisters for something that is no doubt far less worthy of my attention than you are. But go I must, as they are here and you are not.

Do write soon, and with merry news if you can.
Your eternal friend and sister at heart,
Frances Carrington

Mary savoured every word written with such affection from her dear friend. She had decided not to attend the wedding, but Frances' letter caused her to reconsider. In spite of all her activity of late, she missed her friends, and above all, it interested her greatly to see the Augusta that the Carringtons had all come to know. She did not sound at all like the same girl Mary had known from childhood. The infectious and mollifying power of a lively and affectionate family were not, it seemed, to be underestimated.

But if she were to go to the wedding, there would not be time to order a new gown. Whatever would she wear? She opened her wardrobe and scanned its contents. Spying the gown she wore to dinner at Westley Park, she pulled it out and looked it over. She smiled to herself to think how greatly Mr. Ingles had affected her, how mistaken she had been about him. The image of Mr. George Ingles occurred to her, taking her hand and leading her in to dinner. He had not taken Dorothea's hand. She had gone in above him with Lord Marsden. Of course, Dorothea would take the highest place open to her. But George had let her. He had waited for Mary behind everyone. Was this mere compassion, or did he mean more by it? Was he kind to everyone or did she hold some special place for him that inspired him to such thoughtful acts towards her? If he thought of her as she had begun to think of him, it was truly a more tragic case than she had first judged it. She permitted herself a sigh but no tears. A painful tug pulled in her chest, but she refused to indulge it. She hung the gown back in the wardrobe and rang for Davis to dress her. The light in the studio would be good for only a few hours and she was eager to finish her picture. The thrill of seeing the paint wrap itself into beauty and life would suffice to distract and restore her spirit until this wave of feeling passed, and already she felt a growing excitement at the thought of her canvas awaiting her brush.

Chapter Forty-Six

The letter which arrived for Mary a few mornings hence produced quite a different effect from the previous. She had replied to Frances that she would come for the wedding and for Christmas, and expected that this had come from the same friend, expressing the jubilation that would bring Mary such comfort.

It was not.

It was postmarked from the Carrington's house in Surrey, but it was penned by Augusta Hargreaves.

Mary knew its author instantly by the elaborate penmanship which Augusta always employed in her letters, and it made her smile to think how she compensated for her small stature by making everything else about her as large as possible. She set down the chocolate which she had taken to drinking at all hours of the day, in part because they never kept any company anyway, but mostly because she delighted in doing anything that would shock the sensibilities of Mrs. Hawthorne. She suspected that Mr. Clark had begun investing in chocolate as a result of her habit, and possibly in the hope that someone might one day make the product palatable to eat alone as a confection.

She sat by the fire in the smaller drawing room where she loved to repose in the heady languor which only English rain can produce, and she was quite unprepared for the force of Augusta's eternal malcontent, much less the news that in this instance provoked it.

Dear Mary,

I trust you are well and safely returned to Norchester. Everyone here sends their love and greetings. We are all very well and terribly busy with preparations for the wedding. We traveled into London last month to order my wedding clothes. Papa shall simply have to find a way to pay for them, for I was not prepared to be disgraced, which I would have been if I had not ordered something fine. The Carringtons are a very elegant family, and I will not have anyone say that I do not belong among them. As the future Lady Augusta Carrington, it is essential that I have everything befitting my position. Mr. Carrington is so utterly adoring! It would not do to disappoint him with my old rags.

But that is not why I have written. It ought to be. I ought to have the liberty of enjoying my happiness without having it stolen from me by that towering Narcissus. Why must she take everything from me? Why cannot she allow me one minute of sweetness, one respite from her goading superiority? She must always spoil everything for me. It is not fair. Indeed it is the very essence of injustice and tyranny. She has no sisterly feeling, no thought for anyone in the world but herself. She must always have one better than me. I know how it must have eaten her from within, disturbed her unquestioned sense of supremacy, that I should one day be a Lady and she not.

For years I tolerated her exultation, her flaunted betrothal to Mr. George Ingles. It was always such a source of inequality between us— that she was secure in her future and I was not, that she would be part of a noble family and I would not. For once I had an advantage over her. As the wife of Lord Rosborough's third son, she would never have a title. She would have titled relations but would never herself be a Lady.

She could not even wait until I was married! She had to spoil even that for me. She could have waited. There was no cause for making her great announcement before the wedding. She could have given me a few months as a new bride. If she had, I would have rejoiced for her! I am not spiteful like she is. I do not need always to be above everyone. I would not begrudge her making such a good match, not if she would have some decency about it. She might have asked me about it, written to me beforehand, consulted me and sought my opinion on how and when to announce it. One expects such courtesy from a sister, but not Dorothea. We may share parentage but there ends our bond. It is sad perhaps, but I feel my new sisters, Frances and Harriet and Louisa, have become more to me in the space of a few months than she has in the whole course of our lives.

It has just occurred to me that you may not have any idea what I have been going on about. I do not know how much gossip you hear out there in Gloucestershire, and it has not yet gone into the papers. I have only just had it from Father, not even from Dorothea herself. In addition to everything else, she had not even the care to tell me of it. You shall hear of it soon enough, however, from some means or other. Perhaps she will think to write to you, though she did not do as much for me. But I shall take my chance of spoiling for her that privilege if I may and tell you myself. She has thrown off Mr. George Ingles in favour of his brother, Lord Marsden. There, I have said it. She shall be the next Lady Rosborough, and poor George, who was always so good to her, shall be left in the lurch.

Frances says you have decided to come to the wedding after all. We shall have such a merry time and I cannot wait to show you everything that shall one day be mine.

Your humble cousin,

Augusta

Mary put down the letter, then picked it up again, not trusting what her eyes had just read. Having confirmed its contents, she returned it to the table and stood up in agitation. She walked to the door without knowing where she was going, only that she felt she needed to act. What should she do? She needed to think through some course of action, or no course of action. She had just resumed her seat on the sofa, perched at the edge of her seat, when Mrs. Burrows came in to join her and saw instantly that something was amiss.

"Whatever is the matter?" she asked. Mary handed her the letter. Mrs. Burrows at first showed signs of amusement at Augusta's complaining, but her countenance altered suddenly when she reached the last few lines. "I am all amazement," she said. "But, this is good news, is not it?"

"Is it? I was resolved to think of him no more. I was happy. And it is very likely he does not return my feelings. This only leaves me open to uncertainty, to open-ended misery. What am I to do? He is a very eligible gentleman. He is the son of a Lord, and there are many ladies who would not scoff at a thousand a year as Dorothea did. And they shall descend upon him, mark my words. They shall have no shame in taking advantage of the broken heart that he does not have. What if he should marry another before…"

"Before what?"

"I do not know. Am I just to sit idle while he carries on, unaware of my feelings? Is there still nothing I can do? I will not go traipsing about the country in the middle of winter in pursuit of a Mr. Ingles again. I am happy here. I will not make a fool of myself and I will not hang my hopes upon him. He has always been kind to me, but he has never given me cause to hope for more than a pitiful sort of benevolence. Our paths may cross in London in the spring, or at his brother's wedding, perhaps. If he wishes to find me before then, he may seek *me* out."

Just as she spoke, the door to the room opened and the new under-butler, Samson, entered, imitating his idea of a grand butler. Puffing up his chest, he announced in a sonorous voice, "There is a gentleman to see you, madam. I have asked him to wait in the front room. I trust that is satisfactory."

Mary's heart leapt before her head had time to advise it not to. "Do you have his card?" asked Mrs. Burrows.

Samson's face fell at his failure. "No, madam. I forgot to ask."

"Well, what is his name?"

"He did not say, madam."

"And you did not ask?"

"No, madam. I beg pardon, madam."

"Honestly, Samson, you are going to have to do something about your memory if you ever wish to work in a great house in this country. Otherwise, we may need to send you to the Americas. Thank you. You may go." She turned to Mary with raised eyebrows and a grin that spoke of mischief and optimism. "Well, what fresh mystery is this?" she said.

"It is not him," said Mary. "It is Mr. Hawthorne." She rose and passed Mrs. Burrows, who followed her from the room. "It is Mr. Hawthorne, I am sure. I spoke to Mrs. Hawthorne yesterday about sending her a turkey. I told her that I would send it tomorrow, but that if Mr. Hawthorne were passing, he could stop in and collect it instead."

Mrs. Burrows did not argue, but followed behind in curious anticipation. In addition to failing to learn the identity of the caller, Mr. Samson had also left the curtains drawn in the front room so that it was quite dark as they turned into it. They could only make out the figure of a man, facing the fireplace, which had not been lit. As Mary entered the room, the gentleman turned to greet her with the familiar and not wholly unwelcome smile of Mr. Belmont.

Chapter Forty-Seven

"Mr. Belmont!" said Mary with the most sincere surprise. "How pleasant and unexpected this is."

"I am sorry for giving no notice of my coming. I was just in the neighbourhood, passing through, and I thought perhaps you would be so good as to show me your paintings, as we had discussed in Oxfordshire. You did say I would be welcome at any time, and I am most curious to see them, being a great admirer of Mr. Bailey's."

"Of Mr. Bailey's, you say?"

"Yes."

"And you were passing through on your way to…?"

"To London."

"Via Gloucestershire?"

"Yes," said Mr. Belmont with a grin. "It was Mr. Ingles' idea. I am not sure he is so good at geography."

"Mr. Ingles?" Her head was suddenly light and her heart quick as she heard a creak behind her. She turned to see George Ingles rising from a chair in the corner behind the door, where she must have walked right past him in the dark.

"Hello, Miss Markham."

"Mr. Ingles!" Though her heart swelled with feeling, her mind was hopelessly vacant. "I did not see you." His appearance, so long dreamt of and so sudden, was beyond her most fanciful wishes. Had he really come here on purpose to see her? She felt it too much to imagine that his desires might accord with her own, yet what other explanation could there be?

"No." He took a step towards her. "It is rather dim in here." She did not move. She could not tell much in the low light, but it seemed he trembled a little. She had never known him to be anything but blithe and self-assured. This alteration must be her doing, though she could scarce believe it.

Mrs. Burrows stepped briskly forward taking the arm of a grinning Mr. Belmont and whisking him out of the room saying, "Allow me to show you to the studio sir. It is this way."

"You must forgive my surprise; Samson said there was only one gentleman." Her self-possession having only ever been tried by unpleasant happenings, it was not very well adapted to such a happy affliction as this.

Mr. Ingles laughed rigidly. "It is I, or rather Mr. Belmont, who must beg forgiveness there. The surprise was his idea of a joke and quite intentional. I am sorry if I startled you. I would have sent word of our coming, only we left immediately the idea was proposed, and I thought we would arrive before any letter might be delivered, and so here we are. Here I am."

Here he was, indeed! She barely heard his needless apology. "You have just come from Oxfordshire?" Her voice was high and breathless, her hope precarious.

"We have, yes, well, yesterday. You are well, I trust?"

"Yes, very well. And you?" Her nerves would not be steady. "I heard about your disappointment, just now, from Miss Augusta, in fact. I am sorry."

"Are you?" His voice was as strained as hers as he searched her unlit face. "I confess I do not feel any regret. I suppose it is ungentlemanly to say I feel only relief, but to you I think I may speak plainly and true without risk of reproach." It was more question than statement.

"I wish them every happiness," she said. So there *was* cause to hope. Dorothea was right; he did not love her. And if he had come all this way, there could be little doubt as to his intentions towards herself. Yet until he spoke the words, she hardly allowed herself to breathe lest she shatter the delicate perfection of the moment.

"I was never so surprised as when I learned that she had four thousand pounds," he continued. Mary nodded. "I believed her to be penniless." Mary responded with a shake of her head. "Did you–that is–the money, was that you?" Mary nodded again. "I see," he said, dropping his head as though he had received his answer and it was not as he hoped. He looked as if he might turn and leave.

How could he be going? Perhaps she was mistaken after all. Perhaps she only imagined his intentions, for did not Mrs. Burrows say that a man, once bent on proposing, was never deterred? And was she not always right in everything? She must keep him here, encourage him, find a way to assure him of her answer before he had asked the question, before he could walk away.

A mixture of panicked apprehension and heady disbelief had so arrested Mary that she was unsure whether she could produce a sound. As he reached for his hat on the chair, she was just able to rasp, "You were going to marry her anyway."

"What is that?" He turned back to her, straightening, intent. Mary cleared her disobliging throat.

"You intended to marry her without any money, so it made little difference," she said, her voice pleading and thin. "I was merely saving her from embarrassment."

"Then it is not an indication of your indifference, that your feelings–"

"My feelings did not enter into it." Could this possibly be happening? She was immobile with anticipation.

"Then, you are not, that is, you do, or–" He let his arms fall to his sides and drew in a great breath which juddered back out again. "I am sorry. In the carriage I had composed such a pretty and subtle way of expressing myself, but I am afraid I have entirely forgot it now I am here–now that you are here. You must forgive my directness, but Miss Green, Miss Markham that is, I have come here quite on purpose, to speak to you, to ask you, whether I hope in vain, or whether you have ever thought of me as I have for so long now thought of you."

Such elated relief was more than a rational being could withstand. Mary's whole person shook with a fit of either laughter or sobs–she could not say which–and her eyes watered with irrepressible emotion. She nodded her head for she could not speak.

George, now unshackled of his doubt, crossed the room, taking up her hands in his. "Oh, Mary," he said. "I hope I may call you Mary." She nodded and pressed his hands, wishing she could answer him, but entirely unable to do so. She continued nodding her head, and weeping, and quivering, as he asked her to marry him, to love him, to keep him for her own for ever and always.

With his own laughter, born of deep affection and sudden deliverance, he took his handkerchief to her cheek and dried her flowing tears. When at last she recovered from her present seizure, she said, "I am so happy!"

"Are you indeed?" he said. They stood a few moments in mutual, blissful silence, their thoughts and their joy racing faster than words could have hoped to reach. George eventually suggested that they join their respective companions in the studio, remarking that it was shamefully negligent of Mrs. Burrows to have left Mary alone so long with a gentleman of his intentions, and unpardonably cruel of *them* to keep their friends in suspense.

As they made their way through the house, he remarked, "I

thought Marsden would be in for quite a shock, for he is not so high-minded as to marry a lady with no dowry. I was not long in piecing it together, that it must have been your doing. I thought surely I was in vain in coming here. If you would enable her to marry me, then you could not care for me, not as I cared for you. I must have imagined your affection, or exaggerated in my hopeful mind the signs of it which I believed I saw. I had to know, however unlikely my chances. I was certain it was a fool's errand, but the moment I was free, the very day, I had to come."

"The girls have always had a dowry," said Mary. "I would not see them debased."

"Your selflessness has done so much more, spared so much more than their disgrace" he said. "You could not have known how it would liberate her, liberate me. Without your kindness, I would be divided from you forever."

"That is true," said Mary as they arrived at the studio door, "but it was not all disinterested generosity. I am charging Sir Richard four per cent."

He laughed and led her into the room to spread the good news to their friends–friends who, both certain of the outcome, were already two glasses in to the best sherry.

Chapter Forty-Eight

The couple was married from Norchester with very little fuss and almost no advance notice. Neither was willing to risk by delay a happiness so precariously arrived at. Sir Richard attended, though neither of his daughters did. Mary saw them afterwards on frequent occasions–Dorothea when she was in town, and Augusta in Surrey when she visited the Carringtons, with whom she continued a warm and lifelong friendship.

She bore her cousins no resentment. They had treated her as barely above a maid, but then to the servants they had always been rather kind. Certainly they were horrid to her, but so they were horrid to each other. All told, she had little more reason to complain of the sisters than the sisters did of one another.

It was Aunt Preston who had distinguished between her and the Hargreaves girls–Aunt Preston who had kept her in the nursery, prevented her practicing on the pianoforte, and never purchased for her any new clothes despite the significant allowance provided for her. And it is Aunt Preston's fate that is perhaps the most surprising, for she did not help Mr. Ingles to an African bride, as had been so feared, but rather married him herself. He found that Mrs. Burrows had been quite correct. A missionary ought to be married. He was not a man of passion nor of great discernment and was not overly particular about the lady. Her consent to leaving England and to his proposal of marriage were recommendation enough. And it was not so shocking as it may first appear.

Miss Preston had been much younger than her sister the late Mrs. Hargreaves, who herself had married quite young. Mr. Ingles was not a *very* young man, nearly thirty, and so the difference in their ages was barely seven years–not at all unheard of or impossible. Mr. Ingles was not a man of passion, and to have a wife would no doubt be of use to him. How Miss Preston would rejoice at being married at last, and to the son of a Lord! Her jubilation could not be surpassed.

Lady Rosborough lived long enough to hear the news. In fact, there were some who believed the shock of it may well have precipitated her end, though the doctors said she was not long for this world in any event.

Mrs. Burrows eventually returned to London in spite of Mary's repeated and fervent protests. Once in town, she began to pursue a partnership not wholly mercantile in nature with Mr. Graham, whom she already knew to be clever, hard-working and handsome, and whom inside information had taught her was on the way to being a very eligible gentleman.

Norchester saw many incarnations, all of which were begun out of Mary's philanthropy, and most of which were eventually rendered profitable by Mr. Clark's ingenuity. Neither Mary nor the house ever wanted for occupation, art, friends, or most importantly, chocolate.

About The Author

MELANIE KERR studied linguistics, English and theatre at the University of British Columbia and law at the University of Alberta. Kerr is a reckless lover of clotted cream, a staunch defender of the semi-colon and a fierce opponent of unpleasant music. She wooed her current and only husband with false promises of skill at word games and eternally good hair. She lives in Edmonton, where she raises her three young children, sews her own Regency costumes, organizes Regency costume events, blogs on all things old and English, endeavours to take over the world and occasionally practices law.